# DEATH
# STALKS
# DOOR
# COUNTY

## PATRICIA SKALKA

is a former freelance staff writer for *Reader's Digest* specializing in human interest and medical stories. She has worked as a magazine editor, ghost writer, book reviewer and writing instructor. A lifelong mystery fan, Skalka believes that more than simply answer the question *who done it*, a good mystery probes the human spirit and character.

Skalka is a member of the Authors Guild of America, Mystery Writers of America, Sisters in Crime and the International Association of Crime Writers, North American Branch. A Chicago native, she divides her time between her home in the city and family cottage in Door County, Wisconsin.

For more information, please visit her website: PatriciaSkalka.com.

# DEATH STALKS DOOR COUNTY

## PATRICIA SKALKA

**W RLDWIDE®**

TORONTO • NEW YORK • LONDON
AMSTERDAM • PARIS • SYDNEY • HAMBURG
STOCKHOLM • ATHENS • TOKYO • MILAN
MADRID • WARSAW • BUDAPEST • AUCKLAND

Recycling programs
for this product may
not exist in your area.

ISBN-13: 978-0-373-28244-9

Death Stalks Door County

Copyright © 2014 by Patricia Skalka

A Worldwide Library Suspense/September 2017

First published by Terrace Books, a trade imprint of the University of Wisconsin Press

Drawing by Carla-Marie Padvoiskis

Map by Julia Padvoiskis

www.Harlequin.com

**Printed in U.S.A.**

For Ray
In loving memory

"If you wrong us, shall we not revenge?"

Shakespeare,
*The Merchant of Venice*

## Author's Note

Door County is real. While I used the peninsula as the framework for the book, I also altered some details and added others to fit the story. The spirit of this majestic place remains unchanged.

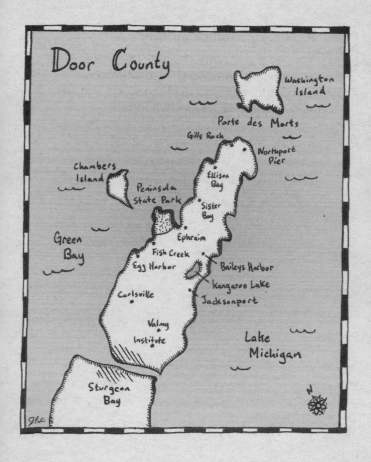

# ONE

---

HE RAN IN the early morning, floating like a specter amid the tall, wet pines of the Wisconsin forest. His thick hair curled from the mist. His lungs burned. His breath stank of beer and cigarettes. At the road, he stopped and swiped his glasses on his baggy sweatshirt. Late June, and the damp, cold spring had yet to give way to summer.

Three months earlier, Dave Cubiak had left Chicago, steering a small rental car north along the Lake Michigan shore, across the Illinois state line, and up two hundred miles to the Door County peninsula. He was forty-two, a former cop undone by the deaths of his wife and daughter, who had been killed in an accident he believed he could have prevented.

The move was supposed to be a fresh start.

Instead, it was a mistake.

Grief stricken, guilt ridden, and often drunk, Cubiak felt like a blot on the tourist landscape, a reclusive misfit among the friendly locals, people who waved even to strangers. He had committed to staying one year and had nine months to go. The time it took to grow a baby, to figure out what next.

Cubiak adjusted his glasses and bent over, his hands on his knees. For a moment, he thought of his mother and felt ashamed. He had failed her; he had failed everyone.

A sharp wail shattered the stillness, and through old habit Cubiak straightened, trying to pinpoint the source. A seagull wheeling over the bay? In his new job as park ranger, he'd sometimes watch the plump birds dive-bombing the water, full of avian bravado. Perhaps the sound had been made by a red fox on the prowl. Or the wind. Silence again. The forest gave away nothing.

He studied the dirt path on the other side of the black-top. The trail was the quickest route to Jensen Station, where the Peninsula State Park rangers lived and worked, but he was in no hurry to return to his temporary home. The longer he stayed out, the longer he could avoid his querulous boss, Otto Johnson, park superintendent.

Cubiak opted for the road.

Turning left, he plodded through a series of gentle curves. Halfway around the final bend, he stopped. Twenty feet ahead, a bleached red pickup idled along-side the pavement. The ranger squeezed his eyes shut. Too late. He'd taken in everything. The truck with the dented door gaped open. Otto Johnson slumped against a corner of Falcon Tower, and a body sprawled at the park super's feet. Male. Average height. Slim, youthful build. Dark hair. Jeans. Shiny black jacket.

As a homicide detective, Cubiak had been exalted for his ability to absorb the details of a crime scene and to play them back with excruciating clarity. Although his photographic memory failed with the printed page, it performed with camera-like accuracy in the places where people did their dirty deeds. Including the seg-ment of pavement half a block from his house where the battered bodies of his wife and daughter had sprawled in twin pools of blood.

Cubiak forced his eyes open. "Fuck," he said.

Johnson started and pushed away from the tower. Rain or was it tears glistened on his weathered face. "Looks like some kid took a nosedive off the top." The park super stuck out his chin as if challenging his new assistant to disagree.

Cubiak said nothing.

"He's cold. I can't find a pulse," Johnson went on. "You want to check?"

"No." Damp with sweat, Cubiak shuddered. He didn't need to look any closer. The odd twist to the victim's neck told him enough.

"Maybe you should."

Cubiak shook his head. He hadn't been near a dead body in two years, not since his family had been killed. "Have you called the sheriff?"

"Can't. Radio's busted. You'll have to get him from the station."

CUBIAK CLIMBED INTO the truck. The pickup wasn't an official departmental vehicle but it was the one the park super insisted on using. The ranger snatched Johnson's cell phone off the seat. The battery was dead. Not that it mattered—it was nearly impossible to get a signal in the park. He tossed the phone down and made a three-point turn. The forest road was deserted. Death pulled the leaden sky lower and peppered the claustrophobic woods with strange whispers of events spinning out of control. Fate was not always kind. A lesson Cubiak knew well.

Away from the tower, the wind came up and swept tendrils of fog across the hood. Squinting into the mist and steering with his knees, Cubiak patted his pockets for a cigarette. He checked twice before realizing he was in his running clothes. Out of habit, he reached toward the dash, but he was in Johnson's vehicle and the super-intendent didn't smoke. "Damn."

At Jensen Station, Cubiak nabbed a half-empty pack from the glove box of his jeep and lit his first of the day, inhaling deeply. The nicotine settled him immediately. He took three long drags, each of them calming him further. When he'd burned down to the filter, he smashed the butt between his fingertips and then stripped it down military style as he walked to the rear door of the former hunting lodge.

The imposing wood and stone refuge had been built by an eccentric millionaire and in its heyday had boasted a ballroom, trophy room, and dining room that could seat thirty comfortably. Indian rugs and portraits of famous chiefs had hung on the walls, and books on Native American lore had filled the third-floor library. Left to the state, the lodge's treasures were replaced with un-imaginative bureaucratic trappings and its grand interior reconfigured into a series of cracker-box offices and stingy, utilitarian rooms.

Cubiak followed a warren of dim passages to the rear staircase and took the steps two by two to his room on the second floor. From his closet he unearthed the second of his vices, a quart of vodka. The ranger had neither the money nor the taste for expensive booze. Rotgut, corrosive liquor, the kind favored by his late and not-dearly-departed father, suited him fine. Drinking as punishment. As effective a penance as sackcloth and ashes. Cubiak took a hearty pull and stripped off his wet clothes. The aroma of freshly baked cinnamon rolls rose up from the kitchen. He gagged and swallowed more vodka, trying hard not to blink because the images of the dead man were most vivid when his eyes were closed.

Dressed in his brown ranger uniform, he drank again and headed for the wide walnut staircase at the front of the house. In the vestibule, his rubber soles squeaked on the black-and-white tile floor. Cubiak glanced up at the noise and caught his reflection in the ornate leaded-glass mirror on the wall, the only piece of original furniture left in the defrocked building. The image was startling. His face was gaunt and lined, his coarse dark hair dusted with flecks of gray. Cubiak had always enjoyed a boyish appearance, but like so much else his youthful good looks had eroded, lost to grief and alcohol.

The radio room was a converted closet behind the stairs, quarters so tight that Cubiak instinctively hunched as he dialed the CB to the emergency channel. He remained in that position, pitched forward, as he waited for the sheriff's office to patch him through to Leo Halverson.

"What? What?" the sheriff yelled over the buzz saw that screeched in the background. "I got a goddamn tree down on Town Line Drive. What are ya calling about?"

The saw stopped abruptly. Cubiak ran through the particulars.

"I'll tell Beck," Halverson said and signed off.

The note on the index card taped to the wall instructed Cubiak to say, "Roger and out." He scowled and flicked the switch to Off. Next door, in Johnson's office, he finger-walked through the superintendent's Rolodex to the coroner's home number.

The connection went through on the fourth ring. "Hello. You have reached the Bathard residence…" The recorded greeting was concise, formal. Cubiak left a message.

At the Emergency Services Department, a woman with a scratchy voice told him that both Sister Bay ambulances were out but that she'd send one up from Sturgeon Bay. "Fine. No hurry." Cubiak dropped the receiver into the cradle and stared out the window at a stand of white pines.

The trees took him back to his first visit to Door County. He'd been a scrawny, ten-year-old city kid, a charity-case Boy Scout stunned by the immensity of the forest. Set free in a world of woods and water, the young Cubiak had imagined himself in paradise. Later, as an adult, after he'd lost everything, it was those childhood memories as much as the urging of his former police partner that drew him back again.

He hadn't expected to find death among the trees. He hadn't anticipated the condo communities and full-service resorts that had spread like a rash on the land. Even the scout camp had been sold to developers who tore down the heavy canvas tents and erected three-story townhouses in their place. The ranger job wasn't what Cubiak had bargained for either. He'd been hired as Johnson's assistant and assured that his duties would keep him outdoors and behind the scenes. Equipment maintenance and grounds keeping were to be his purview.

From the start, however, Johnson made it clear he didn't want or need any help caring for the park. "My park," he'd called it. He installed Cubiak in the front office with orders to handle reservations and to draft a backlog of reports for the Department of Natural Resources. Mostly, the stubborn older man ignored his new employee, barely exchanging a civil word. If it weren't for his promise to Malcolm, Cubiak would have quit after the first few weeks. When he came north, he agreed to try the job and the new location for one year. At the very least, he would keep his word to his friend.

FROM JENSEN STATION, Cubiak took the long way back, following the route that carried him past the Nature Center and the meadow where wild lady's slippers had erupted in bright yellow earlier that spring, past the lowland marsh favored by deer and the grove of quaking aspen near the entrance to Turtle Bay Campground. He noticed none of it, and was aware only of the hum of the tires on the pitted roadway and the need to keep his eyes from shuttering, even for a second.

Door County was a spur of land that jutted at a northeast angle between Lake Michigan and Green Bay. If the state was like a mitten, the peninsula was the thumb and the state park a swollen knuckle that bulged out into the turbulent, cold waters of the bay. Like much of Door County, the nearly four-thousand acre park sat atop the Niagara Cuesta, a horseshoe-shaped bluff that originated in upper New York State where it gave rise to the famous falls. Extending west from there, it skimmed the upper rim of the Great Lakes basin and then arched downward into Wisconsin on a ridge of cliffs that in some spots reached heights of one hundred and fifty feet.

Along the highest rise, Cubiak pulled into a scenic overlook, lit a cigarette, and stared out at the mist-shrouded water. The dead man may have lived nearby, in the direction of his gaze even. Was he a frequent tourist or a first-time visitor? Somewhere out there his family was going about its usual business. Reading the morning paper. Reaching for another doughnut to enjoy with a second cup of coffee. Cubiak imagined them getting the call. Their initial response would be stunned and

protesting. No, there must be a mistake! Dull accep-
tance would come slowly and in its own time, seeping
into their collective consciousness. Like him, they would
spend the rest of their lives wishing they could undo the
day's events, wishing they were God.

CUBIAK CHAIN-SMOKED through the pack. When he finished, he collected the butts and swung the truck onto
the pavement. At the tall wooden tower, he steered onto
the narrow shoulder and coasted to the front bumper of
a black Volvo station wagon.

For a moment he regarded the trio on the other side
of the road. They were lined up like fence posts.

Farthest from the tower, in the adjacent clearing, superintendent Johnson inspected a jumble of upturned
picnic tables.

Next was Leo Halverson in jeans and a red-plaid shirt.
Bouncing on the balls of his feet, the sheriff stood alongside a mud-spattered jeep on the spit of gravel between
the picnic area and the tower and inspected a handful
of small items spread across the hood, probably the victim's personal effects.

A gray-haired man knelt over the body. Cubiak assumed he was the coroner, Evelyn Bathard, whom he'd
not yet met.

Each of them, park super, sheriff, and coroner,
claimed a long family legacy on the peninsula. Unsure
of his role as the newcomer, Cubiak slid from the truck
and trudged across the road, completing the tableau of
four tall men at Falcon Tower.

Johnson ignored him. The sheriff gave a quiet snort of
recognition. Prior to that morning, Cubiak had encountered Halverson twice but only briefly. Both times the

sheriff exuded a jovial, easy-going air, but today he came across as a scared kid dumped inside grown-up skin.

The ranger continued past him toward the man at the tower. "Doctor Bathard? Dave Cubiak. I phoned for the ambulance."

"Good." The coroner's voice was heavy. He glanced up. His face was etched with fatigue. His creased khakis were caked with dirt. He rose with effort and patted his right-hand pocket. "I've taken quite a number of photos. Sufficient, I believe, for the circumstances. Would you mind?" Bathard pulled a pair of latex gloves from his left pocket and held them out to the assistant park superintendent. "I'd like to turn him over."

Cubiak stiffened.

"What's the matter, Dave? Ya must've seen worse than this," Halverson taunted from behind.

"Leave him alone," Bathard snapped. Then, quietly, he added, "Truth is you never get used to it." Cubiak took the gloves.

The dead man's jeans were slit at both knees and his quilted nylon jacket was torn above the left elbow. It was hard to avoid looking at his face. The eyes were wide with terror and the thin lips distorted by fright. Gravel had scraped his nose and cheeks but beneath the bloody gouges, the skin was clear and unlined. He was a young man. Too young to die.

"Well?" Halverson said.

Bathard took a step back. "I don't believe I've ever seen him before."

As he pocketed the gloves, Cubiak walked past the sheriff. "Not roping off the area?" he said without thinking.

"Nah, that's just TV stuff," Halverson drawled, then, on second thought, looked around puzzled. "Should we?"

Cubiak reached the road. "Only if you're on TV."

Halverson colored. "Otto!" he called. "Questions. You found him, making your rounds. So you were first out this morning?"

"No. He was." The park superintendent pointed at Cubiak.

The sheriff whirled around. "What were ya doing out here so early?"

"I run."

"Oh. See anything?"

"No."

"Hear anything?"

"A sound." He didn't want to talk about seagulls. "Someone singing maybe."

"Singing?"

Cubiak looked past the sheriff into the trees. What kind were they? He knew so little about the forest. "Could have been a boat radio. Or the wind," he said.

"Right. Sound travels far out here." Halverson hiked up his pants. "Well, looks like a sure case of suicide to me."

"Or an accident. Wet wood can be treacherous," Bathard said.

Cubiak waited for one of them to suggest homicide. But neither did, and he wondered if murder was considered too unseemly for Door County.

Halverson brandished the victim's wallet in the air. "Anybody know this guy? Name's *Wisby. Lawrence Wisby.* He's from Illinois." The sheriff pronounced it *Ill-a-noise.*

Despite the damp cold, a layer of sweat crystallized on Cubiak's neck. Nausea roiled his gut. He imagined the others watching him, but when he looked, the coroner was again kneeling next to the body and the sheriff was grilling Johnson for details of the gruesome discovery.

Church bells pealed, drowning out what they were saying. The bright blaze of noise ricocheted through the trees, prompting the four men to stare in the direction of Ephraim. It was Sunday and clear from their shared look of surprise that each of them had forgotten. The clarion sound persisted for several minutes and then diminished in slow, measured steps.

In the uneasy lull, Cubiak spoke.

"I recognize the name. Wisby. Lawrence Wisby," He swallowed hard and when he went on, the words came fast, as if they were toxic and had to be spat out quickly. "His brother killed my wife and daughter."

A STUNNED SILENCE FOLLOWED. They hadn't known, Cubiak realized, not even Johnson.

The story hadn't made its way across the state line, though it was major news throughout the Chicago metro area. William Wisby, a convicted felon with an arrest record for robbery and assault as long as the devil's tail, had been out on parole less than ten days when he stole a car and went on a drunken joy ride that ended in the deaths of the beautiful wife and impish daughter of one of the city's top police detectives. For more than a week, reporters and even a few persistent paparazzi dogged Cubiak day and night, eager to mine his pain for their gain. "How does it feel?" one of them had asked. Cubiak remembered taking a swing at the guy.

In the shadow of Falcon Tower, Halverson broke the spell. "I'll be dammed. Ya knew him. What do ya think he was doing here?" he said, scratching his chin.

Before Cubiak could reply, Bathard spoke up. "Dave

did not say he knew the dead man, Sheriff. It's important to keep the facts straight."

"The fact is, there's a connection."

"Tentative," the coroner insisted.

"Yeah, well, we'll see."

The sheriff frowned in a look of smug concentration. Cubiak pictured him connecting the dots, making a case out of conjecture.

Whatever conclusions Halverson drew, he kept to himself. Suddenly animated, he scooped up the victim's wallet and ID and began barking out orders. "You, stay where I can find ya," he said, pointing at Cubiak. "You wait for the evidence technicians and ambulance," he told Bathard. Then to Johnson, "You ride back to the station with me. I need a statement, and a piece of Ruta's pie."

The sheriff's taillights pulled away down the hill, leaving Bathard and Cubiak alone. Despite himself, Cubiak turned back toward the body. "*He's* not the one who should be dead," he said.

"You didn't recognize him?"

"No. He must have been in the courtroom at the trial, but…no." Cubiak looked away. "Do you have a blanket? We should cover him."

They used a patched, gray throw from Bathard's trunk.

"I forgot to thank you, before for… ," Cubiak said as they moved back toward the road.

The coroner put up a hand to stop him. "I was only doing my civic duty. Our esteemed sheriff has been known to shortcut his way to conclusions." He paused. "Not the best circumstances under which to meet, I'm afraid." Bathard glanced at the tower. "This thing's been here some fifty years; I doubt there's been more than a cut lip from a slip on the stairs all that time. It was built as a forest fire observation post originally." Rain glistened on Bathard's hair; his anorak was soaked at the shoulders. He pulled a pipe from his pocket and tapped the bowl on the heel of his hand. "By the way, what do you think happened to the jacket?"

Cubiak was not surprised by the question. The coroner seemed like a man who didn't miss much. "Figure it caught on a nail. Piece tore off," he said. "Halverson must've gotten it when he went up."

Bathard chuckled. "You give our officer of the law a lot of credit. A crow could just as easily have flown away with it. I looked on the ground. It wasn't there."

"It could've been torn already, before he got here," Cubiak said.

"That's a possibility."

A sharp thunder clap boomed, loosening fat drops of rain. They stood for a moment in the drizzle and then Bathard waved Cubiak off.

"You go on. I'll wait for the ambulance. No use both of us getting wet."

As he pulled away, Cubiak glimpsed the coroner in the rearview mirror. Bathard had returned to the tower. Shoulders bent against the rain, the stem of the unlit pipe in his mouth, he kept his silent, lonely vigil.

PARK RECORDS SHOWED that Larry Wisby had reserved a camping spot in Peninsula State Park for the third weekend in June every year for the past five. He also belonged to the Friends of the Park. He was a regular and had probably climbed Falcon Tower many times. Cubiak was convinced Wisby hadn't jumped. His first week on the job, the park ranger had trudged to the top of the seven-story structure. The upper platform, the highest of three decks, was ringed by a chest-high guard railing, with a rail cap that tilted inward for added safety. If Wisby had mounted the barrier, he would have had a hard time keeping his balance and could have tipped over the edge, but it was unlikely he'd jumped. Even when a man leaps with the intention of taking his own life, instinct propels him away from the building or structure from which he's hurling. He doesn't plummet straight down. Judging from the location of the body, Cubiak figured Wisby had either fallen or been pushed. Cubiak didn't particularly care which. Two years prior he'd lost his wife and daughter to the Wisbys' other son. That morning they had lost their younger boy, which didn't settle the score but brought it closer.

Cubiak scanned the records and emailed them to the sheriff. Let Halverson sort it out.

The rest of the day, Cubiak avoided Ruta. He didn't know how much the housekeeper had been told or had overheard about the body at the tower and didn't want to be the one to break the news or fill in the details.

He'd met Ruta in early April on the night he'd arrived in Door County. A spring blizzard had snarled traffic and it was well past midnight when he finally pulled up to Jensen Station with his belongings jammed into a worn army duffel and four battered cardboard boxes secured with twine. Against the backdrop of madly swirling snow, he stood in the doorway like a forlorn refugee in a vintage European war movie. The effect was momentarily heightened when the thick oak slab was opened by a stern, aging woman who announced in a decidedly foreign accent that her name was Ruta Lapkritis. In English, Ruth November, she had said firmly. Ruta had a detached sadness in her countenance that marked her as a fellow traveler in the world of the lost and hurting and immediately made him wary. Cubiak was not wont to share stories.

THAT NIGHT, HE had the dream again. Given the events of the day, how could he not?

The nightmare began, as it always did, with him at home, standing on the front porch on a hot, muggy summer evening and watching as Lauren and Alexis walked hand-in-hand down the street. They were off on an innocent quest for ice cream. He heard Alexis, a spry, freckled wisp of a child, say she wanted vanilla with mint chocolate chips. "Two scoops." He saw Lauren, lithe and deeply tan, glance first at the reddening sky to the west and then down at the blond girl in her teddy bear T-shirt and blue shorts. "Two scoops," she agreed as she tucked a loose strand of long brown hair behind her ear.

Four blocks away, a rusted green car, a monstrous road hog, tore through a red light. The car sported an endless span of metal grille above the front bumper and oversize fins that swept ludicrously up and outward from the rear fenders. As it bore down the street, engine roaring, the vehicle gained speed and momentum.

Cubiak saw the behemoth approach. He wanted to rush out and tackle his wife and daughter and pull them out of harm's way, but he couldn't move. He could only stand riveted to the spot, as the two-ton wreck hurtled out of the twilight. When the car hit, mother and daughter somersaulted through the air like rag dolls and flopped clumsily to the pavement, where they lay with arms and legs twisted at odd angles to their bodies. A pool of blood seeped out from behind Alexis's left ear. Lauren's grasp momentarily tightened around the girl's hand, then fell loose and limp. As they stared upward to heaven, the car sped on.

The block was eerily quiet. Then a neighbor screamed. A screen door slammed, and people raced out into the street. Holding their hands to their faces, they turned away, weeping. Off in the far distance an ambulance siren screeched. Already too late.

Bellowing with rage, Cubiak clawed through the crowd and gathered the lifeless bodies into his arms. He carried them home and upstairs to the second floor. In the master bedroom, he laid them side by side on the king-size bed, gently placing Alexis's tiny bruised hand in her mother's palm. Then he wiped the blood and dirt from their faces and limbs and kissed their suntanned cheeks.

From the bedroom window, he saw the green car idling behind the garage, the driver leaning against the hood, drunken and defiant. Cubiak confronted him in the alley, and they went at each other bare fisted. No one witnessed their battle. It was a brutal, protracted fight. In the end, Cubiak broke the man's neck, cracking the upper vertebrae of his spinal column and severing the carotid connection between brain and heart. Then he hoisted the dead man over his shoulder, carried him up the stairs, and dumped the body on the bare floor of the bedroom.

Lauren woke first and stroked her daughter's cheek until the little girl stirred.

"Daddy, I didn't get my ice cream," Alexis said.

He cupped her chin. "You will," he promised.

The three stood by the body. At a signal from Cubiak,

they dragged the corpse to the open window, heaved it over the sill, and watched it float down, feather-like, into the yard. Before it hit the ground, it vanished. In the alley, the green car crystallized and blew away into oblivion.

Cubiak and his family returned to the accident scene. The neighbors had washed away all traces of blood and dispatched the ambulance driver back to the hospital with vague looks and murmurs of false alarms. The job done, they drifted back into their houses as Cubiak and his wife and child walked past, on their way to the ice cream shop.

THE SOFT HISSING of the radiator near the foot of his bed woke him. It was 4 a.m. The room was overly warm, but Cubiak shivered. He was bone cold. His lungs and limbs ached as if he'd run a great distance in a place with little oxygen. He'd once read that dreams were relatively short, lasting a few minutes at most, but his nightmare had acquired an eternal quality, unfurling at a bitter, languid pace. Each time the dream became more vivid, magnifying the smallest details and drawing them to his attention. Sometimes, it was the tiny yellow flecks in his wife's eyes; this time it had been the fine layer of pale downy hair on his daughter's left forearm.

Cubiak stared into the inky dark. What he'd said earlier at Falcon Tower was only partially correct. True, the elder Wisby brother was the drunk behind the wheel of the car that had run down and killed both mother and child. Legally, the man was guilty; he'd been tried, convicted, and sentenced to what Cubiak considered an insultingly short prison term.

The other half of the story, the rest of the truth, was

the part that Cubiak could acknowledge only to himself. That he, also, was responsible for the deaths of the two people he loved most. This personal guilt was a burden he could not escape.

"Oh, sweet Jesus," he'd wept as he cradled the cold, lifeless flesh that had been his wife and daughter. "Oh, my dear Lord, sweet Jesus, why?"

*Why?* Cubiak knew why. He'd gotten into an argument with Lauren the morning of their long-planned family trip to Great America. When Alexis called the precinct to remind him about the outing, he lied and told her he couldn't leave after his shift, that he had to stay for an important assignment. In fact, he was too embarrassed to face his wife.

"We'll go to the park another day. Tell your mother to take you for ice cream instead," he'd snapped at his darling little girl.

Cubiak yanked the covers to his chin. How could he have been so petty, so small-minded? The confrontation with Lauren started after he saw her talking to a neighbor, a good-looking stud of a guy, recently divorced, who owned a string of successful Laundromats that gave him plenty of money and free time.

"What's he sniffing around for?" Cubiak had said.

"What do you mean?"

"You know what I mean."

Lauren was incensed. "How dare you," she said.

Things escalated from there, his anger fed more by his insecurities than by any mistrust of Lauren. In the morning, she offered him a cup of coffee, but he turned his back on her, unable to utter a simple thanks. Too proud to say *I'm sorry. I love you.*

How could he ever forgive himself?

# TWO

*Monday*

FUELED BY TOO much coffee and too little sleep, Cubiak headed south to Sturgeon Bay. After a tortured night, he'd risen early and singed his lungs on a grueling five-mile run. Besides alcohol, which helped him forget, physical activity was his only other defense against the remorse that defined his life. He needed to keep moving. At breakfast he finished a stack of Ruta's pancakes and then volunteered to spend the day clearing trails or cutting firewood.

"Bathard and Halverson are meeting at ten at the coroner's office to go over the tower incident. You need to be there," Johnson said, pushing back from the kitchen table.

"Me? Why?"

"'Cause Bathard asked for someone from the park to come, and I choose you," the super said as he walked out the door.

Situated on the western edge of Door County, the city of Sturgeon Bay had grown up on either side of a deep fingerling of water that bled off Green Bay into a long, natural harbor. Sturgeon Bay's historic geography matched its contemporary dual personality, with one segment of residents working the shipyards and the other serving the tourists. When Cubiak turned off the highway, the industrial sites were already deep into the first shift while the tourist shops remained shuttered and dark. He drove mindlessly, well above the limit, and braked hard to keep from sliding past the stop sign by the Kozy Kafe, one of the few businesses in town that catered to both tourists and locals. A luxury-edition Mercedes, license JDB-1, hugged the curb outside the restaurant. Cubiak recognized the car. The silver sedan belonged to J. Dugan Beck, a local big wheel and head of the Peninsula State Park citizens advisory board. A few weeks after he arrived on the peninsula Cubiak learned that Beck had pressured Otto Johnson into taking on an assistant. The ranger felt that made him indirectly beholden to Beck for his job and he didn't like that. For that matter, he didn't like the man, period—too slick and pompous. Cubiak scanned the café's breakfast crowd for a glimpse of Beck's distinctive shock of gray hair but came up empty. He was halfway through the intersection when he saw Beck exiting the office of the *Door County Herald*. Close behind was *Herald* editor in chief Floyd Touhy. Cubiak didn't owe anything to Touhy but he didn't like him either.

The weekly newspaper was scheduled to come out the next morning. With the Fourth of July Festival starting in nine days, Cubiak could imagine the discussion that had taken place between the two men. Touhy would suggest that the unfortunate doings at Falcon Tower could not be ignored in the name of journalistic integrity, and Beck would concur, while insisting that, for the sake of the county's reputation, the accident be mentioned in the context of the park's long safety record. Both men would agree to focus the banner headline on the upcoming festival. If Cubiak were a betting man and he had anyone to bet against, he'd lay a wager on it.

The prospect of the festival, with thousands of happy tourists invading the peninsula, depressed Cubiak. He doubted if there were some corner of the park where he could hide from the cheerful families and manic joie de vivre. Maybe the rain would continue and no one would come.

BUOYED BY THE THOUGHT, Cubiak crossed the old iron bridge to the west side of the bay. There were a couple of upscale condo developments along the harbor but few tourist shops. The west side traditionally represented the nuts and bolts of Sturgeon Bay: the county co-op, two dry cleaners, a hardware store, and businesses that sold appliances and paint. Bathard's office was tucked between an electrical repair shop and a pizzeria and marked by a simple bronze sign. Cubiak followed a narrow hallway, redolent with garlic and oregano to a small waiting room outfitted with several spindly zebra plants, a bamboo magazine rack and four wooden chairs. Opposite the chairs was a pale blue door with another discreet sign. On one side, the world of life; on the other, the universe of things dead and dying. Reluctant to cross the line, Cubiak knocked softly, as if hoping not to be heard.

"It's open. Enter, please." The coroner's quiet formality drew the park ranger across the threshold and into a tiny closet of a room. Cubiak hadn't anticipated such economy of space. Still the compact office was neat and precise and carried a subtle sense of authority that was reinforced by the half dozen diplomas and certificates hung on the walls.

"I don't see why you need me here," Cubiak said, sounding harsher than he wanted.

Bathard looked up from his reading. "I don't, yet.

However, Wisby died in the park, and Halverson may have questions I can't answer. I requested that someone from the staff be present. Don't blame me that Otto nominated you."

The coroner pointed to a chair, one of two on the front side of the desk. Cubiak shook his head.

"Suit yourself," Bathard said, studying a rack of pipes on his desk. He chose one with a square bowl and slender cherry stem.

Moments later, Halverson sputtered in, not bothering to knock. He glared at Cubiak and then he plopped into a chair, self-consciously shifting his considerable weight.

"You got my email?" Cubiak said.

"Yeah, I got it."

Cubiak told Bathard about the park records. "Wisby may have known people on the peninsula. Rubbed someone the wrong way."

"Good point," the coroner said.

Halverson grimaced. "Doubt it. Tourists pretty much keep to themselves." The sheriff stifled a yawn. He'd been up half the night playing poker with his deputies, he said, as he pulled a slim pen and small, worn notebook from his breast pocket.

"May as well get right to it," he went on, simultaneously popping the cap on the pen and flipping open the pad. "Suicide?" he ventured.

"Broken neck," the coroner said.

"Yeah, but suicide, right?" Halverson's pen was poised above the blank page.

Bathard straightened his shoulders and scrutinized his visitor. "That's for the inquest to decide." The coroner tried to keep the annoyance from his voice. "At this point, I can tell you the young man is dead and give you a fairly accurate estimate of the time of his demise. I can tell you the cause of death, but I cannot presume to guess at what precipitated the unhappy event."

"What are ya going to put on the death certificate?"

"Intercerebral hemorrhage. Large subgaleal hemorrhage. Multiple comminuted fractures of the skull. Multiple contusions of the brain and lungs. Fractures of the left humerus, left iliac bone, left kidney, and ribs. Bilateral hemothorax. Hemopcritoneum."

Halverson blinked hard. "Right." His hand floated uncertainly above the notebook, and then he abruptly shoved paper and pen into his pocket and pushed up, snagging his cuff on the arm of the chair. Tipped off balance, the sheriff grabbed the edge of the desk and righted himself. Red-faced, Halverson glanced from Bathard to Cubiak and then back to the coroner.

"How's Cornelia?" he said as he maneuvered toward the door.

"Doing well, thank you. And Frank?"

Halverson gripped the knob. "He's fine. Good. Under the circumstances." The answer was automatic, well practiced.

After the sheriff's footsteps faded and the outside door banged, Bathard spoke quietly. "Cornelia, my wife, is currently undergoing treatment for uterine cancer. Frank, Halverson's father, has been paralyzed for nearly thirty years. For the past decade, he has resided in a convalescent home on the other side of Fish Creek." The coroner waited a discreet interval. "Neither of them is fine."

RETRACING HIS PATH over the bridge, Cubiak felt calm for the first time that day. He'd made sure the sheriff knew Wisby's history of visits to Door County, as far as park records went. Now it was up to Halverson. What the sheriff did with the information was none of the ranger's business.

The road north was flat and straight. Taking advantage of the light traffic, Cubiak accelerated along the high Niagara bluff toward Fish Creek. Inside the village limits, the highway hooked left and plunged precipitously off the edge of the plateau, curving down into the bayside community. If pushed, Cubiak would have to admit that there were a couple of things about Door County that he enjoyed and driving into Fish Creek from the south was one. Barreling into town between the sheer rock wall on one side and the sea of treetops on the other, there was no room for error and barely time to catch a breath before the pavement leveled off and cut a ninety-degree angle to the right onto the main drag. Miss the turn, and it was a short hop into the water. Every time Cubiak flew down the incline, he imagined a winter storm and what it would be like to be the first kid sledding down the slope, the one carving fresh tracks in the snow.

Fish Creek stretched along the bottom of a wide, boxy bay in such a way that little in the pencil-thin town was more than two blocks from the water. At the southern end, the cluster of picturesque historic buildings at Founders Square formed a bulbous tip, like an eraser, but the bulk of the businesses lined up in tidy symmetry along the main thoroughfare. A few of the shops weren't open yet for the season, and several motels and lodges posted vacancy signs out front. The street was void of people except for a woman loading a large bundle of wooden dowels into the trunk of a car outside Caruthers Hardware. At breakfast, Ruta had asked Cubiak to buy stamps and a loaf of limpa bread on his way back. There were no lines at the post office or the bakery, and Cubiak wrapped up the errands in minutes. The jeep was pointed in the direction of the park, but when he climbed back in he remembered the sheriff telling him to stay where he could be found. Fuck that, Cubiak thought, as he swung around and drove back to the old part of town.

At one time, the antique frame structures had housed Fish Creek's city hall, school, and early businesses, including one of the peninsula's oldest resorts. Now, gathered together under the overarching branches of ancient maples, they served the tourist trade, historical cover for restaurants, a T shirt emporium, confectionary shop, ice cream parlor, and stores that specialized in stained glass, wheat weaving, pottery, and watercolors. Dominating the historic center was Sarah Humble's, a grand three-story, white clapboard hotel that had originally been located on the other side of Green Bay in Marinette, some forty-eight miles away. In 1906, the owner of a fledgling Fish Creek health spa and resort bought the building and had it dismantled. The following winter, the pieces were loaded on massive wooden sleds that were pulled over the ice by three teams of specially shod horses.

Past the Sarah, Cubiak turned toward the water and the Little Snug Harbor Diner. He'd been to the restaurant half a dozen times and was accustomed to finding it empty save for the proprietor, Evangeline Davis, and the occasional customer. That morning two old men bent over a chessboard in the middle booth. Startled by the blast of bracing air that came in with Cubiak, they looked up in alarm and then settled back to their game.

Cubiak dropped onto the end stool. He was suddenly exhausted.

"Coffee?" Evangeline filled a white porcelain mug and set it before him. She was a grandmotherly type with coarse gray hair pulled into a neat bun. "I heard about that kid, in the park. So sad."

"Yes."

"Jumping, I mean. At least that's what I heard."

Evangeline sighed and moved cream and sugar within his reach. Then she crossed to the booth and poured refills for the other two customers.

Cradling the mug, Cubiak swiveled toward the plate glass window. The cloud cover had thickened and sunk toward the horizon, creating a strange claustrophobic atmosphere in the great outdoors. In the squeezed light, the distant trees looked black, as if sketched in charcoal. A solitary fishing boat, scuffed and in need of paint, bobbled near the end of the pier. The only spot of color was Johnson's pale red pickup nestled in a small clearing at the southern edge of Peninsula State Park. The park superintendent was out there working alone, probably chilled to the bone. Cubiak felt a stab of conscience. Maybe he should go help. Or at least call. The ranger felt for his phone. He'd forgotten it. The hell with him, he thought. Every time Cubiak offered to do outdoor work, Johnson turned him down. Anything, it seemed, to establish distance between them. So here they were, one out in the cold, the other warm and comfortable. Not my problem, Cubiak thought and spun back toward the counter.

"I got pie. Cherry and blueberry." Evangeline made the announcement in a no-nonsense voice. "Which do you want?"

"I'm really not hungry," Cubiak said.

"Cherry or blueberry?" The proprietress waited.

"Cherry."

A piece of pie the size of Rhode Island appeared in front of the park ranger. He ate down to the crust. Still thinking about Johnson, he pivoted toward the bay again just as a wrinkled bulldog of a man tottered around the corner and planted himself in front of the restaurant window. A nubby wool watch cap was pulled down tight over his ears. Coal black eyes scowled from his leathery face. A stub of cigar was stuck between teeth that were startlingly white. The man grinned. Evangeline stepped up to the counter behind Cubiak and tittered softly.

"Ben Macklin," she said gaily and waved.

Macklin saluted sharply before continuing his un-steady march toward the dock. The old codger was clearly drunk.

Evangeline set a platter of cake doughnuts near Cu-biak. "There's a tough old bird for you," she said as she sifted powdered sugar over the breakfast treats. "Good ol' Benny. Love him or hate him."

Across the room, the chess players mumbled their assent.

"Know him?" she said to Cubiak.

"No."

Benny was born during the Armistice Day Blizzard of 1940, Evangeline explained, her voice thick with memory. The day he plopped into the world, three cargo ships went down in Lake Michigan and all the men on them drowned. "Benny was a strong baby, a wild young man, and ornery as a goat when he grew up. Did what he pleased, what he thought was right. Anyone else could go to the devil for all he cared."

A fisherman, he lived on Chambers Island. Never married. No family. Once when no airplane or helicopter could fly and no other boat would attempt the crossing because of a storm, Benny transported a desperately ill child to the mainland. Got her to the hospital in time to save her life and became a hero. To some, that is. Folks who took exception to his drinking or had been publicly lambasted by his quick, merciless tongue dismissed Benny's bravery as a fluke. It was all just as well with Macklin. He never cared much for a fuss. Then, as now, Evangeline said, he wanted to be left alone.

Reaching back to set down the still-hot mug, Cubiak watched Macklin. Is that how he was going to end up? A lonely drunk?

At the end of the dock, the fisherman scrambled onto his boat.

Cubiak squinted but the name was too faint to decipher. "What is it?" he said.

Evangeline cackled. "His true love, the *Betsy Ross*."

Cubiak was about to comment but something in Evangeline's tone stopped him. They continued to watch as Macklin bent down and picked up something off the floorboards. Whatever it was, he looked at it and tossed it to the deck.

Then he lit a match.

The explosion blew a crater into the water and rocked the diner. Under a cascade of splintering glass, Cubiak dove to the floor. He counted to ten out of military habit and then scrambled to his feet. "You okay?" he called to Evangeline, who was plastered ghostlike against the back wall. The chess players were drained of all color but still seated upright and unhurt.

Cubiak bolted out the door and raced toward the ugly orange ball of fire dancing on the water. Thick black smoke barreled upward from the flames, releasing the sharp smell of creosote into the air.

Evangeline stumbled behind the ranger. She ran awkwardly on thick legs and stiff ankles, her apron whipping hard around her solid hips. When she finally caught up with him, the boat was gone. Evangeline sobbed and swayed. Cubiak gripped her shoulder, and the two braced against each other as charred slivers of wood and scorched flesh rained down into the shallow harbor. Tsst...tsst...tsst. The hot scraps sizzled as they hit the cold water.

A small crowd quickly assembled on the dock. Les Caruthers looking shell shocked. The woman with the dowels in her trunk, somber and unreadable. The clerk from the front lobby of Sarah Humble's, her black mascara mixed with tears against paper-white skin. The men from the diner, shivering inside matching red-and-black checked mackinaws.

Amid the stunned onlookers, Cubiak remained a man apart. Though he recognized and understood their pain, he felt unable to share in it, not because he was insensitive by nature—far from it—but because unrelenting grief had drained him of empathy and rendered him numb to any sorrow but his own.

Seagulls wheeled overhead, gliding through the spreading plume of smoke like greedy water vultures drawn to the carnage.

Cubiak squeezed Evangeline's shoulder and then let go and hurried back to the café. The most he could do to help was step inside and call the sheriff.

NIGHTFALL BROUGHT A hard rain. The downpour pummeled the tall pines and stately maples and oaks that

filled Peninsula State Park and the vast tracts of pastureland and forest that gave the peninsula its richness
of color and sweet-scented air. In the carefully tended
gardens of the year-round residents, the deluge destroyed
roses, late-blooming lilacs, and the tulips that had stub-
bornly refused to die, strewing the ground with their
dislodged petals. On the county's western rim, angry
rivulets swelled the creeks that fed Green Bay, while on
the east side, the runoff cut miniature canyons into the
soft sand along the Lake Michigan shore.

At Pechta's Tap in Fish Creek, Cubiak slumped on a
stool and nursed a beer, waiting for a break in the storm.

The rain drummed the metal canopy over the entrance, but the only noise Cubiak heard was the loud
boom of Ben Macklin's boat exploding. Two days. Two
deaths. It almost seemed as if there was a jinx on the
peninsula. Was it him, dragging bad karma?

Cubiak drained his glass and studied the drawing of
Door County tacked to the facing wall. Were the deaths
linked? Larry Wisby had died on the north edge of Peninsula Park, Macklin little more than a day later and
some three miles away near the park's southern bound-
ary. To get from Ephraim to Chambers Island where he
had lived, Macklin would have to cut through Falcon
Harbor along the ridge where the tower stood. What if
the old fisherman had been on the water the morning
Wisby died, motoring from home to town or vice versa?
Would he have seen anything other than trees if he'd
looked up toward the tower?

From the service side of the bar, Amelia Pechta ran a
tattered rag around Cubiak's empty glass and followed
his gaze to the map. "Lots of water out there and Benny

knew it all. He could get around these parts with his eyelids taped shut," she said.

"You know where he usually went?"

"Benny? Benny went wherever there was fish, women, or whiskey!" Amelia poured two shots and slid one across the bar, the wood worn smooth from use, toward her solitary customer, indicating that while Cubiak might still be considered a newcomer on most of the peninsula, at the bar he qualified as a regular. "Or maybe it was fish, whiskey, or women." She raised her glass. "Skoal," she said, and they tossed the drinks down together.

"He deserved better." Amelia slipped her glass under the bar and took up the rag again. Shuffling away, she continued talking over her shoulder. "The place'll fill soon. People'll come for Benny." She made a sound like a whimper. "They used to come for fun. On Sundays, there was fried chicken and potato salad, sometimes a game of bingo. We had dancing, too, once a month. My cousin played waltzes and polkas on an accordion. Ancient history."

Amelia floated back toward Cubiak. She was bent and wrinkled, her skin sallow in the pale yellow-green light from the fluorescent ceiling fixtures. Whether from habit or the need for more conversation, she drew his attention to the massive gray-black fish that hung on the wall behind her. "A muskie," she said by way of explanation. "My father caught it. Ugly son of a bitch."

"Your father? Or the fish?"

Amelia chortled and then she turned and pointed to a torn, black-and-white snapshot stuck along the bottom edge of the cracked mirror. "There's Benny's boat, the *Betsy Ross*." Cubiak guessed that the picture was another bit of ancient history. The young man Benny wasn't in the photo, but the *Ross* was as sleek and lovely as a fishing trawler could be. Taped alongside the picture were bedraggled snapshots of other boats and of fishermen brandishing strings of bass and perch, their happy faces out of context in the dreary pub.

As the proprietress limped away again, the front door banged open. Evelyn Bathard walked in, followed closely by a tall, elegant woman whom Cubiak recognized as the lone person he'd seen that morning by the hardware store and again at the bay following the explosion.

"Dave Cubiak, new assistant park superintendent. Ruby Schumacher, a longtime friend," Bathard said, introducing them. Shaking hands, Cubiak sensed an air of that intangible otherness that comes from money and breeding.

In short order, Pechta's was packed, just as Amelia had predicted. Otto Johnson joined Bathard and Ruby at a back table, and Cubiak recognized a few of the others as well. Les Caruthers. Martha Smithson, owner of the Ephraim Bakery. Floyd Touhy. Evangeline Davis. One of the chess players from the diner. As if by some unseen accord, the more genteel folks occupied the tables or stood in awkward clusters along the windows and billiard area. Around the bar, a different sort had gathered, somber men with leathery faces and thick, rough hands, all of them in heavy work clothes. Fishermen, Cubiak assumed.

"I don't see Beck," he said.

"And you won't neither. Bastard's too good for the likes of Benny."

"I didn't know Macklin," Cubiak said and started to stand.

"Don't matter. Here, help me with these."

She handed him a fresh bottle of cognac and two of cold cherry wine. While he opened the bottles, she loaded a tray with shot glasses. Then the bottles and tray were circulated around the room. Cubiak watched the ritual unfold. One by one, every person in the room poured a drink and passed the rest on. While this was happening, Amelia pulled an old wooden stool from behind the bar.

Like Moses parting the Red Sea, she pushed through the crowd, dragging the stool behind. At her approach, people fell back on either side. Someone turned off the jukebox and the crowd slowly quieted. When Amelia reached the far wall, she tipped the stool forward against a large patch of chipped paint and then stepped away.

A man at the end of the bar slid off his perch. "To Benny," he called out gruffly and raised his drink toward the forlorn chair. The others lifted their glasses. "To Benny," they chimed in tribute to the dead man.

In the ensuing silence, Les Caruthers cleared his throat. "I hear there'll be no official investigation," he announced to no one in particular. "Benny was drunk at the time. It was an accident."

Nearby, Martha Smithson gestured carelessly with her right hand. "These things come in threes," she shrilled ominously, splashing wine on the floor.

At their table, Evelyn Bathard, Ruby Schumacher, and Otto Johnson refilled their glasses from their own bottle of cognac, Macklin's favorite brand. Ruby looked from one man to the other. "To Benny," she said firmly.

They nodded and drank.

"To life," Bathard whispered. Then, white faced, he turned to Ruby. "There wasn't enough left for a post mortem."

In the back room, Buddy Entwhistle sprawled on a narrow, worn cot. He was unshaven and slovenly. Entwhistle had started drinking heavily two days prior, and by the time he had hooked up with Macklin late that morning, he was barely cogent. Listening to Benny go on about what he'd seen Sunday morning at Falcon Tower, he took in a staggering amount of beer and then passed out. Unaware of his friend's tragic demise, Entwhistle slept soundly, a crooked grin etched on his dissipated face.

# THREE

---

*Tuesday*

IN THE MULTIETHNIC European neighborhood where Cubiak grew up, death was a powerful magnet. When someone reached the end, both close friends and casual acquaintances endured the wake as a show of respect. From the receiving line, mourners moved to the lounge for a roast beef sandwich or a slice of homemade cake and then to a private back room for a shot and a beer if they were so inclined, and most were. But generally only family, intimates, and the usual cadre of professional mourners—people in need of either the company or the free lunch—participated in the funeral.

By coincidence, Cubiak had witnessed Ben Macklin's death and been a party to the unofficial wake. He had no intention of attending the funeral, but Ruta had baked a chocolate pound cake for the postservice coffee and asked him to drop it off at the Holy Light Moravian Church in Ephraim. Cubiak reluctantly agreed, intending to arrive after the ceremony was underway. It was his bad luck that a quartet of disapproving parishioners had detained the pastor, the Reverend Waldo Thorenson, in the small yard between the parsonage and the church, thus delaying the start of the service.

As Cubiak approached, the women aired their grievances. "Benjamin Macklin was not a man of God. He doesn't deserve church burial," they insisted all of a voice.

"What will people think?" trumpeted one, the obvious ringleader, whom he would later learn was Anne Cooper.

"They will think we are good Christians," Thorenson replied evenly.

The women fell into a shocked silence, though Miss Cooper was quick to recover. "You're an avowed abstainer. How can you eulogize a confirmed drunk?" she said, tossing down the gauntlet.

"Why don't you come in and see?" Thorenson said.

The invitation sent the women off in a collective huff but piqued Cubiak's curiosity. After depositing the cake on a table brimming with baked goods in the basement hall, he slipped upstairs to the rear vestibule.

The little church was full. The fishing communities from the peninsula and surrounding areas filled the fifteen pews on one side. Ruby Schumacher, Evelyn Bathard, Martha Smithson, Otto Johnson, and Leo Halverson sat opposite with the townies, old friends, and neighbors, people whose lives had been touched by this one man.

Thorenson was brief. He spoke about goodness and beauty and Door County. "Natural beauty is a reflection of God. It is our duty to respect and preserve the world which we inhabit. Doing so, we honor our Creator and come close to continuing his work upon earth. Our world is a small peninsula and we, each of us, must act as its caretaker. For all his faults, Ben Macklin knew this."

THE INQUESTS FOR Lawrence Wisby and Benjamin Macklin were held later that afternoon. Coroner Bathard had

wanted to set a separate date for reviewing the circumstances surrounding Macklin's death, but Halverson and
Beck had prevailed. "No use draggin' this stuff out, 'specially with the festival coming 'n' all. Just puts everyone
in a bad way," the sheriff said.

The Falcon Tower incident was first on the docket.
Bathard reported that Wisby had expired at least one
hour before his body was discovered. He also read a
statement from the victim's doctor stating that the young
man suffered from vertigo. Given the diagnosis and lacking any witnesses to the event, the coroner ruled the
death accidental.

From a corner spot near the rear of the small assem-
blage, Cubiak watched the deceased's parents, who were
seated at the far end of the second row. The Wisbys were
a diminutive pair, matched pillars of sorrow bundled in
drab, charcoal-gray trench coats. They looked sickly,
with their sallow complexions and their rheumy eyes that
flickered behind the thick lenses of gold, wire-rimmed
glasses each time they turned to confer with or console
each other. As the coroner described their son's injuries they clutched each other's hands and looked down.
Mrs. Wisby's thin shoulders quivered in time with her
soft sobs. The room grew even more still until the only
sounds were the gentle cadence of Bathard's voice and
the weeping of the mournful mother. Cubiak sensed the
rising tide of compassion among those in attendance
but he felt no sympathy for the two. If anything, he was
heartened by their emotional torment. Now they know
what it's like, what it will always be like, he thought.

When the proceedings ended, he left the hearing room
and took up a position near the exterior exit. He didn't
intend to confront the Wisbys but he wanted them to see

him. They were among the final few to leave and approached with hands clutched and eyes averted. At the last moment, the husband glanced up and saw Cubiak. The man's momentary confusion turned to shock. As the jolt of anguished recognition flowed from him to his wife, she looked up. All color drained from her face and then unexpectedly she opened her mouth as if to speak. Cubiak spun away and went out into the rising wind. He would not give her the satisfaction.

Thirty minutes later, the parties reassembled for the second hearing. Fortified with vodka, Cubiak returned. Through a haze of alcohol and shame, he heard Halverson report that on the day Macklin died, he had arrived in Fish Creek directly from Sturgeon Bay. His movements on the previous day were not mentioned, and Cubiak assumed that they had been traced and dismissed as irrelevant. As Les Caruthers had predicted, Macklin's death was attributed to an accident, an undetected leak in one of the boat's two gas tanks. Case closed.

BY EARLY EVENING, with the unpleasant events of the day wrapped up, the county once again turned its attention to the important business of summer tourism. In the first floor foyer of Jensen Station, Cubiak stood inspection under the bright glow of a small but freshly polished chandelier as Ruta plucked a piece of lint from the sleeve of his charcoal corduroy sports coat.

"You look good," she said, giving a final tug to his lapel. "You have good time."

Cubiak glimpsed himself in the hall mirror. He didn't look good. His skin was pallid. He needed a haircut. His jacket pulled across the shoulders. His twill pants had long since lost their crease; his black turtleneck was pilled and limp from numerous launderings. But he didn't care; he intended to keep drinking for the next several hours but not to enjoy himself.

That morning Johnson had tossed an invitation on his desk and appointed him the park's official representative to the evening's festivities at Beck's house. "Command performance. Someone has to go. You have the honors," the superintendent said. The announcement was not subtle. The party was Beck's annual fete for local merchants and county officials. A rah-rah, get-the-juices-flowing party before the big Fourth of July celebration that kicked off the official summer season on the "Cape Cod of the Midwest."

Like its East Coast big sister, Door County courted tourists. In case anyone forgot, Beck spelled it out: Some two million visitors a year. More than 60 percent of the peninsula's economy dependent on the summer trade. A bad season, a bad year all around. More people on welfare during the winter. Fewer taxes and user fees for state and local agencies.

Two tragic deaths in one week weren't going to derail the resort area's summer plans. Would anyone at the party mention Wisby or Macklin? Cubiak doubted it.

The ranger squinted at the jeep's windshield. Under heavy cloud cover, the premature twilight made it hard to distinguish landmarks along the road. Waning night vision, his ophthalmologist had called it. Another sign he was slipping too quickly through midlife. Cubiak supposed he should feel some angst. But there was none, just a vague sense that nothing mattered much except the next drink.

Nearing Sturgeon Bay, he nearly missed the turnoff to Bay Shore Drive, the gently curving road that ran along the well-manicured, waterfront estates of Door County's prominent families.

Cubiak pulled up behind a row of cars, as a sporty red convertible swung out of a nearby yard. The car screeched to a stop on the opposite shoulder.

"Hey!" It was Barry Beck, the teenage son of Door County's leading industrialist. "Do I get the job?"

"Yeah." The position was part-time and minimum wage, an aide-de-camp at the Nature Center during the two busiest summer months. Cubiak suspected there were kids in the area who needed the job, but taking Barry on hadn't been his decision. Politics being what they were, the park's oversight committee had given a thumbs-up to the boy's application.

"Cool. Enjoy the party," Barry said, waving with youthful enthusiasm as he sped away.

On foot, Cubiak followed a wide driveway to Beck's mansion. The house was three stories of gray granite punctuated with oversize-windows and topped with a slate roof. A dark lace ruffle of neatly trimmed hedges hugged the perimeter, a quiet understatement of the language of power and money spoken within these walls. It was the kind of place where Cubiak's mother would have worked had she not cleaned hotel rooms. He'd been in places like this in Chicago, houses where the front hall was larger than most kitchens on the side of tracks where he'd grown up. In one case, the splendid surroundings hadn't done anything for the owner, who had been found lying next to an in-ground swimming pool with a bullet hole in his chest, as lifeless as the terra cotta tiles beneath him.

Standing outside Beck's front door, Cubiak heard a dim murmur of voices, accented by an occasional burst of laughter. He put on his best blank face and pressed the buzzer.

The door opened to a rush of noise and light and the impressive figure of a young female Viking. Cubiak blinked. The apparition transformed into a tall, blond teenage girl flashing a bright, practiced smile.

"Hi. Good evening." The salutation was crisp, well rehearsed.

Cubiak pulled a crumpled invitation from his right pocket.

"Oh, that's not really necessary." A giggle ruffled the girl's routine. Her white jumpsuit shimmered. Around her neck, a string of glass cherries sparkled. When she turned to show him the way, Cubiak noticed the cherry tree branch silk-screened across the back of her outfit. "Like it? They're ordered special for the greeters. We act as the official hospitality staff for all the different summer events on the peninsula. Mr. Beck's prefest party is always the first job we work and the first time we get to wear our new outfits." Her exuberance bounced the words toward Cubiak.

"You know everyone?" she said, gesturing toward the living room, a sprawling arena decorated with white gardenias and buzzing with local civic and business honchos.

Cubiak didn't recognize a soul. "Sure."

"Great. Otherwise my instructions are to introduce you around. Mr. Beck likes people to mingle." The greeter gave him another vacuous grin and then stepped aside to let him pass.

Thirsty, Cubiak approached the nearest bar and asked for a beer.

"No beer." A muscled young man in white pants and

starched, nautical shirt—no cherries—handed him a flute of champagne.

The glass was chilled, the bubbles cold. Cubiak drank it in one gulp. He helped himself to another and slowly wove his way around the periphery of the room. The west wall was plate glass; the others were hung with soft abstract paintings. A pair of low-slung white leather couches faced each other in front of an enormous field-stone fireplace. Scattered elsewhere were several group-ings of comfortable low chairs in rich gray-green. Tables were mahogany. Rugs thick, probably hand-knotted Ori-entals. Cubiak scanned the crowd for Bathard.

"Glad you made it." Out of nowhere, Beck appeared at Cubiak's side. The scion of Door County was deeply tanned and nautically dressed. He studied the ranger's appearance critically. "That the best you can do?"

Cubiak shrugged.

Beck gripped the ranger's elbow. "These are the mov-ers and shakers, the people who count," he said, as he turned his guest around the room. "My job is to make Door County prosper and to do that I have to keep them happy. Your job is to help me do mine well." He released his hold. "Got it?"

"My job's at the park," Cubiak said and finished off his third glass of champagne.

"Precisely." Beck beamed. "The park is pivotal."

"Whatever," Cubiak said.

Beck looked at him and laughed. "Chitchat's not your forte, is it?"

"Nope."

From across the room, someone important raised a hand and caught the host's attention. Beck saluted over the crowd. "Buy yourself some new clothes," he said as he moved away.

Cubiak grunted and downed more champagne. Little more than supercharged soda water as far as he was concerned. A drink for women, effete socialites, and wedding toasts. He checked his watch and felt a familiar stab of anguish. The watch had been a gift from his wife on their first Christmas together. He tugged his cuff down. Only fifteen minutes since he'd arrived. He figured another fifteen and he could leave. Maybe stop on the way back and have a real drink.

"Eloise Beck. We haven't met."

A petite, dark-haired woman offered her hand to Cubiak. She wore a slim-fitting silver cocktail dress and was extremely well put together, almost artfully enough to hide the slight puffiness in her cheeks and the fine network of lines that radiated from the corners of her mouth.

"Oh," she said when she heard his name. "Beck's boy."

He colored slightly, and she giggled and moved closer. "Don't worry. Everyone here is a Beck's boy, and besides I'm a little looped."

Eloise tittered again and slipped away.

A waiter materialized, offering a tray laden with food. Cubiak sampled the smoked salmon and cherry canapés and looked out at Green Bay and the last shreds of daylight. An impressive expanse of manicured lawn separated the house from the water. On the right, a white stone walkway led to a dock outlined with tiny white lights. A luxury cabin cruiser, a boat large enough to qualify as a yacht, was tied up alongside, bobbling gently with the chop.

Cubiak guzzled several more glasses of champagne. Anesthetized and with a full glass in hand, he zigzagged between the guests and down a rear hall into a contemporary family room, more vaulted space tastefully grafted onto the house. Three people he didn't recognize huddled inside the doorway and laughed at a private joke.

He eased past them. The noise level dropped dramatically, and Cubiak sank into a low small couch, feeling surprisingly calm. Whether it was the effect of the alcohol or simple exhaustion he didn't know. Beyond Beck's twinkling dock, an ore boat similarly ablaze with lights and riding high in the water slid silently toward the harbor at Sturgeon Bay. Cubiak decided he would leave when the boat reached port.

"May I join you?"

Startled, Cubiak looked up. The ore boat had vanished.

A woman perched on the arm of a chair studied him over the rim of her glass. She was startlingly good looking, long and lanky, dressed completely in black, with tangerine hair.

Despite himself, Cubiak sat up straight.

"Cate Wagner," she said. "Ruby Schumacher's niece. I noticed you this morning at Benny's funeral, figured you must be new. I served coffee after the service, but I don't think you came down." She looked past him and blinked hard several times before going on. "Poor Benny. He loved that old boat. I can't believe he'd do something stupid like that. Must've been losing it."

"He was pretty drunk."

Cate grinned. "His natural state. You know, he used to take me out fishing when I was a kid. Made me bait my own hook. 'Just 'cause you're a girl, don't mean nothing,'" she said, mimicking a husky voice. "Guess I can't begrudge him the pecan rolls."

"Pecan rolls?"

"Sunday special at the Ephraim Bakery. You are new, aren't you?" Cate said. "Every Sunday morning, Martha Smithson makes pecan rolls that are very popular with the locals. This past Sunday, Ruby and I stopped in around ten, hoping to snag a dozen, but they were already gone. Martha said Benny had been in bright and early and bought a sack full."

Cate tilted toward him. She wore perfume and had the same sculpted cheekbones and thick, straight brows as her aunt. "Wouldn't happen to have a cigarette would you... ?"

"Dave Cubiak. I quit."

"Right." Cate unwound herself from the chair. "Give me a sec," she said.

As Cubiak watched, she strode up to a trio of men who were pretending they hadn't noticed her. When she returned, two cigarettes lay across the palm of her hand. She passed one to him, cutting short his protest. "Look at your fingers, for god's sake."

Silent, he struck a match for them to share.

Cate inhaled deeply. "Mister Cubiak. You are a... painter? No, hands too unsullied, save for the nicotine. Woodcarver? Owner of a gift shoppe?" She pronounced the final *e*.

"Park Service," he said stiffly.

"Oh. You work for Johnson then." Cate searched the bumpy, thick carpet at the base of the chair until she found a place to put her empty glass. "Strange man.

You know he used to date Beck's sister Claire. Hard to imagine, the park super with a sweetheart."

"Love is strange."

Cate laughed. She was nonchalant and at ease in the room. It struck Cubiak that she fit in about as well as he did not. "Greeters." She indicated one of the young girls in white. "It's a fun job when you're sixteen."

Right, Cubiak thought. The summer he was sixteen, he had worked in a wet-end extrusion factory on South Kedzie. One morning, a fat-faced foreman with a cheap toupee made him stick his right hand through the intake of a plugged dryer. Blood and worse dripped out as Cubiak tugged at a tangled blob of sausage casings. When he finally pulled his arm free, he noticed that the hair had been burned off up to the elbow. He quit on the spot.

"You always this glum?"

"You always this chipper?" Her question had been posed lightly. His, delivered like a sledge hammer.

"Well, touché!" Cate said.

She ignored him for several minutes. Then she snatched two flutes of champagne from a passing tray. "Maybe this will mellow you out," she said, handing one to Cubiak. "Ruby was supposed to meet me here. Guess she got tied up. You know her?"

"Not really. Met once."

"Bit of a character. Local treasure. Dedicated environmentalist. Nationally known fabric artist. Like a second mother to me. You don't mind my chatting, do you? It's just, you're going to live here you may as well know some of the folklore."

When she was eleven, Cate told him, she and Ruby had hiked up the bay side from Ephraim to the tip of the peninsula. Door County was different then. Just a few condos. Mostly cottages and houses and a couple rustic resorts dotting the waterfront.

"Ruby knew all the Indian tricks. How to walk without making a sound or leaving a trail, but I couldn't do it, not as well as she did. I'd step on twigs and muss up the trail."

After three days of walking, they camped on a high wooded bluff overlooking Porte des Morts, the deep channel where the waters from the bay and the lake converged.

"Death's Door is a treacherous stretch of water," she said. Hundreds of ships had gone down there. Nobody knew how many people have drowned. Probably thousands.

"Legend has it that the currents trap the ghosts of the dead, and on moonless nights, you can hear their cries." She looked past him again. "You believe in ghosts?"

He fidgeted. "No."

But didn't he? Lying in bed one night a week after the accident, he'd sensed Lauren behind him in the dark and understood that her presence was a gift and that turning around, insisting on seeing her, was blasphemous. He'd willed himself still and waited. After a bit, he'd felt her breath warm his neck. She'd come to say goodbye.

Cate swallowed a yawn. It was late, and she was tired. Could she impose on him for a ride back to her aunt's house? "It's a bit of a haul, I'm afraid."

Cubiak was glad for an excuse to leave.

They were silent on the way to the jeep and then north through Egg Harbor, Fish Creek, Ephraim, and beyond. As he drove, Cubiak relaxed into the engine's steady hum and the insignificance that the immense darkness conferred upon them. At Gills Rock, a tiny fishing village near the tip of the peninsula, the road narrowed and curved sharply to the right. Thick pines crowded on either side. A crescent moon hung above the tree line, creating a patchwork of shadows on the undulating roadway. Inhaling the cool night air, the ranger felt settled and calm.

"So, you married or what?"

Cubiak started. His passenger had been quiet so long he thought she was asleep. In the dappled dark, the familiar agitation returned and he shook his head.

"No? Divorced? Single?"

"Widowed." The word caught in his throat.

"Oh. Sorry." There was an awkward pause. "I'm divorced, myself. Six months," she said at last. Cate pointed in the dark. "Left at the next driveway."

Cubiak careened between the trunks of two large trees and coasted into a wide clearing where a sprawling one-story ranch and several outbuildings hunkered in the sparse moonlight. The aroma of magnolias hung over the yard, and in the distance a dog yelped. He rolled to a stop where an old-fashioned fixture threw a tight splotch of light on the rear steps.

"Sucks, don't it," Cate said.

"What?"

"Life." She popped the door and slipped out. "Maybe we can get together sometime, for coffee or something, and, you know, talk." She ducked down toward him, one hand on the back of the seat, waiting for a reply. When none came, she pulled herself straight. "Or not," she said and banged the door. "Bastard."

# FOUR

CUBIAK DROVE WITH the front windows down, hoping the cool night air would keep him alert and blow away the remnants of Cate's perfume. He was glad he'd annoyed her. He didn't want to think of her because she made him think of Lauren, and he missed his wife to the point of pain.

More sober than drunk, he rolled into the park entrance. It was well past midnight and a wall of clouds had blotted out the moon. He stopped alongside the maintenance shed and fished a pack of cigarettes from his pocket. He was halfway to the station door when a vehicle peeled off the road and tore up the drive, momentarily blinding him with its headlights before the yard went black once more.

"Who's there?" Cubiak called out.

A door slammed.

"Get out of the truck." Otto Johnson's brusque voice cut through the dark.

Cubiak flipped a switch on the yard pole and a cone of light fell over the gravel lot. From the shadows, the park superintendent pulled Barry Beck from the passenger seat of the pickup and dragged him center stage. The boy was pasty white and wobbly. A thick trail of something that looked like vomit ran down his shirt. His hands were streaked with something that looked like blood.

"I found him like this near Turtle Bay. I think he's in shock," Johnson said.

Barry stank of piss and fear. The two men maneuvered the boy through the back door, into the kitchen, and onto a chair.

Cubiak handed him a glass of water. "What happened?" he said.

Barry choked on the water and began to cough and cry at the same time.

Cubiak waited for him to recover. "Were you alone?" he said finally.

The boy's eyes glazed over.

"You were with a girl?"

Barry nodded. His breathing was rapid and shallow.

"What were you doing, messing around?"

Barry nodded again. "Yeah."

The story came out in spurts. He'd taken a girl named Alice to the hilltop clearing behind Turtle Bay Campground. After about an hour or so, they ran out of beer. Alice said she was cold so Barry gave her his jacket and the flashlight and left to get another six-pack from the car. Coming back he got lost, and when he finally located the spot where they'd been hanging out, he found her. He looked at them in panic as if they should know the rest without his having to spell out the details.

"What happened?" Johnson shouted. He tried to shake the boy but Barry swatted at his hand.

"Is she okay? Is Alice all right?" Cubiak said quietly, tamping down his own fear. What could harm someone in the woods? A hungry bear? Wolves?

Barry shuddered and doubled over. "She...she... ,"

the rest dissolved into sobs as he rocked back and forth, sputtering saliva at the floor.

Cubiak snatched a coat from the hall and dropped it over the boy's shoulders. "You better call Beck and Halverson," he told Johnson. "I'll go and check. Maybe she's hurt."

IN THE BLACKENED FOREST, Cubiak felt the same cold dread he'd experienced as a cop answering a call in the most violent urban neighborhood. No matter how much information the police had going into a situation, there was always the unknown factor: the door knob wired to a bomb, the guy at the bottom of the basement stairs waiting to slam a nail-studded board into the face of the first person down. Maybe Alice had passed out from drinking. Then how to explain the blood on Barry's hands? A nosebleed, animal bite?

Cubiak missed the campground cutoff and had to double back. On the second go-round, the headlights caught the marker. He parked at the bottom of the trail, flipped on the flashers as a signal for Halverson, and climbed up the path, spurred on by the nervous click-click of the emergency lights.

The sound ebbed away and a cobweb brushed Cubiak's face. A ridge of sweat rose on his spine.

The woods were familiar in the daylight. At night, they were changed, at once vibrant and soulless, alert and sleeping. Darkness reshaped the landscape until time and distance lost their meaning. He was a man accustomed to sodium-vapor streetlamps. In the dark forest, even with the flashlight, he felt powerless.

An owl hooted. Cubiak spun toward the sound. Behind and to his right, the wind whistled through the trees. He turned again and through a thicket of wild blackberry bushes spied a faint yellow glimmer.

As he pushed through the brush, he caught a whiff of wood smoke. It was cold in the woods, and he figured the two had disregarded park regulations and made a fire. Cubiak expected to find Alice curled up alongside it. But she wasn't anywhere near the mound of embers. She was sitting at the far side of the small clearing, braced against the trunk of a young white birch tree. A blue-and-yellow plaid blanket draped her head and torso. Her lap was heaped with empty beer cans and her bare legs extended straight out toward him. She was shoeless, and the soles of her feet glistened winter-white in the light from the lantern that lay near her thin canvas slip-ons. The forest was oddly quiet.

"Alice?"

There was no answer.

A sense of rage pulsed through Cubiak as he crossed the patch of trampled grass. Was this some kind of sick joke? Or a prank, an initiation into an adolescent club that Barry wanted to join?

Cubiak trained the flashlight down and lifted the blanket, scattering the empty cans. Alice was slumped forward. Her hands were clasped over her stomach, the long nails, one of them broken, were painted the same bright red as her shorts. Her face was hidden by her hair, and her neck obscured by the jacket's crumpled blood-soaked hood. Alice's skull had been neatly dissected, both the frontal and parietal bones split down the middle from front to back.

A BATTERY OF klieg lights ringed the crime scene, illuminating the individual pebbles and blades of grass and

keeping the spooky shadows at bay. Bathed in the unnatural glow, Bathard went about his methodical work.
In the surrounding darkness, three deputies searched the
underbrush for the murder weapon. Cubiak listened to
them call out to each other as they thrashed through the
undergrowth. He and Halverson stood on opposite sides
of the clearing, each man half in light and half in darkness, each lost in thought. Had Barry murdered the girl?
The sheriff had dared whisper the question earlier. "Oh,
Jesus, God, I hope not," he'd said, paling at the prospect.
Cubiak couldn't see it. The boy wanted to fuck Alice,
not kill her. Why was she attacked here? Why the park
again? Cubiak scrubbed his scalp, trying to blur the images of the dead girl. He needed a drink.

LATE IN THE MORNING, Beck phoned Jensen Station. Three
hours' sleep didn't go far, and Cubiak struggled to follow the man's compulsive patter. "Why are you telling
me this?" he said. Beck didn't reply, just kept on with
the story of how Halverson had questioned Barry for
an hour, with the family lawyer present, until a fuller
picture emerged of the previous evening's events. The
victim was Alice Jones, sixteen going on seventeen that
month, a local girl who'd just finished her junior year at
Door County High and was known largely for being a
regular at Kingo's Resort.

"Kingo's," Beck said, spitting out the word.

"Never heard of it."

"Count yourself lucky. Kingo's is a goddamn genuine biker bar on Kangaroo Lake."

Cubiak had heard of the lake, the peninsula's larg-
est inland body of water. Kingo's, according to Beck,
was a colossal thorn in his side and an affront to all that

Door County represented. Unfortunately for the Tourism Board, the resort was a legitimate business, handed down by a drunken father to a druggie son.

"Tourists don't generally frequent the joint but Petey Kingovich, the owner, is pretty lax about checking IDs, a policy that cultivates a certain clientele among the younger locals," Beck said.

"That why your son goes there?"

Beck swore. "Barry claims he'd only been to the bar the one time, the night he met Alice Jones. It wouldn't surprise me at all," Beck went on, "if Alice wasn't one of Petey's girls. He's known to like his ladies on the young side."

In fact, Beck allowed, he and Halverson figured that Barry had probably frequented the bar often enough to goad Petey into a jealous attack on Alice. The murder weapon had not been found in the woods. The sheriff was laying odds it might show up at Kingo's.

"Halverson's going there later to check things out. I want you with him," Beck said.

"Why? There's no reason I should go."

"She was killed in the park. That's reason enough," Beck said and slammed the receiver down. "Son of a bitch," he growled.

On the wall behind Beck's desk, four generations of family history were documented in an array of photos, certificates, and news clips. Beck knew each one by heart. Understood their progression, their testimony to the one-upmanship of the generations. "Son of a bitch," he said again.

THE SHERIFF'S ENTOURAGE picked up Cubiak at dusk. From the park the caravan sped east across the peninsula. The ranger rode in the rear of Halverson's jeep, which was driven by the First Deputy. Six more men followed in three additional vehicles, an excessive show of force in Cubiak's opinion, but he said nothing. This was the sheriff's call, not his.

As the convoy approached Kingo's, Halverson ordered the men to cut their lights and pull off the road. "You sure you don't want one of these?" he asked Cubiak, indicating the extra pistol tucked into his belt. "I could deputize you right here. Make it all legal like." Cubiak shook his head. He didn't want to be armed and didn't need Halverson's permission to carry a weapon.

"Whatever." The sheriff directed the officers to silence their phones and motioned for them to move around to the back of the tavern.

"The bastards are all here," Halverson said, peering through the supply room window into the saloon. "That's him." He pointed at a skinny, scar-faced man slouched against the bar. Lining the stools were Kingovich's cousin and three running buddies, all of them greasy and unsavory. Halverson didn't know their names. Behind them, a sixth man aimed the eight ball at the right side pocket of a pristine, tournament-sized pool table. He was short and squat and built like a wrestler. "Look at those scum," Halverson whispered. "Filthy, no good scum."

The sheriff was wired. He had been on the case since Johnson's call the previous night. Beck had given him twenty-four hours to find the killer, and he told Cubiak that he intended to get the job done on time. That morning Halverson's men had interviewed a half dozen people who had placed Alice Jones in or around Kingo's at 6 p.m. Tuesday, just hours before she was found murdered. The sheriff didn't need to know any more than that.

Leaving the other troopers to watch the bar, he led Cubiak and his First Deputy on a search of the remaining buildings. "We'll find something," he said.

In the bedroom of Petey's one-story frame house, the men discovered four small bags of cocaine and marijuana at the back of a sock drawer. The six cabins yielded only dust and stale air. The toolshed was empty except for a gas-powered lawn mower and a shelf lined with cardboard file boxes.

The sheriff was jogging toward the small boathouse when his deputy popped out of the garage. "Jumpin' jeepers Christ hey. Leo, over here," he called out cheerfully and then led them inside. In a dark corner, the deputy pointed to a stack of discarded tires and behind it a bloody axe propped against the wall.

Halverson and four of his men barged into Kingo's. Cubiak trailed behind. Gagging on air heavy with the odors of sour beer and something coming from a backed-up toilet, he stayed near the door, determined to remain an observer.

"For shit." At the bar, the cousin regarded the officers with their drawn weapons and raised his right hand in a five-finger salute. "For crying out fucking shit."

Petey Kingovich waved him quiet.

"Who's he?" Petey said, with a glance at Cubiak.

"None of your fucking business," the sheriff said.

The man at the pool table jeered as he flipped his cue and clutched it like a club, fat end up.

The deputy moved into his face. "You got two options, buddy," he said quietly. "Either you put that stick down or I'll ram it up your ass so hard you'll have a blue chalk mark on the inside of your fucking skull."

"Do it. Now," Petey said.

The stick thudded against the floor.

They were all high and too stupid to be dangerous, thought Cubiak. Except Petey. It showed in his eyes. He was too smart to do something dumb like kill Alice and leave the murder weapon lying around but borderline crazy enough to commit murder and assume he could get away with the crime.

Halverson signaled his men to spread out along the length of the room. While one of the detail droned the Miranda litany, Petey glanced at the roach in the ashtray. "That the problem, Sheriff?" Petey had both hands on the bar. He knew the routine well.

Halverson ignored him.

"For chrissake," the cousin bellowed.

"Shut up," Petey said. His eyes flicked to Cubiak then pinned on Halverson.

"There's more just like us waiting outside," the sheriff said quietly. "Only they got even bigger guns. So I suggest you come with us nice and easy. Just ease out from behind the bar nice and slow."

"Not till I know why. I gotta right to ask why."

"Why?" Halverson mocked him. "Maybe because you're the scum of the earth and we're having a litter drive. Murder, that's why."

The room hushed suddenly. A dark shadow played across Petey's face. "Whose?"

"Alice Jones."

"Alice! You ain't gonna pin that one on me." Petey spoke with casual disdain.

The sheriff opened his jacket and pointed to the

search warrant in the inside breast pocket. "We got a bloody axe in the trunk of my car that says we are," he said evenly.

The men at the bar looked at Petey. "Don't worry," he said.

Cubiak watched Halverson test the weight of the gun in his hand. The sheriff had seen the girl. Cubiak knew what he was thinking. Knew how much he wanted to blow the place apart. How he'd like it if Petey or one of the others made a quick move and he and his men could open up on them.

"Let's go." The sheriff waved Petey forward.

A heavy mist had risen from Kangaroo Lake and rolled out over the resort, obscuring trees and buildings alike. A mixed chorus of frogs and crickets sang in the soup, and then fell silent as the men filed past to the cruisers along the road. Cubiak shared the back seat with Petey.

"Got a cigarette?" the prisoner said.

"Nope."

Up front, Halverson was busy with self-congratulations. Cubiak knew the sheriff was waiting for acknowledgment and praise from him, the former big city cop, but he refused to play the hypocrite. To him, Petey's arrest wasn't noteworthy, merely convenient.

Cubiak lowered his window, hoping to catch strains of the animal concert. But he could hear nothing over the harsh screech of sirens wailing through the fog.

# FIVE

*Thursday*

ALICE JONES WAS buried quickly and with little fanfare. Funeral services were held in a modest, cement-block evangelical church, a few blocks from the shipyards. The walls and ceiling of the claustrophobic sanctuary were desperate for a fresh coat of paint. And despite the best efforts of two tall radiators that hissed quietly in the background, an aura of dampness and mildew permeated the air.

The prompt arrest of Petey Kingovich sent a tangible ripple of relief through Door County. People rationalized that Alice—cheap, tawdry Alice—had contributed to her own doom. They regretted that her death had been so gruesome but assured themselves that they—being so unlike her—were immune to such horror. Barely recovered from the deaths of Wisby and Macklin and now both wary of negative publicity and shamed by the brutal killing, the locals were eager to put this tragedy behind them.

Even the minister talked euphemistically of Alice's passing, as if her death had been little more than an unanticipated tumble through a doorway. The victim's beleaguered parents, faced with the daunting task of rearing five younger children, fumbled through the service dazed and resigned, uncomfortable in the new attire purchased for the day. Besides the siblings, who cried throughout the brief ceremony, there were few mourners, only a handful, scattered amidst the scratched wooden pews: several disheveled young men, in worn denim jackets, clustered together, sharing a mutual hangover; two old-biddy neighbors, smug and disapproving, whispered conspiratorially across from them. To one side, Alice's posse of girlfriends dabbed mascara-stained tissues at their tears, unaware that the outfits they wore, indeed their very best, were inappropriate funeral attire.

Eloise had come, too, in open defiance of her husband's wishes. Wrapped in a plain brown wool coat and with a beige scarf covering her hair, she'd braved Beck's wrath as well as the stiff northeast wind that lambasted the peninsula and piled tall gray clouds up against the horizon. Seated quietly to one side, she witnessed the suffering of this family of strangers, allowed their pain to supplement her own. Barry remained at home, forbidden by his father to attend the funeral. Beck had allowed his son to talk a second time with Halverson about the murder, again with the family lawyer present, and had kept the boy's name out of the paper.

Cubiak slouched in the rear of the bleak chapel. That morning Johnson had woken sick with flu, and the junior assistant had been delegated to attend the service. He agreed to go only as a show of respect because Alice had made her transition—another of the minister's euphemisms—in the park.

It was worse than Cubiak had expected. Alice's casket was white, like Alexis's. Unsettled by the sight of the coffin, he bore a look of such grim intensity that no one dared approach him. Afterward, as the other well-wishers followed the procession through the front door, Cubiak ducked out a side entrance.

He rushed full throttle toward the fresh liquor bottle in the back of his closet, but never made it past Pechta's. In true Pavlovian style, he swung into the driveway, only vaguely aware that the lot was empty and the window displays dark. His mouth burned with the remembered taste of vodka as he pushed the door in. The interior lights were off and he hesitated. Had Amelia forgotten to lock up the night before? He hadn't noticed her at the funeral but perhaps she'd sat on the far side and was among the mourners on the way to the cemetery. Cubiak turned to leave.

"Dave, that you? Come on in." Amelia beckoned from the shadows at the far end of the bar.

He moved toward her.

"Pull up a stool and join us," she added.

Too late, he realized Amelia was not alone.

"You two know each other?"

Cate Wagner glanced up. Her hair, pulled back severely off her face, had turned dark, black like her sweatshirt and pants. They acknowledged each other warily.

"You at Alice's service?" Amelia went on as she reached for an extra glass and poured three shots.

"Yeah."

"Well, at least they caught the bastard," she said, shoving one drink at Cubiak and another at Cate. "To Alice," she said, proffering a toast. "Poor kid." The whiskey went down warm and smooth. Amelia poured a second round, passing over her own glass, then pushed the bottle to Cubiak.

"Help yourselves. I'm going to lie down. Bum knee's killing me," she said and shuffled toward the back room.

Above the bar, a neon beer display sputtered on. Cubiak refilled his glass and offered the bottle to Cate.

"I'm okay," she said.

He tossed down his drink and started to get up.

"Wait, please," Cate said.

He hesitated and then eased onto the edge of the stool, poised for flight. Cate reached for his arm but stopped short and rested her fingers on the counter. "I want to apologize for the other night. I didn't mean anything by it, just trying to be friendly."

Cubiak tensed. He didn't want to have this conversation.

"You never mentioned you had a daughter."

Their eyes met in the cracked mirror. His were steel hard; hers soft with sympathy and something else Cubiak couldn't read. He looked away.

"Ruby told me. Last night."

Cubiak swallowed another shot. The story was getting around.

"You want to tell me about it?"

"No."

"I understand." Cate hunched over the bar, hugging herself. Cubiak was uncertain what to do.

After a moment, she looked up. "I miscarried. Twice," she said. Her stricken reflection stared back from the mirror. Cubiak didn't know what to say.

The first pregnancy ended before she had time to adjust to the idea of having a child, Cate told him. But the second time was different. She carried the baby for three months before things went wrong. "I was convinced I was going to have a baby girl. I had a name picked out and started a list of all the things we'd do together as she grew up."

Cubiak turned away. He didn't need to hear this.

Fetal development inexplicably ceased, Cate explained, and the baby died in the womb. "It changed who I am," she said.

"Yes," Cubiak said finally, unable to manage any more than a solitary word. He steadied himself against the bar. He knew the power of death. It had robbed him of his purpose in life and his passion for living.

"I named her Polly. My pretty Polly."

"Alexis," Cubiak said finally. "And Lauren. My wife." Having misinterpreted silence for loyalty, he had not spoken their names out loud since the funeral; in naming them, he realized how mistaken he'd been.

THEY SAT TOGETHER through the afternoon. Cubiak did most of the drinking and Cate most of the talking. The only links they shared were growing up as only children and in cities on the shore of Lake Michigan. Her childhood had been as plush and easy as his had been stingy and mean. She'd gone to Smith and lived in Cushing House, the oldest residency hall on the quad; he'd ridden the L to the University of Illinois Circle Campus just south of the Loop. She had a trust fund; he did not. Cubiak had known women like her and had found them to be shallow and callous, but Cate seemed kind and vulnerable, and he found himself drawn to her.

They were half through the bottle and three-quarters through a pack of cigarettes when Amelia reappeared with a tray of sandwiches and coffee. "Figured you could both use some of this about now," she said.

The sandwiches were ham and swiss on rye, heavy

on butter and mustard. The coffee was black and strong. "Not like at that café by the dock. You can always tell when it's tourist season. Evangeline starts watering down the coffee," Amelia said as she flipped on the bar lights.

A single, framed, black-and-white photo hung near the switch. She lifted it off the wall and set it on the counter. A small cadre of fiercely handsome young people dressed in traditional outdoor gear stared back at them.

"The Door County High School Survivalist Club." Amelia's voice swelled with pride. "Kids trained in hunting, trapping, all the tough skills. Not like kids today. Fat slobs, most of them." The club had had Jocko Connelly for an instructor, the best. Amelia jabbed a crooked finger at the imposing figure on the right.

"You know all these folks," she said to Cate. For Cubiak's benefit, she tapped her index finger across the glass. "Beck. Les Caruthers. Cate's uncle, Dutch Schumacher. Used to be sheriff. Handsome as the devil, ain't he? Otto Johnson. Frank Halverson, Leo's father." A shadow crossed the barkeeper's face. "Real shame, what happened to him." One girl stood amidst the boys. She was lithe and strong, with a halo of curls and a saucy, devil-may-care look on her face.

"Who's that?" Cubiak said.

Amelia smiled ruefully. "That's me," she said in a whisper.

Cate continued staring at the photo. "Dutch died a couple years ago. Ruby took it real hard. I…"

The front door banged open, shattering the afternoon's intimacy. As if guided by the narrow beam of afternoon sunshine that sliced through the dim interior,

Beck strode toward the trio. He was a noisy intruder, jangling his keys and slapping the leather soles of his shoes against the hardwood floor.

"Asshole," Amelia murmured, sweeping the photo off the bar.

"Ladies. Gentlemen," Beck said. Dressed in a navy wool blazer and charcoal pants, his pale blue shirt open at the collar, he looked like an upscale tourist who'd wandered off the beaten path.

Amelia dodged a peck on the cheek. Cate shuddered through a kiss and a quick hug. Cubiak ignored the outstretched hand.

Beck pretended not to notice and rested his elbow on the bar. "I've been looking all over for you. Got a minute?" he said.

Cubiak seemed to consider the question. Then he tipped his hand to his two companions, slid from the stool, and followed Beck out the door to the side porch where half a dozen mismatched chairs stood in a row along the outside wall. Beck choose the two sturdiest, twirled them to face each other, and sat. Cubiak claimed the other, determined to act sober.

"No time to waste on pleasantries," Beck said, leaning in confidentially. "The Conservation League is meeting tomorrow evening and Johnson's on tap to talk about the park. Probably up to his usual bag of tricks. I need to know what he has to say and what kind of reception he gets from those crazy tree huggers. I'd go myself but I have critical business elsewhere. Besides, those people don't like me much. On the other hand, you show up, and it's kind of like you're just doing your job."

Cubiak caught little more than half of the rapid-fire prattle.

Beck thrummed his manicured fingers on the arms of the chair. "You know, Halverson says he doesn't trust you because you have nothing to say. But I believe the old adage about still water running deep. The question is: what's down there?"

He paused, waiting for a response. Then he went on. "Okay, it doesn't matter. You don't want to talk to me, fine. Just so long as you listen. There are people up here who can't think beyond today. They have no vision. I'm not like that, and I'm sure you're not like that. Some of these people will be at the meeting. I need to keep tabs on them and what they're thinking. The festival is coming up fast and it's important it goes off without a hitch. It's always important, but this year more than usual. Make sure you understand that."

"Right."

Beck winked. "Good things are going to be happening and you could benefit," he said, as he stood and brushed himself off. "Better have some more coffee, before you get behind the wheel."

As Beck walked away, Cubiak offered a one finger salute.

# SIX

*Friday*

CUBIAK WAS IRKED that he'd acquiesced to Beck, but he'd been too numbed by alcohol and sadness to argue. Grudgingly, he coasted downhill into Ephraim, trailing the remnants of an early evening storm. Low, wind-driven clouds scudded inland over the sleepy village, backdrop for a pale rainbow that arched over the gray chop of the town's U-shaped harbor. At the base of the incline, the road leveled and followed the bottom rim of the shoreline, running past vacant cottages and under giant sugar maples that shivered raindrops over the jeep's windshield, enough to require an occasional swipe of the wipers. One of the oldest communities in Door County, Ephraim was quixotically laid out, with a hodgepodge of spider-leg lanes that radiated out from the old Village Hall and ran steeply uphill to the top of an inland ridge. The village's genteel, fairy-tale look was enhanced by whitewashed shops and cottages nestled amid miniature flower gardens and elfin lawns. Ephraim banned the sale of liquor and imposed strict limitations on live music, yet despite its prudish demeanor, it was one of the most popular resort towns on the peninsula.

Tourists adored the waterfront village, and the faithful returned every summer without regard to lake levels, gas prices, or weather. On his way to the Conservation

League meeting, Cubiak passed the ever-popular Milton's Ice Cream Shoppe where a man and a woman in heavy sweaters huddled under a red-and-white striped umbrella on the roadside patio and dipped long-handled spoons into enormous whipped cream–topped sundaes as new clouds gathered on the horizon. In the fading light, a lone sailboat bobbed alongside the long wooden dock, its halyard clips chiming rhythmically against the metal mast, and a handful of fishermen in sturdy slickers cast for bass and perch off a low wall of large gray rocks. Behind the young lovers—for what else could they be in that setting—smatterings of cars and bicycles peppered the parking lots of the surrounding B&Bs. Only the Christiana, a grand, clapboard hotel near the town's center, was deserted. Clinging to an old custom, snobbish in a way few could comprehend, the Chris waited until summer was well underway to begin the annual season, opening its doors with a fresh coat of white paint and setting out the rocking chairs along its famed porch in time for the Fourth of July Festival.

Uphill from the Chris was the Holy Light Moravian Church, where the league met. In direct counterpoint to its name, the church was a bleak, cold edifice. A granite plaque near the front door honored the founding minister, who, it explained, made the church of simple measure so as not to compete with the natural surrounding beauty. A paper sign directed meeting attendees downstairs to the social hall where Reverend Thorenson manned a small table inside the entrance.

The minister's warm greeting embarrassed Cubiak, who had no interest in the organization and was attending the event under false pretenses. He took a seat in the last row. Among the sparse crowd were Bathard and Les

Caruthers. On one side, Evangeline Davis and Martha Smithson sat shoulder-to-shoulder. A stern Anne Cooper perched nearby, notebook in her hand, talking to herself. Cubiak listened to the hum of voices. In the five days prior, three people had died within a ten-minutes' drive of the church. One of the funerals had been held upstairs. He found it unsettling how quickly life returned to normal for those on the outskirts of loss. For a week after Lauren and Alexis died, he'd failed to pick up the morning newspapers from the front porch, not because he forgot but because everything commonplace seemed superfluous. His perspective had been so altered by death, he could not comprehend a world in which someone would continue to drop a daily paper at his door. He was only beginning to understand that for those not directly touched by it, death was a transient event.

Thorenson banged the gavel. Cubiak looked up. Six people he'd never seen before sat two rows ahead. Thorenson called the meeting to order and gave the lectern to Ruby. The room quieted instantly. Following the minutes and treasurer's report, Ruby spoke about the future of Door County and the need to balance development with conservation. "The league does not stand in the path of progress. We are its partners. The challenge to protect the natural environment is one we take very seriously." Ruby paused. "However, our resources are not limitless. We have finite time and only modest funds for our noble work. So we choose our battles carefully."

Otto Johnson, she explained, had developed a proposal regarding the future of Peninsula State Park. Ruby looked across the room to the superintendent, who stood framed in the rear doorway. "Otto, do share your thoughts with us."

Johnson was the antithesis of Ruby, as nervous and unsure of himself at the podium as she had been calm and confident. Speaking so quietly the audience had to strain to hear him, Johnson reminded his listeners that for years he had lobbied for ways to reduce tourist amenities in the park. Due in large part to support from the league, the park had fewer cross-country trails per acre than other public-use lands. Snowmobiling was banned. Campsites were limited. The previous year, bow hunting had been sharply curtailed, a first for any state facility.

Now, Johnson wanted them to go further. He cleared his throat and raised his voice. "I challenge the Conservation League to declare Peninsula State Park a wilderness area."

A gasp went up in the room. Martha Smithson and Evangeline Davis exchanged worried looks. Three of the young people cheered.

Johnson continued. "All nature programs will cease. All trails, campsites, and facilities will be dismantled. The park would revert to its natural state and be operated as an animal refuge. Public access to the park will cease. Only Jensen Station, restructured as a nature museum, would be open to the public."

Caruthers jumped up and shook a finger at the park superintendent. "That's the most absurd idea I've ever heard. You close the park and you bankrupt the peninsula. People are going to think we don't want tourists up here. I say no. Absolutely. Positively."

Ruby rapped the podium with the gavel. "Otto has the floor."

Caruthers shot an angry look around and plopped back down.

Johnson had found his stride. "Since 1952, we've lost

more than twenty-three species of insects and plants in the park. These are not my figures. The data are based on studies by state biologists and botanists. The inner fibers of the park's ecosystem are being broken down and eroded. Just by way of example, garlic mustard is spreading through the undergrowth, choking out native plants and even disrupting tree reproduction. We pull out as much as we can every year, but the seeds are carried in on muddy shoes and tires from cars and bicycles. It's a losing battle." The larger picture was exceedingly more ominous, he explained, predicting eventual damage to trees and the demise of the deer population from pollution.

"What's happening here in miniature is what's happening to the great national wildernesses out west. We either conserve or destroy. There is no middle ground."

"There's always a middle ground," Caruthers protested. The rest of the room was silent. Cubiak waited to see what came next.

"At least a committee to study the idea. It would be a start," Johnson said.

Ruby called a fifteen-minute recess. When the board filed back into the meeting room, she was somber faced. "Unfortunately, this is simply not a fight we can win," she said, speaking directly to the park director. The board, she explained, had voted to table the motion indefinitely.

Johnson blanched and spun away, nearly tripping in his rush to leave. In the doorway, he turned back and shouted at the group: "You'll be sorry. You'll all be sorry!"

# SEVEN

*Saturday*

UNDER COVER OF NIGHT, Door County got its miracle. The prayers said, the candles lit, the silent supplications to the gods of land and sea paid off. In the impenetrable dark, an invisible force lifted the shroud of gloom from the peninsula and from among the general populace vanquished the last lingering concerns about death and bad weather. Daylight ushered in an upbeat attitude along with the sweetness of summer and the requisite accouterments of tourism: blue sky, warm sun, gentle breezes.

Up and down the peninsula, business owners and residents whose livelihoods rode the tide of the visitors' trade quivered with expectation. The festival—and the season—would be saved.

Even as the lingering shards of bad weather dissipated over the Great Lakes, cars and vans throughout the region were being readied for the trek to Door County. Suitcases and duffels were packed with swimsuits and stylish resort wear. Bicycles and golf clubs were pulled from hibernation. For those intent on living outdoors, tents, sleeping bags, air mattresses, cookstoves, even mosquito netting—every piece of camping equipment imaginable—were checked off lists and stuffed into vehicles for the trip to the peninsula.

The Fourth of July Festival kicked off in four days,

and the compulsive early birds, eager to claim their share of fun, were already on the road. By late morning, Interstate 43 from the south and Wisconsin 57 from the west were liquid rivers funneling traffic to the Midwest's magnificent answer to Cape Cod.

By contrast, the mood in the kitchen at Jensen Station was somber. Johnson remained visibly upset over the league meeting. He tapped his thick fingers on the oak table and worked his jaw as if he were delivering his speech to a new, more enlightened audience. Having witnessed the superintendent's humiliation, Cubiak found it hard to face him.

Ruta scurried around the two silent men, pouring coffee and piling hot buttered toast on their plates.

"Eat," she said to both and no one in particular.

Cubiak blinked and pinched the bridge of his nose. A branch scraping against his bedroom window had kept him awake half the night. Lying in bed, he'd listened to the stiff wind and remembered the time a late spring thunderstorm had knocked out the electricity in his Chicago neighborhood, frightening four-year-old Alexis. Nothing he or Lauren did would console the child. Finally, Lauren announced that she was going to make a picnic and asked Alexis and Cubiak to help. Father and daughter stood in the kitchen training flashlights on the counter and singing "Twinkle, Twinkle Little Star" while Lauren prepared peanut butter and jelly sandwiches. When she finished, they spread a blanket on the living room floor and ate by candlelight. It had been one of their happiest meals as a family, Cubiak thought, as he looked at the toast cooling on his plate. He wanted that life back.

Johnson pushed away from the table. Cubiak looked

up. The superintendent hadn't shaved, and stubble lay thick on his jowls. His hair was surprisingly lacking in gray for a man his age. Only his arthritic limbs betrayed him. His movements were stiff and clumsy. In the doorway, Ruta reached out to help him with his jacket, but he pulled away from her.

"I'm checking for claim jumpers," he said, glancing back into the room.

Claim jumpers: campers who snuck in early without permits and established camp in areas marked off limits.

As Johnson's footsteps receded, Cubiak returned to the DNR bulletin on invasive plant species that he'd brought to the table, pretending to read. At ten, he'd start check-in procedures at the main entrance, and he knew that once the first wave of vacationers rolled past, there'd be no hiding in dim corners for the next two months. But first he had to call Beck and tell him about the meeting. Whatever bad blood ran between him and Johnson, Cubiak sensed that it was dark and deep and wondered if it had anything to do with Beck's sister.

At the sink Ruta spritzed water on a row of dark-leafed plants that lined the deep windowsill.

"African violets?" Cubiak said.

"Yah. Yes. You know these flowers?"

"My mother liked them."

"Ah," the housekeeper said with a single, knowing sigh.

When she finished with the plants, Ruta carried a bowl of apples to the table and began peeling the fruit. "Otto works too hard. He is not a young man," she said after a while.

Cubiak murmured in agreement, and they fell back into a comfortable silence, the only sound the steady swish, swish of the blade against the dense pulp as Ruta stripped the apples and cut the fruit into uniform slices. She seemed to operate by radar, barely looking at what she was doing.

"The superintendent likes apple pie, not cherry," she said, apropos of nothing.

So did he. Cubiak reached for a piece of toast. He was considering a third cup of coffee when a burst of static rattled through the half-open door.

As abruptly as it started, the buzzing stopped and the kitchen was quiet again, but only for a moment.

"Oh, God!" A sob swallowed the words that followed but they both recognized the voice. It was Johnson, from somewhere in the huge park, shouting to them over the pickup's recently repaired radio.

Ruta dropped the paring knife and clutched her fist to her chest, mimicking what they were both thinking.

Then, "Dave!"

Cubiak was already on his feet. He sprinted down the hall to the radio room, Ruta on his heels.

"Dave. Come. Dave. Come."

"Otto? What's wrong?"

"Dave. Come."

"Where are you?"

"Help me." The rest of the response was garbled.

"Otto? Are you okay? Where are you?"

There was clicking on the wire and then the transmission cleared. "Lighthouse. Garrity Point."

"I'm on my way."

Cubiak pulled Ruta in from the hall and plunked her down in front of the radio. She was to wait there until she heard from him. He showed her how to operate the mike and the dial. "You may need to call Halverson," he said from the doorway.

SINCE 1868, THE powerful lantern in the William Garrity Lighthouse had flashed its special code of one second on, six seconds off to guide passenger and cargo vessels past the Strawberry Islands and the rocky shoals that paralleled the western edge of Peninsula State Park. When the facility was automated in 1926, the last lighthouse keeper moved out and the building slowly fell into disrepair. Packs of small brown field mice built nests in the empty cupboards. The roof began to leak, paint bubbled, and entire sections of wall began spalling. Several civic leaders labeled the vacant building a potential hazard and agitated to have it razed. The Conservation League, under Johnson's tutelage, won the fight to restore and preserve the historic edifice. Its glory regained, the beige brick structure became a popular attraction. School groups came from as far away as Green Bay on field trips. Families picnicked on the carefully mowed lawn. Amateur and professional artists alike stood in its shadow and produced widely varying renditions of the tower in oils, chalks, and watercolors.

It was still early enough that morning that the grounds were deserted. Cubiak found Johnson on a log bench near the lighthouse path. The super was shivering and breathing heavily with his mouth open.

"Are you hurt?" Cubiak said.

Johnson shook his head. Unclenching a swollen hand, he pointed toward the lighthouse. "There," he said.

Cubiak jogged up the trail. The forest was hushed, void of the usual early-morning chatter of birds and squirrels. At the top of the rise, the path emerged in a small clearing and the view opened to the tower. From a distance of fifty feet, Cubiak confronted the madness that had stilled the forest and frightened his boss.

A man, tall and angular, in worn jeans and torn sweat-shirt, was skewered to the shiny oak door of the building. An arrow pierced his chest. Blood flowed down his torso and legs and pooled on the ground.

Was the sun playing tricks? Cubiak looked away and then back. The terrible image endured. Johnson appeared at his elbow, trembling.

"Do you recognize him?" Cubiak said.

"No." Then. "A visitor, I think."

As the two approached the lighthouse, the horror became more riveting. The man's lips parted in agony, his hazel eyes wide with fright, his palms red smeared with blood from rabid, vain attempts to free himself.

"Is he dead?" Johnson said.

"Yes." The man had to be dead—no one could lose that much blood and survive. Cubiak registered the dark liquid on the ground, the navy wool cap that sat like an island in the center of the pool.

Johnson lunged past his assistant and wrapped one arm around the man, lifting him off the ground. With his free hand, he jerked hard at the arrow.

"No," Cubiak said, struggling to restrain his boss.

Johnson shook off Cubiak and tugged on the arrow again. The shaft pulled free and the dead man toppled forward into the superintendent's embrace. In a grotesque mockery of dancing partners, they reeled several yards before Johnson regained his balance and reverently lowered the body to the grass. When the superintendent stood up, his face was contorted and glistened with sweat. A tattoo of the dead man's torso was imprinted in red across the front of his jacket. Johnson swatted at the fabric in wild panic.

Cubiak grabbed the super by the wrists and held firm. "We need to go, get help," he said.

"We can't..." Words failed Johnson.

"We'll put him inside." Under the circumstances, it was the only solution. Cubiak couldn't trust Johnson to get back to the station on his own and hesitated to leave him alone with the body.

The ranger forced the door open. When the two men finished moving the victim, Cubiak rolled a white decorative boulder from the walkway and wedged it against the door, as if sealing a makeshift tomb.

Driving back, he radioed Ruta and told her to contact the sheriff. "Tell him there's been an incident at the lighthouse at Garrity Point."

Near the bottom of Ricochet Hill, the park rangers encountered the morning's second circle of hell. At the base of the steep incline, two touring bicycles lay in the patches of wild chicory at the edge of the woods. Wheels bent. Handlebars askew. Cubiak pressed his full weight into the brake bringing the jeep to a skidding stop inches from a single strand of piano wire stretched across the lane.

The ranger glanced at Johnson. The superintendent had aged a decade in the last thirty minutes.

"Stay here," said Cubiak as he jumped from the vehicle.

A patchwork of sunlight filtered through the forest canopy. Squinting against the crazy-quilt pattern of light that illuminated the scene, Cubiak ducked under the wire and walked past the twisted bike frames toward the two riders who sprawled on either side of the road. They wore shiny black helmets, biking shorts, and covered toe sandals, and their arms were flung out as if they had meant to fly through the trees. The cyclist on the right, a young man, lay on his back, his expression frozen in terror and surprise and his lips parted as if to call out a warning. The victim's throat was slashed, almost sliced through. Trails of blood smeared the front of his yellow jersey. His left incisor was missing. Cubiak felt the bitter taste of bile rise in his throat. He swallowed hard and checked for a pulse. Nothing.

The other victim was a young woman. Eighteen? Nineteen? She'd matched her lipstick to her magenta jersey. Now horror distorted her features and blood splattered her top. Her helmet strap had snagged the silver hoop in her left ear and pulled it askew. Her throat was cut and she was dead as well.

Two riders, but only one set of skid marks. They had ridden down the incline one behind the other, Cubiak realized. With their heads lowered against the wind, the visors on their helmets would have blocked their view of the wire until it was too late. The first rider was caught unawares. The second unable to stop in time.

Not daring to look at Johnson, Cubiak walked back to the jeep, pulled a blanket and canvas tarp from the cargo area, and covered the bodies. Then he returned to the vehicle for wire cutters. There were none in the tool box. There were no gloves either. Not thinking, he approached one of the trees and tried to untwist the piano wire anchored to it with his bare hands. The steel strand sliced a deep gash in his right palm. Cubiak winced and wrapped his kerchief around the wound. Still without a word to Johnson, he opened the passenger door, reached past the superintendent, and rummaged through the glove box, coming away with a roll of bright orange tape. With his teeth, Cubiak tore off a long strip and wound it around the wire. Then he ripped off five more pieces and dangled them from the wire as a warning to anyone unfortunate enough to venture down the lane.

Unable to reach Halverson, Cubiak eased the jeep under the wire. Wordlessly the rangers continued through the park. They reached the main entrance as the sheriff was turning in. Cubiak flagged him down.

"What do I do?" Halverson wailed after hearing about the cyclists.

"Cordon off the road and set up a detour through the access lane at Turtle Bay Campground. I'll take Otto back and tell Bathard to meet me at the lighthouse."

With Johnson left in Ruta's care, Cubiak grabbed a coil of rope from the garage and doubled back to Garrity Point.

When Bathard arrived, the rock had been rolled away from the door and the area strung with the brown rope.

"You okay?"

"Yeah." Cubiak stood at the edge of the bluff, smoking. He was suddenly very tired.

"I stopped and administered sedatives to both Otto and Ruta. Nothing too strong." Bathard paused. "How about I tend to your hand as well?"

Cubiak looked down, surprised by the red blotch on the handkerchief. The doctor rebandaged the wound and then turned toward the lighthouse. "Why don't you come in? I don't mind, and you might notice something of import," Bathard said.

"I've seen enough," Cubiak said. Six people dead in one week. In the city, the number would not be considered cause for alarm, but on the peninsula it was ominous, even if some of the fatalities had been accidental. The problem was that the pattern had no pattern.

A somber Bathard finally emerged from the dark interior. His shoulders drooped in defeat and the paper whiteness of his face intensified. Cubiak wired the door shut, and they went on to the scene of the dead bicyclists.

Halverson's men had tromped around the area with such abandon, they'd obliterated any clues that might have helped reconstruct the sequence of events that had led to these two deaths. Two deputies were rinsing blood off the road when Cubiak and the coroner pulled up. From the jeep, Cubiak watched Halverson bully Bathard through his examination. When the coroner was done, the sheriff ordered the bodies removed, at the same time dispatching a team to the lighthouse on a similar errand.

While the county ambulances moved in and out of the park, Halverson kept the police presence to a minimum. Rumors flitted through the campgrounds, but these were quickly dismissed as signs of the double tragedies were erased. The festival campers already in place were busy staking out territory against the onslaught of new arrivals who were streaming into the park, with only one goal in mind: to make the most of their week in the great outdoors.

THAT AFTERNOON, DOOR COUNTY officials gathered around the conference table in the third-floor library at Jensen Station. They were a solemn group, the morning's elation gone and their commingled high hopes shattered. The warm sunshine that poured through the windows had become a source of mockery. They were not in the room to admire the few remaining portraits of Indian chiefs that hung on the walls or to rue the depleted inventory of books left on the walnut shelves. They had come together to discuss the morning's tragic events and develop a plan forward: the mayor of Sturgeon Bay, the village administrator of Ephraim, the town board chairman of Fish Creek; Door County Tourism Board president Les Caruthers; Sheriff Leo Halverson; *Herald* editor Floyd Touhy; coroner Evelyn Bathard, park superintendent Otto Johnson; and chair of the Door County Arts Coalition Ruby Schumacher, the only woman in the group. Halverson drummed his fingers on the table. The Ephraim representative cleared his throat. Otherwise the room was silent. Below them on the first floor, a clock chimed, but no one noticed. They kept their eyes down and their thoughts to themselves. The coffee and cookies that Ruta had set out were untouched.

Cubiak lingered at the window, his back toward the others. The top of Falcon Tower was directly in his line of sight. One week earlier Larry Wisby had tumbled off the observation deck, making him the first of six people to die in seven days. One murder and two deaths officially ruled accidents. That morning, three tourists killed under gruesome circumstances. Cubiak focused on the different greens of the forest to avoid seeing the red of blood. He assumed most of the assembled officials would be unwilling to recognize the crisis they faced and instead would favor interpreting the recent events as a continuation of bad luck. From their perspective, that was the only option that made sense, and without any hard evidence to the contrary, who was he to argue? He was an outsider and if he disagreed with their assessment, he'd be dismissed as a troublemaker.

Door County was known for charm, not murder. Fifty thousand visitors were expected over the next couple of days; this first batch would be followed by waves of tourists right up until school started. Some came to sample the wondrous place they'd heard so much about. For others, a Door County summer vacation was an annual tradition. Year after year, generations of families rented the same cottages or campsites, hiked familiar trails, and told their well-worn stories. Spring and fall and even winter drew people to the area but summer was the season that defined the peninsula, and summer would proceed normally if the people gathered in the library didn't overreact.

The meeting was scheduled for four. At a quarter past, Beck blew into the room. Reaching past Ruby, he poured a cup of coffee and grabbed a cookie. "I've given the situation considerable thought," he said as he moved to the head of the table. He set the mug down in front of the empty chair but remained standing, forcing the others to look up at him.

"We proceed as planned," the civic leader announced brusquely. His eyes on his audience, Beck paced the room and tested the waters, striving for a conciliatory but controlling tone. "If we curtail activities or cancel, people will panic. We don't just destroy this year's festival, we threaten the entire season and put a black mark on the peninsula that will endure for years. We can't afford that." Beck's voice tightened, emulating the economic noose closing around their necks.

"I know this morning's tragic events are hard to reconcile. But we must act responsibly. The hiker's death was accidental. Horrific, but an accident nonetheless. Who would shoot an arrow through a human being, for god's sake? It was probably some stupid tourist aiming at a deer. We all know about the deer problem in the park." The comment fell flat.

"The bikers, well, it's harder to see but it had to have

been the result of a prank gone awry. Nothing else makes sense…"

"Frederick Delacroix, Timothy Anders, Suzanne Pithy." Bathard spoke, interrupting Beck. "The victims have names. Let us at least have the decency to acknowledge them as individuals rather than identify them with labels."

The group squirmed and several of those at the table exchanged anxious glances. Beck listened politely and glanced in the coroner's direction. Then he continued blathering on, his manner growing increasingly folksy. "We all know that people come up here and put their brains in their back pockets. Nothing against tourists, but they do pull some pretty crazy antics. I remember the time those kids from UW paddled through the canal in barrels. They could've all been drowned. Stupid piss-ant stunt like that. They did it on a dare. Floyd, that's before your time. But Les, you remember?"

Caruthers bobbed obligingly, a minnow gumming the bait.

"It's probably the same kind of thing that killed those two," Beck went on. "Someone's idea of a practical joke. Only it went tragically wrong."

"That's a big assumption," Bathard interjected.

"But a legitimate one nonetheless." Beck pulled at his cuffs. When he spoke again his tone was deliberately light. "Like I said before, people go on vacation, they put their brains on hold, don't think things through. Leo's got several men combing the campgrounds now, asking questions. This'll all be cleared up by evening. Tomorrow at the latest."

There was a strained silence.

Beck looked directly at Bathard. "Well? Do you agree or disagree?"

The coroner stood. He had the advantage of age, height, and dignity and brought all to bear in his response. "I will say for the record that I disagree. I would even go so far as to suggest we consider calling in the FBI if it seems necessary." At the mention of the agency, panicked looks flew back and forth across the table. Bathard went on unperturbed. "I also acknowledge that, unfortunately, my suggestions most likely will not make any difference."

Beck smiled. "Of course, if it seems necessary we will consider all options, no matter how extreme they might be."

"I say we stay the course." Caruthers cast his vote with his usual smug bravado.

"Yes. We have many other guests. We must not forget our obligation to them," the gentleman from Fish Creek said.

Ephraim's administrator concurred. "The best approach is to continue as usual."

The Sturgeon Bay mayor, a man handpicked for the office by Beck, voiced his assent.

As Bathard sat down again, Ruby Schumacher raised a hand. "I vote with the majority but only with the understanding that adequate steps are being taken to ensure the safety of both guests and residents alike. You have taken precautions?" she said to Beck.

"Yes, of course," he said impatiently. "Leo's deputized twelve extra men to monitor festival activities, and I've got a half dozen private security guards coming in from Milwaukee. They'll be in plainclothes with orders to blend in with the crowds and keep a careful watch on things."

"Good," Ruby said and sat back in her chair.

"And you? What's your take on all this?" The chief cheerleader bounced the ball across the room to Cubiak, turning all heads in his direction.

The ranger raised both hands in a mock gesture of helplessness. He would not be drawn in to their argument.

"Floyd?"

"Never give in to terrorists," the newsman blurted. Beck hesitated only as long as it took for Touhy's meaning to sink in. He wasn't going to argue with a non sequitur that bolstered the tally in his favor.

"Leo?"

To Cubiak's surprise, the sheriff didn't seem eager for the spotlight.

"I'm not real sure about the nature of the deaths," Halverson said, directing his attention to a picture of Sitting Bull. A row of perspiration formed across his brow. He cracked his knuckles. "I mean, I'm sure you're right about keeping the park open. Just not the reason." The sheriff grimaced and chanced a fleeting glance at the kingpin of Door County. "I mean, I think there's another explanation and that we can get at it probably by the end of the day."

"Go on." Beck's voice was barbed ice.

"I think it's more of Petey's buddies. Reinforcements, like. I spotted a gang of them this morning on their bikes—big fucking Harleys and such—maybe ten or twelve guys roaring toward the park. I know how these punks think. They figure if someone gets killed while

Petey's in jail, then he's in the clear. So they do this to help their friend out."

Beck feigned interest. The adolescent theory played into his hands, and had other advantages as well.

Halverson pulled his shoulders back smartly. "I think I ought to go out to Kingovich's again with my men and poke around. No telling what I'd find."

"And the park?" Beck led him on.

"Ain't nothing more going to happen here now. The park stays open."

"No." Johnson lumbered to his feet. "It's not your decision."

"Hell it's not!" Beck shot back.

"You have no jurisdiction over the park."

"The fuck I don't. I run the damn advisory board."

"The park should be closed immediately." Johnson took a deep rattling breath and looked around, settling his gaze on the sheriff. "I have the authority to order you to vacate the grounds," he said.

Halverson shifted uneasily but Beck came to his rescue. "You do that and folks will be mighty unhappy."

"This is not a popularity contest," Johnson boomed.

Beck gripped the back of his chair. "Everything's a popularity contest! The park, the festival—everything." He gestured at Cubiak. "Ask your junior ranger over there about politics in the big city. Ask Les. Ask the fucking town reps." Beck stabbed his finger toward Johnson. "You don't understand anything, do you? Never did. Never will. You fucking mess with this park, you tell the sheriff to close it up, and I'll be on the phone to the governor so fast it'll make your head spin. And then you see what happens."

So it came to this, Cubiak thought. A standoff between established enemies. A power play with the outcome obvious from the start. And another public humiliation for the park superintendent.

His hands curled into tight fists, Johnson lurched toward Beck. Although the forester was taller and on his own turf, Beck was more fierce, more adept at getting his way. After a moment's silent confrontation, Johnson crumpled. Stifling a sound that was half sob and half groan, he dropped his arms helplessly to his sides and fled from the room.

Beck quickly dispensed with the remaining business. Halverson was to check out his theory about Petey's friends. Touhy would see to it that the *Herald* would print a minimum of information about the deaths, attributing all three to accidents. Caruthers would issue a terse statement to the same effect to the merchants. Cubiak would initiate no announcements to park visitors. Nothing on Twitter or Facebook. Should anyone press for details, the official line was regret over the unfortunate events. The bottom line: no comment pending further investigation.

"I'll ask the state medical examiner to assist with the autopsies. With the holiday that buys us enough extra time until—bingo, festival's over. No problemo." Beck gave a snappy salute. The meeting was adjourned.

BATHARD TRAILED CUBIAK into his office. "What are you going to do?" the coroner demanded.

Cubiak didn't answer.

"Something must be done. Surely you realize that with your experience, you can be of tremendous assistance."

"I can't do anything," Cubiak said.

"Can't or won't? You have a responsibility."

"I have my own problems. I have nothing to offer anyone here!" Cubiak slammed his bandaged fist on the desk. "What's it matter anyhow?" he said, blanching as he turned away. He'd meant the response to sound inconsequential but in the abrupt silence, it rang harsh and forlorn.

"What's it matter?" Bathard rose to his full height. Though his voice was strained thin with despair, it remained rich in authority. "More often than we think, a great deal."

# EIGHT

*Week Two: Sunday Morning*

CUBIAK WOKE WITH a bad feeling and an even worse hangover. Dragging himself from bed he tried to burn away both afflictions with a punishing hot shower. He knew Bathard was disappointed with him. Wasn't everyone? He'd fallen far short of his mother's expectations, failed his wife and daughter in the worst possible way, and walked out on his partner. Malcolm had meant well, sending him to Door County, not realizing that it was Cubiak's fate to be a major fuck-up.

Toweling off, the ranger caught his blurred image in the clouded mirror. He'd become slovenly and dissolute. A broken man, like his father. If failure was destiny, then Cubiak had fulfilled his.

Engulfed in gloom, he descended to the kitchen. Johnson's upturned mug was already in the drainer, a stern, silent affront. Ruta frowned and slapped a ball of dough on the counter. After brushing flour from her hands, she shoved a steaming mug at him.

"You drink," she said. Her comment was either a directive or a bitter critique of his behavior.

"Yes, I drink," Cubiak said and swallowed a mouthful of scalding coffee.

LATE FOR ROUNDS, he skipped eating and chain-smoked three cigarettes. Driving through Peninsula Park was like playing dodge ball with human targets. Enthusiastic day visitors streamed in through the entrance, their vehicles piled with picnic supplies and weighted down with bikes and kayaks. Happy campers thronged the park's overnight facilities. Their tents and awnings and tarps fluttered open and transformed the forest into a sparkling kaleidoscope of shape and color. The park as playground. Precisely what Johnson loathed.

Eight days earlier Larry Wisby had died at Falcon Tower. Terrible as his death was, it had been eclipsed by more recent events. Ultimately all six deaths were overshadowed by Beck's single-minded determination to save the festival and the summer, a decision the other officials embraced with little hesitation. A mistake? Surely. And yet, Cubiak grudgingly admitted, the county depended on the tourist economy; hysteria served no good purpose.

CUBIAK FOUND BECK waiting at Jensen Station. His hair was mussed and his clothes had a slept-in look. "We need to talk," he said, pushing away from the Mercedes and steering the ranger into a stand of maples behind the garage.

"The day Ben Macklin died, he hooked up with an old drunk named Buddy Entwhistle. You know who he is?" Beck's tone was low key but infused with a hard-to-miss undercurrent of urgency. He didn't wait for an answer. "Doesn't matter. The two were drinking at Pechta's for a couple, two-three hours before Macklin's boat blew up. Later, Entwhistle told Amelia that Benny said there were two people on Falcon Tower the morning of the business with Wisby."

Macklin had been out fishing, Beck explained, and was heading home after selling his haul when he'd seen them. Beck glanced around, making sure he hadn't been overheard. "Well?" he said finally.

Cubiak conjured up the map he'd noticed at Pechta's the night of Macklin's unofficial wake. Could he have been right? "Well, what?" he said.

Beck scoffed. "You're a real dick, you know that? Anyways, Entwhistle tells Amelia, and Amelia passes the info on to Halverson. Not that I think two drunks ever say anything much worth repeating, but according to Entwhistle, Macklin thought they was both fucking nuts. Here's a nasty-looking set of clouds rolling in and these two dopes are up there. One on top, waving like all get out, and the other coming up the stairs."

He pressed two fingers to the ranger's shirt.

"Remember, this was the day the kid flew off the tower. Leo thinks this could mean maybe Wisby didn't jump but was pushed. I still say he slipped and fell. Heavy dew made the wood treacherous. He climbed the railing to show off, lost his balance, and tumbled off. So what if there was a friend up there with him? The friend got scared and ran away."

Problem was, Beck went on, Entwhistle was nowhere to be found and it wouldn't do to have him pop up and start blathering some cockeyed version of the story. "Most likely he's sleeping off another binge in some hidey-hole no one knows about. Ah fuck, it probably doesn't mean a thing. Amelia's been known to tie one on occasionally, too. She may have gotten the whole story ass-backward."

Another uneasy silence sprang up. Beck waited as long as he could and then went on.

"I just found all this out and figured it should be looked into." He pretended an easy, confident air as if the story was little more than a misunderstanding between friends that could easily be resolved.

"What matters is finding out what really happened to Wisby on the tower." And the rest, too, Beck added after a pause. Halverson's been looking into it, he said, but besides arresting Petey, the sheriff hadn't come up with anything solid. "He's too stupid to find his own asshole with two hands." Beck was fidgeting again. "I need someone I can rely on to check out Entwhistle's story," he said, as he raked his fingers through his silver mane.

Cubiak laughed. "And you're asking me? Halverson would like nothing better than to prove that I had something to do with Wisby falling from the tower, and you want me to investigate how the kid died?"

"Leo's an idiot. If you were going to go after anyone it wouldn't have been the younger brother."

"You got that right," Cubiak said. Given half the chance, he would have killed the entire family. "Why don't you call the governor? Ask him to send in the National Guard."

"I don't want any outsiders involved."

Cubiak snickered. Amid the cozy peninsula crowd, he was the consummate outsider.

"You know, Dave," Beck went on quietly, "I've got friends in the Windy City and have learned so many interesting things about you. The wife, the kid. Bad luck. My sympathies. But then going off the deep end like you did. All those messy details. And people will talk.

"There'd be plenty of sympathy for you, at first. But

before long people would start wondering. Maybe you decided to get your revenge on the Wisby family any way you could. Maybe you found out the younger kid came up here and that's the only reason you even took this fucking job. That happens, people start thinking like that, and you become a liability, bad for business. A persona non grata."

"You threatening my job?"

"I'm trying to protect your job." Beck paused. "It would be unofficial, of course. Leo is the sheriff by rights. You'd be freelance, a consultant answerable directly to me."

Squares of sunlight pierced the bower and blinked like fireflies amidst the fluttering branches and whorls of fresh green shoots. "If I won't?"

"Then it's adios."

Cubiak flexed the fingers on his bandaged hand. Tension along the cut meant it was healing. He couldn't let Beck fire him. He'd made a mess of everything. He'd lost his family, his job, his home. The only thing that he had to hold onto was his promise to Malcolm. It was what kept him going, and to keep his word, he had to keep his job for another few months, even if that meant going through the motions of cooperating with Beck.

"I'll do it," Cubiak said, finally. "But just so you know, I'm not doing it for any of the reasons you think."

"Yeah, well, I don't give a damn why you're doing it." Beck juggled his keys. "Entwhistle has a room somewhere in Ephraim. You can start there. Come on, I'll give you a ride."

"I can get myself into town."

"Not in this thing you can't." Beck kicked the right rear tire of the jeep as they walked past. "Flat as a smashed nickel. You must have picked up a nail on your way back."

Cubiak cursed under his breath. There was only one working jack between the two park vehicles and the last place he'd seen it was in the rear of Otto's truck. "Give me a minute to change, anyway."

"Don't bother. The uniform makes you look official."

"Yeah? And what's a park ranger doing in town looking for one of the local lowlifes?"

"You'll think of something. Now, you coming or not?"

"What about the park? I've got work I'm supposed to do today."

"Don't worry about that. I'll take care of it. Otto can find someone else to babysit the campers."

Fine and fuck you, Cubiak thought, as he got in the Mercedes and slammed the door.

# NINE

*Sunday Afternoon*

UNDER A CLOUDLESS SKY, the bay at Ephraim assumed a blue tint of breath-taking intensity. In the calm and near perfect conditions, a flotilla of sailboats, kayaks, and one lone canoe was on the water. When the canoe disappeared around an outcropping of rocks, Cubiak stepped off the dock. He didn't like the way Beck had manipulated the meeting the previous afternoon and had no intention of helping him find Entwhistle. He'd hang around town for a couple hours and then say he hadn't had any luck.

Up and down the narrow waterfront, artists and vendors were setting up their stands, hoping to get a jump on business. Outside the Village Hall, volunteers hammered together craft booths where pioneer skills would be demonstrated throughout the five-day fest. Tourists wandered the narrow streets, inhaling the aroma of brats, grilled onions, and popcorn.

At the entertainment stage, Cubiak watched the Bay City Cloggers' rehearsal. The men wore white shirts and sky blue pants; their partners were dressed in white blouses and skirts that did little to flatter their soft, middle-aged frames. Faces furrowed in serious concentration, the cloggers focused on their leader, a plump, gleeful woman with red starched hair and fleshy arms. When she let loose with a shrill hoot, the dancers slammed their steel-cleated shoes into the wooden platform in an ear-splitting crash. A group of onlookers roared its approval and hand-clapped in time.

As the cacophonous din drew more people, the ranger walked away.

The laughter and happy chatter that suffused the village was an affront to Cubiak. Every family reminded him of what he had lost. Every couple reinforced the gnawing emptiness inside. He wandered aimlessly, occasionally nipping at the bottle tucked in his pants pocket. In a sea of determined revelers, he was a piece of floating debris a solitary lost and despondent soul. He had felt that way before. When Lauren and Alexis died, his friends, the other cops and their wives, tried to console him. But they, too, felt defeated and helpless. Nothing they said comforted him. Nothing they did lightened the burden or eased the pain. Nothing assuaged the guilt.

COUNSELING HADN'T HELPED EITHER.

*Session one.*

Therapist: "How are you holding up?"

Patient: "Fine."

"Problems at work?"

"No."

"Tell me about your dreams."

"I don't dream." He had nightmares. Cubiak knew he was playing word games and didn't care. The therapist trained his sad brown eyes on Cubiak, who in turn studied the psychologist's soft Italian loafers and muted argyle socks.

*Session two.*

Therapist: "What would you like to talk about?"

Patient: [*Shrug.*]

The therapist didn't work hard to disguise his impatience. Halfway through the second appointment, Cubiak stood up, thanked him, and walked out. Stone faced. Emotions pummeled into a thimble, ingested whole. Alone. Alone with his guilt. He sped recklessly down dimly lit side streets until he reached the shabby neighborhood tavern where his father's ghost waited. "Ah, now you know," Papa uttered in grim satisfaction as his son inhaled a triple shot of vodka and ordered another.

HE HAD TO accept and move on. Intellectually, Cubiak knew this was true. But emotionally, he couldn't. He tried, but every attempt failed. Eventually he tired of the angry inner voice and turned a deaf ear to the ranting. In denial he found some relief, and for a long time he convinced himself he had dealt with the loss. But he hadn't bargained for the enduring pain and the relentless ache that became his constant companions.

His work suffered. He skipped shifts or showed up intoxicated. Pressured by his superiors, he eventually agreed to resign. Though he was several months short of being fully vested, police officials made helpful accommodations that resolved the issue in his favor and allowed him to leave the force with a substantial lump sum. The money could have paid off the house. Instead, it bought boatloads of vodka. He clambered on board, capsized, and lost everything, except the pain and guilt that were seared into his heart.

In the bright sunlight of a Door County afternoon, Cubiak blinked and remembered the day his world disintegrated, the day his blind stupidity prevented him from keeping his word and sent his wife and daughter off by themselves to endure death by battering.

"HEY, SARGE, WHAT *is* that *smell*. Man, that's *terrible*."

Cubiak chuckled.

*"What you laughing at?"*

"Nothing."

"Man sitting in a *frying pan* getting *poached* and *laughing while it's happening is* either going crazy or he's laughing at *something*."

Cubiak appraised his reflection in his partner's mirrored sunglasses. "I'm laughing at you. Not at you. With you," he said. "It's the way you talk."

A Bible-thumping, hand-clapping Pentecostal who took not the Lord's name in vain, who persisted, even in hell's most abominable holes on earth, to keep his language, his mind, and his soul pure, Malcolm spoke only in italics.

"Oh, *that*."

"Yeah."

"Well, all *right*. Least you's laughing at *something*." The temperature in the stakeout car jumped up a notch as a rough-edged, desertlike breeze swirled the stink past Malcolm again. *"So?"*

"It's a dead skunk. Probably killed by a stray dog. Or a stray bullet."

*"Here?* We are sitting in the *middle of Chicago* and you're telling me there's skunks around *here*?"

"There's all kinds of animals in the city." Cubiak glanced back to the smeared windshield and the local drug house under their surveillance. "You're just too used to dealing with the two-legged variety."

Malcolm started to close the car window and then

reconsidered. With the sun frying the blotched roof of the rusty black Mustang, the heat inside the car might be more oppressive than any odor. He slumped farther into the driver's seat. They were one of several dozen undercover police teams that, operating under the extra precaution of radio silence, were scattered across the tattered Lawndale neighborhood in the mayor's latest assault on narcotics. These much ballyhooed crackdowns came as regularly as local elections. The downtown spin doctors had dubbed this one "Operation Clean Sweep." So far, lots of brooms, very little sweep.

Cubiak worked his shoulders. Sweat spread a delicate, liquid spider web down his back. He momentarily projected himself into a cool shower and fancied a cold beer in hand. Or ice cream. He squinted down the street. It wasn't a pleasant vista. They were in deep on the West Side, an area torched during the King riots and then left to wither in slow decay. There were four buildings on the entire block. Three were vacant and in danger of imploding where entire sections of masonry had been worked loose and removed. One was a run-down tenement, a lifeless facade save for a torn, yellowed sheet in an open second-floor window. From inside, a high-pitched, grating Motown refrain boomed into the street.

The Loop was four and a half miles directly east, the city skyline a shining symbol of power and wealth stark against the blue sky. On the corner, a pack of boys, probably five or six years old, swung metal pipes through the heavy heat haze. They alternately jeered and taunted each other with cries of motherfucker, shithead, and other attributes Cubiak couldn't decipher but could imagine. He looked from the ragtag group to the

cityscape and felt an immeasurable sadness. How the
hell do you get from here to there? he wondered.

To the vice and narcotics cops who regularly worked
the area, Lawndale was just another segment of blighted
city landscape. Cubiak hated it, viewed it as an aberra-
tion of the American ideal, a sore that festered up and
down the urban backbone.

*"Sweet Jesus, help us."*

Startled, Cubiak looked up where Malcolm was pointing.

Less than ten feet away, a scrawny teenage girl in a
dirty cotton dress lurched toward them. Somnambulant
and balanced on thin birdlike legs, she cautiously negotiated the cracked, uneven sidewalk, unremarkable in the
setting, save for the naked baby haphazardly cradled in
her frail arms. The infant was grotesquely malnourished,
with a swollen belly and an incongruous black smudge
across its forehead. The jagged smear reminded Cubiak
of Ash Wednesday, how he'd always tried to duck the
priest's thumb.

Was the child hers?

The baby slipped. The girl snapped to and struggled
to secure her human cargo against her bony chest. In her
momentary alarm, she looked up, and Cubiak caught her
frightened gaze. *Help me* she seemed to be pleading. He
felt suddenly overwhelmed by the impulse to leap from
the car, grab the child from her arms, and snatch them
both into the safety of another world. He blinked and
the moment passed. The infant settled into place, and
the girl's hooded eyes swung down again to the broken
pavement. She drifted forward, as he watched, empty
with relief.

The scream of police sirens shattered the air. One

blue-and-white came in from the alley. Another wailed directly down Madison and jumped the curb. Flying past the girl with the baby, the vehicle screeched to a sliding stop in front of the Mustang. Three uniforms jumped out and ran to the stakeout car.

Malcolm jolted upright. "What the *heck*?" he sputtered.

A beefy, red-faced cop shoved his face through Malcolm's window and whispered in his ear. Malcolm blanched. *"Sweet Jesus."*

The other two opened Cubiak's door. The lieutenant grabbed his arm and pulled him from the seat. Cubiak did not share Malcolm's predilection for sanitized speech. "Hey. What the fuck, man! You're blowing our stakeout. What about the mayor, for chrissake. Clean Sweep?"

The lieutenant responded in well-practiced cop cadence—"Fuck them/Fuck him/Fuck it"—and kicked the door shut. "You got trouble at home, buddy. Let's go."

MONTHS LATER, IN a freezing spring rain, Malcolm found Cubiak near a strip of abandoned factories on the far South Side near Indiana and 119th, just off the Ryan. He was huddled under a viaduct like discarded trash, his hands trembling from either too much or too little to drink.

*"Jesus Christ."* The interjection became a prayer as, with tears brimming and his face hard-set, Malcolm half-carried, half-dragged his former partner through a slimy, sucking mixture of mud and animal excrement to his car and brought him back to his home on a quiet street of black, middle-class respectability in Chatham.

Malcolm kept him there, sat stoic and unmoved while

Cubiak ranted and beat holes in the pink rose patterns of the neatly papered walls, waited patiently until the demons gave up. Then he hauled the broken shell of Dave Cubiak into a straight-back chair, pushed his chin up off his chest, and said, "They *see* you from up *there*. You ain't got *no right* to break their hearts, too."

When he finished lecturing, Malcolm offered himself up as the crutch that Cubiak would finally use to begin his long, painful climb back up. Encouraged badgered—by his friend, Cubiak rented a room at the Lawson YMCA, parked cars for a few dollars a day, and wrenched his gut to stay reasonably sober. One day Malcolm arrived with a newspaper opened to an inside page and handed it over.

"You *need* something like this. It'll give you a *new* direction." Malcolm was insistent.

Cubiak shoved away the paper with its ad for continuing education, but his friend wouldn't relent. Malcolm kept on cajoling until he elicited a promise. Then he showed up the next morning to help Cubiak fill out the application.

Two weeks later, apprehensive and shy, his face raw from a clumsy shave, Cubiak folded his too-tall frame into a lecture hall seat at Truman College. On a whim, he'd signed on for forestry, a vocation as far removed from his former life as he could imagine. Several weeks into the class, Cubiak grudgingly admitted that Malcolm had been right, and though he feared failing and disappointing his former partner, he did well—not at first but slowly and steadily. When Cubiak graduated, Malcolm brought his entire family to the ceremony. Dressed for church, they stood and applauded their friend. His smile for them was the first in a long time.

Cubiak was working for the Cook County Forest Preserve when Malcolm came across a notice about a job in Door County. "It's *there*," Malcolm said, laying a map of Wisconsin on the table and pointing to the peninsula. "A *new* world."

All Cubiak saw was the great expanse of blue Lake Michigan water. In high school, he'd sat by the inland sea and read *Moby-Dick*, convinced he understood Ishmael's pain.

"Didn't you tell me you went up there when you were a *kid*? *Boy Scouts* or something?" Malcolm said.

Yes, Cubiak said, he had.

"Well, then, what are you waiting for?"

FUCK BECK, FUCK EVERYTHING, Cubiak thought, reaching for the bottle. He felt a tug at his sleeve and looked down into the tear-stained face of a little girl with long brown bangs and a crescent of freckles across her nose. The child sniffled and said something in a panicky voice. Unable to hear her above the crowd, Cubiak bent down.

"I lost my mommy," the little girl whimpered into the side of his chin. A ketchup stain smeared the shoulder of her orange top.

"Shit." He spoke louder than he intended and several reproachful looks came his way.

Even the child turned an accusatory look at him, her plight momentarily overshadowed. "You shouldn't say that word."

"Yeah, well." Cubiak scanned the horde for the face of an anxious parent and nearly drowned in an ocean of good cheer.

He tilted toward the child again. "Where were you before?"

She shivered.

"Think," he insisted.

The girl pinned her red-rimmed, puffy eyes on him. "I don't know," she wailed.

It came to him slowly that the child had sought him out because of his uniform; she had done what her mother had told her to do if ever she was lost or needed help. Find a policeman. Tell the store clerk. Look for someone official, the person in charge.

"It's okay," he said gruffly. "We'll walk around together. You look for anything familiar." He'd take her to the church. Find a cherry-decked greeter and leave the girl with her.

The simpering child latched onto Cubiak's arm. But when he stepped forward, she didn't move.

"Come on," he said impatiently.

"I can't."

Before Cubiak could stop her, the girl pulled off her right shoe and bloody sock. A large blister on her heel had broken. The skin underneath was fiery red and raw. She hopped unsteadily on her good foot and started toppling over when Cubiak grabbed her. Without thinking he swung her up against his chest and, in the automatic reflex of a child being rescued by an adult, she wrapped her thin legs around his waist and her arms around his neck. The feather-touch of her hands on his shoulders stabbed his heart.

Cubiak thought he would weep.

"I think we were there." She pointed toward an ice cream stand fifty feet away. "Or maybe there." She looked toward the stage.

Steadying himself, Cubiak waded into the frolicking throng. He struggled to keep the clinging child at arm's length, but the crowd kept jostling at them and the frightened child responded by pulling closer and tightening her grip.

Cubiak stopped abruptly. He was light headed; his heart drummed wildly in his chest. He loosed the child's grasp on his collar and dropped her to the ground.

She wobbled and grabbed his arm. "I'm sorry. I'll walk, I'm too heavy," she said as tears trickled down her face.

"No. It's okay," he said, but he remained motionless.

He had fooled himself into thinking he had erased all image of voice and touch. He hadn't.

Memories washed over him. He was at the petting zoo with Alexis. Still a toddler, she wore one black leather Mary Jane and one white ballet slipper. Trailed by a spotted baby goat, she twirled through the miniature farmyard in her favorite yellow sundress, her laughter the purest expression of innocence and joy he could imagine. The next instant, he was lying on the living room rug, exhausted from working three straight shifts, while Alexis bent over a puzzle nearby. From the kitchen, Lauren admonished the child to leave Daddy alone and urged him to go up to bed. But he'd been too exhausted to move and so Alexis knelt by him and sang a lullaby. While she serenaded him, her fingertips brushed lightly up and down his arm. Then she dipped and kissed him. "Good night, Daddy," she whispered.

Cubiak had met Lauren at a party. He'd almost not gone. She had looked tall from across the room, and he was surprised when he stood next to her to find she barely reached his shoulder. She was a kindred spirit. She cooked chili and talked to him about books. She loosened the ties of his spiritual straitjacket and freed him from the pain of his soldier's soul. She eased his guilt at not having saved his parents from themselves.

When Lauren's life seeped away into a puddle of blood on a pot-marked street, Cubiak lost more than his love. He lost his way.

"Are you okay? Sir?" The child's voice cracked.

"Yes." Cubiak squeezed her stubby fingers.

RAGE AND ANGUISH had driven him to drink. Crazed with alcohol, he plotted ways to kill the elder Wisby son in prison; it would be easy enough to bribe a guard to poison the man or to hire another inmate to stab him. Other nights, he thought about ways to take his own life; the method he preferred was carbon monoxide poisoning — so simple to lock the garage and leave the car running. Dying like that, he thought, evoked a sense of ironic justice. In the end, he didn't do anything to harm either the DUI or himself. Years before, he'd decided that there was too much death and killing in the world. That's why he became a cop in the first place, to try to stop the slaughter. He couldn't add to it.

At the same time, he was consumed by pain and loneliness. The psychologist suggested that in addition to grieving the loss of his wife and daughter, he was also experiencing delayed grief for the deaths of his father and mother. Cubiak had ridiculed the notion. His father was a bum, an abusive alcoholic. Good riddance. No tears for his mother either, a rigid, domineering woman who had smothered him with her anxieties and petty ideals. "I was relieved they were gone," he'd said fiercely, blind to the complexities of familial ties and the long tendrils of grief.

"Mister, please, let go. It's not your fault." The child struggled to pull free.

Startled, Cubiak looked at her and then released her hand. "What did you say?"

"I'll find her. It's okay."

"No, what did you say before?" Cubiak crouched down, eye level with the little girl. He was suddenly calm, and his manner quieted her as well.

The lost child looked at him. "I said *it's not your fault.*"

How many millions of times had Cubiak heard that simple statement, and how many times had he rejected it and instead embraced guilt as punishment for his inability to keep his wife and daughter safe from harm. *It's not your fault.* The child had infused the words with an authority and strength that pierced his emotional armor.

The little girl smiled, and a hairline fracture shuddered through Cubiak's mantle of hubris and despair.

He stared at her.

"Sir?"

A crushing weight slid from his shoulders. Humbled, he wanted to weep but from joy, not sorrow. Hundreds of miles from any of the places he had ever called home and in a blinding midday light, redemption came. Delivered by a child.

Time will do its work, the shrink had said. The question was: would he let it.

Cubiak smiled. "What's your name?"

"Mara."

"That's a beautiful name."

A new mass of pleasure seekers surged toward them, and Cubiak suddenly saw the situation in a new light. Bathard was right. Door County faced a dangerous

threat, and if he did nothing to find the killer, others—
this child perhaps—could die.

He picked up Mara and plunged into the throng. "I'd
say it's time we found your mother," he said.

They traveled the length of the beach, up and down
the docks, and past the souvenir stands. Near the church,
a greeter tried to intervene, but Cubiak waved her away
He bought Mara an ice cream cone and stopped twice to
retrieve her shoe when she dropped it, finally shoving
it into his pocket. They rested long enough for Mara to
drink a bottle of grape soda, and then Cubiak lifted her
onto his shoulders again for a better view and walked
on, his hands on her knees to keep her steady, her suntanned legs dangling down his chest.

"Mommy!"

A petite, athletic woman shoved through the crowd toward them. Her body was tense, alert. Her face sculpted
by panic. Loosely braided hair tumbled over her shoulders. Cubiak dropped Mara into her mother's arms. The
woman's face was ashen. The kind of fear she had experienced dissipates slowly. It would, he knew, haunt her
again in unsuspecting moments for a long time to come.
She put a hand in his and gripped hard.

"Thank you. She's all I've got."

Mara looked up. Safe in her mother's embrace, she
grinned at the handsome man in the wrinkled uniform.
He tousled her hair. "You stay with your mother now,
you hear."

Cubiak watched them walk away, hand in hand. Mara
and her mother. Alexis and Lauren.

"This is for you," he said and tossed the half pint into
a blue-and-white checkered trash barrel.

# TEN

*Monday Morning*

CUBIAK CRAWLED OUT of a soft canyon of sleep and for a long while remained motionless as if stitched to the bed by threads of slumber. He had forgotten the weighty luxuriousness of such intense repose. When the final remnants of inertia dissipated, he rolled onto his side, swung his feet to the floor, and pushed upright. The room took a moment to settle, but even in the dim light and without his glasses, he was able to make out the two empty quart bottles that leaned against the wall under the window. For a moment he feared that he had drunk them dry and thought that the sleep he had so enjoyed had come as a result, but then he remembered pouring out the contents the previous evening after the long climb back from Ephraim.

After reuniting Mara and her mother, he'd hiked the village's shoreline and hilly terrain in search of Ben Macklin's elusive drinking pal. The festival drew vendors from throughout the region, and although many worked the event every year, most had never encountered Buddy Entwhistle. Even many local business owners didn't recognize the name. Three hotel managers remembered hiring the old drunk for odd jobs the previous fall and in late winter but none had seen him since. The boardinghouses that provided cheap temporary rooms were filled with summer staff from area resorts. Maybe Beck was wrong about Entwhistle living in Ephraim. If he was around, he was keeping a very low profile. A smart move, thought Cubiak, as he massaged his right knee. Macklin died after telling his friend about a mysterious second person on the tower with Wisby. Maybe Entwhistle figured he knew too much and went into hiding. Or he fled, scared for his life. Which meant he could be anywhere.

Cubiak looked out the window. The view was all forest. He envisioned Falcon Tower looming above the tree line. At that early hour its upper reaches would appear smudged and black against the bright blue of the sky. That's where it all began, he thought. But why and how had Wisby died? And what about the others? Cubiak craved coffee, but even more urgent was the need to organize his thoughts.

On a dresser mounded with books and clothes, he pulled a yellow notepad from under a pile of socks. Perched on the edge of the bed, he flipped to a blank page and jotted the names of the dead across the top, listing them in chronological order: Wisby, Macklin, Jones, Delacroix, and Anders and Pithy. Down the left margin, he noted five topics—PI or personal information; LC, local contacts; COD, cause of death; Opportunity; and Motive. Separating the headings with vertical and horizontal lines, he fashioned a crude chart and started to fill in the blanks.

Other than Wisby, Cubiak knew very little about the people who'd died or why anyone would want them dead. Initially, Halverson insisted that Wisby had leapt off the tower platform, but Bathard had ruled the death accidental. Not just because of the proximity of the body to the tower, although Johnson admitted he might have moved the victim in the initial confusion of trying to revive him. But because, according to the family physician, Wisby was fearful of heights. The coroner understood that suicides valued control and chose a method of dying that allowed them to guide every step of the process, avoiding any factor that jeopardized their tragic goal. A woman scared of guns wouldn't use a pistol to take her own life; she'd worry that she might pull the trigger too soon or not aim correctly. A young man afraid of heights would not climb a tower with the intention of jumping off. He'd worry about losing his nerve or his footing at the wrong moment. Wisby either accidentally slipped to his death or was shoved off the tower by someone intent on murder and strong enough to heave him over the railing. Macklin supposedly saw someone with Wisby. Was the unknown second person the killer? Did Macklin die because he saw Wisby pushed to his death and could identify the attacker? Jones, the third to die, had been murdered. But by whom and why?

Delacroix, the next victim to be discovered, was an insurance agent from Iowa. His death could have been an accident, but again that was improbable. Anders and Pithy, the final two, were students from UW–La Crosse. It was unlikely that they died as the result of a prank, as Beck insisted. That left two possibilities: either the three visitors were known to someone who wanted them dead, or they were random victims targeted for a reason or reasons unknown.

Had one person killed Wisby and Macklin? Another, the three tourists? And Petey, Alice Jones? Or were there two killers: Petey and the person responsible for the other five deaths? Possible but not likely, thought Cubiak. Despite the different MO's, simple logic pointed to one killer, which meant the six incidents were connected. But how? He hoped the evidence gathered at the crime scenes would provide a clue.

SHERIFF'S HEADQUARTERS WAS in the new Justice Center outside Sturgeon Bay. From the jeep, Cubiak watched the herd of Holsteins across the road. One of the black-and-white cows occasionally tossed its massive head and another flicked its tail, but most focused on eating. They seemed a contented lot, unlike the shifty raccoons that foraged for food in the Dumpsters behind his old Chicago precinct center. Cubiak hadn't been inside a police station in a year and a half, and the proximity alone was enough to remind him how much he missed his former job. He'd been a good policeman, and along with regret for his vanquished life came confusion over his present role. What exactly was he? A cop masquerading as a park ranger, or a park ranger pretending to be an officer of the law? This morning, with a half-day off from work, he wore jeans and a T-shirt and could have passed for a tourist.

Cubiak sensed a reckoning waiting and reached for the key. Then he remembered Mara and realized it didn't matter if he was a cop or a ranger or just a civilian; he'd vowed, if only to himself, to see this through.

Inside, he stepped into a familiar past. Door County sheriff's headquarters was modern and quiet yet he felt instantly at home. He had a job to do and he knew how to do it.

Behind a glass wall, a young receptionist looked up.

"Dave Cubiak for Sheriff Halverson," he said.

She tugged at the heavy green cardigan draped

around her shoulders and hit a button on the phone console. "Somebody to see you," she said, then buzzed him in and pointed down a long hallway.

The sheriff was ruddy from the sun. "Hey, what are you doing here? How come you ain't in uniform?" he said, waving his visitor to a chair in his corner office.

Cubiak swore under his breath and pulled the door closed. "My morning off," he said. Then, "You talk to Beck?"

"Not since the meeting. I been busy arresting more of them bikers."

Cubiak approached Halverson's desk. Halverson. "We got a new situation, which I'm sure you can appreciate. And whether you like it or not or whether I like it or not, it's what we're dealing with. So we need to come to some sort of accommodation on this."

The sheriff looked confused. "What do ya mean? Why you talking so much, anyways?"

"Beck wants me to help with the investigation. You have questions, you have to take them up with him."

Halverson picked up a bundle of reports. "Meaning?" he said as he tapped the documents on the desk, taking care to align the edges.

"You'd be in charge officially, of course. You do what you think needs doing, long as it doesn't interfere with what I'm doing or want done. If I ask for men, I get them. If I want you somewhere, you go." Cubiak paused. "Think of me as kind of a consultant."

"This 'cause of what Macklin told Entwhistle?"

"Yes. New ball game."

"But I got all them bikers under control. I thought we agreed they were the troublemakers."

"And you may be right, Leo."

Halverson flushed a deep crimson. "Kind of an unusual arrangement," he said after a moment, his voice flat.

"It is."

Again, the sheriff took his time responding. "You mess up, it's your ass."

"My ass."

Halverson cleared his throat. "I still don't like it."

"Didn't think you would."

"This all going to be real quiet-like?"

"Absolutely."

"Sure hope you know what the hell you're doing," the sheriff said resignedly. He had recruited another five men that morning, he told Cubiak. "They can help with traffic or whatever."

"Good. We'll need them," Cubiak said. His biggest concern, he told the sheriff, was for public events like the water show on the festival's opening day.

"I got twenty years in with the county, one way or another. Five more to my pension," Halverson said.

"Understood. No one's going to mess with you on that. Now, if you'd be so kind, I need the salvage from Macklin's tug."

"What do ya want with that stuff?" Leo tried to sound breezy.

"Just fishing."

The sheriff led Cubiak to a vacant office and then barked an order to a gangly, boyish officer who retrieved two plastic bags from the evidence room and dropped them on a table along with a pair of latex gloves.

"Help yourself," Halverson said.

Cubiak pulled the gloves on. He disliked the clammy feel of the material, but he knew the rules. There wasn't much to inspect in the first bag. A few scraps of wood, the pathetic remnants of the *Betsy Ross*, smelled of fish and gasoline.

The other bag gave off the same bad odor. It held the detritus scooped from the water where the boat had been moored. Cubiak sifted through the bits and pieces: chopsticks that had once been part of fishing poles, scraps of netting, a dented aluminum pot, a shredded cushion, shards of cloth, a twelve-inch length of rope, and a baseball-sized chunk of black plastic. He set the remnants of rope and plastic on the table. The rope fragment was charred at one end and neatly sheared on the other. From the diner, Cubiak had had a clear view of Macklin on the boat. He'd seen the old man bend down and retrieve something from the deck. A vague image of a sinewy, gray object flashed through Cubiak's memory, and he realized that Macklin had picked up a fragment of rope. There'd be lines and ropes all over an old fishing trawler. Why would one particular piece catch Macklin's eye?

Cubiak studied the hunk of plastic. The piece was slightly rounded and embossed with clear white markings near the ragged upper edge. He rolled it in his palm, thinking.

"They were good ones. Strong."

Cubiak started. He hadn't realized the junior officer was still in the room.

"The old man's binoculars. The numbers give the rating."

"Sure?"

The deputy blushed. "I'm an amateur astronomer."

Probably not the kind that studies the night sky, Cubiak thought. What about Macklin? Was he a star gazer or a voyeur? Had he seen something he shouldn't have through the lenses?

Cubiak jotted down the number rating. Then he looked at the rope again. "Let me see what you've got from Delacroix, the guy at the lighthouse," he said.

There were three clear plastic bags, the contents black with dried blood. When he unzipped the clothing bag, a sharp, musty odor filled the room. The deputy gagged but Cubiak didn't react. He pulled out the cap and fingered the stub of yarn that extended from the peak. He'd once had a cap similar to this one.

"No tassel?" he said.

The officer looked around as if he expected the missing piece to suddenly materialize in the room. "We ain't got it," he said after a moment.

The tassel could have fallen off long before Delacroix was pinned to the door of the lighthouse. Or, Cubiak thought, the killer was collecting souvenirs.

"One more, if you would. Suzanne Pithy. Just the personal stuff." He didn't need to see more blood.

From the back room, the deputy returned with a single bag, pitiful in its size and contents. The young cyclist hadn't had much with her the morning she died: driver's license, credit card, two dollars and some change, sports watch, high school graduation ring, and a single, silver hoop earring. Women lost earrings all the time. Lauren had kept a small box full of what she called earring orphans. A missing earring might not mean a thing.

Halverson was dozing in his chair when Cubiak returned. He coughed and the sheriff bolted upright. "You done?"

"For now."

CUBIAK TRIED TWO stores in downtown Sturgeon Bay before he found a pair of binoculars comparable to those salvaged from Macklin's boat.

"On a clear night, you'll see the rings of Saturn," the shopkeeper promised.

Cubiak pulled out his wallet. He didn't need to see that far.

To avoid traffic, he used the peninsula's interior county roads and came to Jensen Station the back way. He made a quick call, changed into his ranger outfit, and hurried to the docks at Ephraim. It was late morning and the bay was dotted with recreational boaters.

John Breuder was waiting on the last wharf north of the village center, a clunky cabin cruiser at the ready. "Tank's full," the dock manager announced after Cubiak introduced himself and flashed his ID. "Get you where you want to go and back, assuming you ain't going too far or staying too long."

"Just around the cove."

"Fishing?"

"No."

Breuder pointedly surveyed the pier, noting the absence of any appropriate equipment. "Didn't think so. Traveling light if you was." Slightly bowlegged, he nudged the boat out with the toe of his boot and remained silent until it drifted back into the rubber bumper. "Be surprised, the stuff folks bring out with them. Enough to sink a battleship." He grinned at his own wit. "So where you off to?"

The sleeves of Breuder's blue workmen's shirt were rolled neatly to the elbow. He wore a gold wedding band on his left hand and dangled the contract in his right. He hadn't yet offered it up for a signature. Cubiak said something about writing up an official report about the incident at the tower and told him his itinerary. He was happy he had.

The boat handler knew the precise route Macklin took from Ephraim to Chambers Island after he'd drop off his catch. The fisherman religiously followed the same path, hadn't varied it in years, Breuder explained, as he squinted over the glistening water and pointed the way. From the fishery north of town, he'd steer along the top of Horseshoe Island and then hang a left and make a direct run west to his pier on Chambers Island.

"Why go around Horseshoe? Isn't it closer to cut along this side of the island?"

"Aye." Breuder blinked into the sun. "Shorter distance for sure, but takes longer 'cause of the currents." As he talked, he handed over the contract and watched Cubiak scrawl his name.

When the formalities were complete, Cubiak stepped into the boat, regaining his balance as the bottom shifted underfoot.

"Course you're talking about Sunday, and on Sunday Benny would've gone into town first, before heading back," Breuder drawled on, pretending not to notice Cubiak's clumsy attempt at righting himself. "Martha Smithson over the bakery makes her fresh pecan rolls every Sunday morning starting in early June. Benny had a soft spot for them. Some say for her, too." He hesitated. "It was Sunday, wasn't it?"

Breuder was right, Cubiak realized. At Beck's party, Cate had told him that Benny had gone into Ephraim early for pecan rolls. If he was on the water, returning home, around the time Wisby was on the tower, he might have seen what happened.

Cubiak was suddenly self-conscious about engaging the motor in front of Breuder, but the old man seemed to have forgotten him. While Cubiak fiddled with the controls, the pier manager stared past the boat toward the park and Falcon Tower. Was he thinking the same thing? Before Cubiak could ask, Breuder turned on his heel and shuffled back toward his shanty office.

Cubiak was grateful that the water was calm. Dodging a cluster of small pleasure craft, he retraced Macklin's path as best he could. According to Breuder, Macklin would have moored at the Christiana's private pier. It was near the bakery and since the season wasn't officially underway, he wouldn't have worried about trespass warnings—not that Macklin would have heeded the signs even during season, Breuder added. Cubiak didn't share that luck. The Chris's water access was cordoned off for swimming and the dock hopscotched with guests' floating jetsam, making it impossible for him to get within one hundred feet of land. Offshore, he idled the engine and let the boat coast to an easy stop. As it rocked beneath him, Cubiak pulled out the binoculars.

They were deceptively light. He draped the thin strap around his neck and, for a quick test, scanned Ephraim. The lens power surprised him. The village's narrow lanes ran at his feet. Uphill, the cottages were an arm's length distant. In one garden, he watched a young woman carefully snip roses, both the flowers and her face visible in vivid detail, down to the delicately scalloped edges of the petals and the mole on her right cheek.

Comfortable with the heft and manipulation of the binoculars, Cubiak reengaged the motor and pivoted the boat 180 degrees. He moved at a trolling speed, taking his time as he pictured Macklin doing with the *Betsy Ross* that Sunday morning. Like Benny, he crossed the cove, running parallel to the park and occasionally scanning the cliff face with the binoculars. He made several passes, each one equally frustrating. No matter where he was when he looked up, the bluff blocked Falcon Tower from view. He was approaching Horseshoe Island before he got a clear view of the upper portion of the structure through the lenses. Even then the result was disappointing. There were several people moving about on the platform and two people ascending. Cubiak could make out the people on top but the faces of those on the stairs were blocked by the steps and hidden in shadow. Assuming Benny had noticed a second person coming up the tower after Wisby, he wouldn't have known who it was.

Breuder was out when Cubiak returned the boat. A lanky, suntanned teenager haphazardly hung the key on a pegboard inside the office door, scribbled his initials on the receipt, and returned Cubiak's driver's license. Breuder would have asked how it went. The boy didn't bother.

Cubiak headed back to square one. Falcon Tower.

Falcon Tower loomed over the surrounding trees, a symbol of humanity's dominion over nature. The trapezoidal structure was supported by thick corner beams that gradually tapered inward as they rose up seven floors. Cubiak climbed to the first platform and then trudged past the second.

The last flight carried him above the treetops. He'd seen the view before but it still grabbed him. This was Door County at its purest: water, land, forest.

Two adults and a teenage girl stood at the railing. "Horseshoe Island and the Strawberry Islands," the man said, pivoting from right to left and stabbing his index finger in the air. "Come and look," he said to two children, a boy and girl, who huddled in the center of the deck.

"Stop acting so silly. There's nothing to be scared about," the woman said, her tone mean and dismissive. Was she the mother, the stepmom, or maybe Dad's new girlfriend?

Cubiak grinned reassuringly at the youngsters. "It's okay to be afraid. Lots of people are," he said.

The woman started to say something, then noticed Cubiak's uniform and clamped shut, settling for a raspy throat noise instead of a snappy retort.

Finally, they left and Cubiak was alone on the tower. He scanned the inlet. Most of the cove was visible. There were even more boats out now, two of them proximate to the route Macklin would have taken. Without the binoculars, the vessels were little more than smudges against the blue water. Cubiak could discern color and, on several, humped shapes at the helms but nothing else. Certainly not enough detail to allow for a positive identification. The same was true looking out from the stairs.

If Macklin couldn't make out who'd been on the steps the morning Wisby had dropped off the top, what could he have told Entwhistle that would make any difference? And if the alleged second person couldn't ID Macklin's boat, where was the motive for murdering him? Could the fisherman's death really have been an accident? Cate said Macklin loved his boat and that even drunk he wouldn't be reckless around the *Betsy Ross*. Which brought Cubiak back to the unknown figure Macklin saw climbing Falcon Tower the morning Wisby died.

From the water, Macklin could distinguish two people on the tower but he couldn't say more than that. If the second person, the one on the stairs, knew Macklin was in the bay that morning, then the old man might have been killed as a precaution, making the death look like an accident. But who, other than a local, would know anything about Macklin's routines? Was it possible the fisherman was killed by someone he knew?

According to Beck, Macklin told Entwhistle he saw two people on the tower that morning, "one on top, waving like all get out, and the other coming up the stairs." That put Wisby facing toward the bay. With his back to the stairs, he wouldn't see anyone below still on the steps. If he was on his own, he wouldn't even realize that someone had followed him up.

Cubiak imagined three different scenarios. One: The person on the stairs was a young woman known to Wisby. They'd started the climb together but he reached the top first. Spotting Macklin's boat, he waved. Then, foolishly hoping to impress his female friend when she finally reached the upper platform, he climbed the railing and slipped off just as she got to the top. Two: They were lovers. Perhaps he intended to propose atop the tower. When she announced that she was leaving him for another man, Wisby became overwhelmed with despair. Threatening to do himself in if she left him, he scrambled onto the railing and accidently plunged to his death. Three: Wisby had climbed the tower alone. Waving and shouting at Macklin, he was taken by surprise, knocked off balance, and hurled over the ledge by the mystery climber. Why? And who was the unknown assailant?

From Falcon Tower, Cubiak proceeded to the other sites, following the order in which he'd listed the victims' names: the dock at Fish Creek, Turtle Bay Campground, William Garrity Lighthouse, Ricochet Hill. At each one, dozens of images materialized. He sank into them, hoping some new detail would emerge.

Nothing did. Still, he couldn't shake the feeling that he was missing something important. But what?

Driving back to Jensen Station, Cubiak drew a mental map of the route he'd followed that afternoon. The image reinforced what he already knew, that each victim had died in or near the park. But it also revealed something else. Each death had occurred in a locale that was readily accessible to someone familiar with the surrounding area and yet isolated enough that it could be reached by a killer intent on not being seen. There were probably dozens of people with that kind of intimate knowledge of the park but only one Cubiak could name who had a motive as well.

Whom to trust with his suspicions?

In a different life, when Cubiak was a real cop, he'd learned to follow his instincts, and instinct told him to confide in Bathard.

There was no answer at the coroner's office. Cubiak tried Bathard's house and caught the housekeeper as she was about to leave. She told him that the doctor and his wife were out to an early dinner and, yes, she knew where they had gone.

# ELEVEN

*Monday Evening*

FISH CREEK WAS thick with tourists, and, in the hubbub, Cubiak nearly missed seeing the coroner near the side entrance of Babe and Ray's, one of the town's most popular supper clubs. Bathard had his arm around the shoulder of one woman and was talking to another. The ranger ditched the jeep behind Evangeline Davis's diner and caught up with the three as they slowly progressed toward Sarah Humble's.

Cubiak had never met Cornelia. A photo in the coroner's office showed her petite and waiflike even in good health. Cancer had diminished her to a wisp of flesh and bone. She was a sliver, hung on the arms of her companions, both of them hard pressed to mask their alarm. "So pleased to meet you," she said. Her hand was a feather in Cubiak's calloused palm.

The other woman looked like Cornelia's robust twin. "My sister-in-law, Helen," Bathard said, introducing her to Cubiak.

"I'm on a roll," Cornelia chirped as the two shook hands.

Cubiak lowered his glance, barely able to look at her. "I need to talk to you," he told the physician.

The two men settled Cornelia in the car with Helen and then followed the bike path to Pechta's. This far from the town center, the only sounds were the buzz of mosquitoes and the hard crunch of gravel underfoot. The wind off the bay smelled faintly of fish. The duo was quiet, each man caught up in his own thoughts. Inside the bar, they took a rear booth. The coroner ordered a whiskey, neat. Cubiak asked for tonic with lime. At that, Bathard allowed a slight rise of the eyebrows.

"Things change," Cubiak said as Amelia went to pour their drinks.

"Indeed. Certainly did for me." Bathard concentrated on filling his pipe. "I'm not just a country rube, you know. I worked in the big city, too. Until the day I got a parking citation for exceeding the time at the meter."

"You give up easily."

"The reason I overstayed my allotted time involved a medical emergency. I was in the library reference center when a middle-aged patron went into cardiac arrest. Fortunately, I was able to resuscitate the man before the paramedics arrived. Afterward, as a matter of principle, I accompanied him to the ER and waited for authorities to locate a family member. As you might assume, this took quite a while and I returned to the library to find not one but several citations slapped on the windshield. The patient recovered and called me several weeks later. It turns out he'd been ticketed as well. We considered going to court together and explaining the circumstance, but we never did. For some reason, I remained fixated on the travesty of the tickets and finally decided that this incident was probably the first in a long list of indignities and injustices I'd be forced to endure simply because of the nature of the city. Too big. Too impersonal. Six months later, I returned to Door County and I've been here since."

"Do you ever regret it?"

Bathard furrowed his brow and tamped the bowl. "Sometimes. But mostly not. Life was very good for many years, before Cornelia became ill." The coroner looked past Cubiak. "Tuesdays are the worst. That's when the obituaries appear. She reads them all and recites the details to me when I get home. If the cause of death is not included, she gets annoyed, as if she's been cheated out of some necessary data. Age is important, too. Dying young upsets her. On one visit to the hospital, she saw a child leaving chemotherapy. Diminished to a shadow, poor chap, and crying. She refused to enter the department until he was gone. Next trip, she wore headphones—not that they were plugged in to anything. Just to block sound. She said she simply could not tolerate the thought of a child's soul ascending to heaven."

Cubiak saw Alexis with wings.

Bathard scowled at his unlit pipe. "The awful dilemma is that I could intercede and accelerate the process," he began again. "We've discussed it, many times, but her ultimate decision, which I respect, is to let nature take its course. 'You are burdened as my witness,' she said, 'but it is the lighter burden.'" The coroner signaled for another round. "She's been in excruciating pain for days. Hence her sister's arrival."

"I'm sorry."

"Thank you." For several minutes they sat in a companionable silence, both of them watching Amelia work the bar across the room.

"You'd think she'd hire some help," Cubiak said at last.

"Not enough business to justify an employee—full or part time. Reluctant to part with any more money than necessary. Too stubborn to admit she can't do it alone. Any number of reasons she'd give not to."

Amelia limped toward them and set their drinks on the table. "Gentlemen." She forced a tired smile, and then moved away.

Bathard took a hearty swallow. "Well, what is it?"

Cubiak related his conversation with Beck.

The doctor was quiet a moment. "It's as I feared, then. More than we thought and certainly more than our sheriff can handle." Bathard looked at the ranger. "What made you change your mind?"

"Things you said." Cubiak paused. "Things that happened."

"Well, I for one am happy to know you're on the job. Did Leo acquiesce gracefully?"

"As well as could be expected, I guess. Beck was supposed to tell him but I ended up having to lay everything out this morning. I've been going over the evidence and trying to track down Buddy Entwhistle."

"Try Thorenson. Buddy sometimes does odd jobs around the church. The reverend might know something about his whereabouts."

"I will, thanks."

"Anything else?"

"Halverson's locked up more bikers but I don't think that's going to mean anything."

"Too random."

"And too easy." Cubiak shifted uncomfortably. "I don't think Petey is involved either. Alice's death wasn't a crime of passion. This is someone with a plan. At this point, Peninsula Park is the only common thread. There has to be a reason for everything happening there or near there, in Macklin's case." He hesitated, and when he finally spoke, it was with caution. "It might be Otto."

Bathard looked at him with disdain. "That's preposterous. Utterly and completely preposterous. I can't believe that you would even consider Otto a suspect."

"He has no alibi for any of the murders."

"Or so you assume."

"He discovered Wisby's body and was close enough that he could easily have been the first person on the scene for the others as well. More often than not, that scenario alone points to the killer. The person who finds a body is often the one responsible for its being there in the first place."

"You're referring to police statistics. There are always exceptions. At any rate, you were at the dock when Macklin's boat blew up and with Johnson when the bicyclists were discovered."

"Otto's truck was in the park not far from the pier where Macklin had docked his boat. He might have been working in the woods or skulking around the pier. On Saturday, he could have been out for hours before I saw him at breakfast and then pretended the lighthouse was his first stop. When I went back there with him, he did his best to contaminate the scene."

The two men were quiet a moment.

"Otto has a motive," Cubiak said, finally.

"Too transparent."

"You think so? He wants to close the park. Make it off limits to people and transform it into some kind of nature preserve. He said so in public. At the meeting, he told everyone they'd be sorry for not backing his plan."

Bathard looked doubtful. Cubiak went on. "In the late fifties, three young women were murdered in an Illinois state park. The place was near Chicago and popular with tourists. It took them a decade to recoup the numbers. People panic. They get scared. I think Otto's counting on that happening here and helping him realize this crazy scheme he has."

"He'd never kill Benny. They were friends."

"He had to, to protect himself. Remember, Macklin saw the second person on the tower."

"He claims he saw someone. He didn't actually identify anyone, did he? If Benny thought the second person was Otto, why didn't he tell Entwhistle?"

Cubiak had already considered the question. "Loyalty."

"I don't buy it."

Amelia appeared with pretzels and fresh drinks. "On the house. In honor of the festival," she trilled.

"Otto couldn't have done it," Bathard said when they were alone again.

"Convince me."

Meticulous in his preparation, Bathard refilled his pipe and struck a match. "We're near an open window. Amelia doesn't mind," he said. When the tobacco grabbed at the flame, the coroner took two long draws. "Just how knowledgeable are you about Quakers?"

"I know that they're pacifists."

"It goes further than that. Pacifists don't kill, end of definition? To call a Quaker a pacifist is comparable to labeling Itzhak Perlman a violinist. It doesn't even begin to convey the entire picture."

Bathard inhaled another puff. Can't smoke at home now, he explained matter-of-factly. After several more draws, the coroner went on. "Most people around here are Catholic, Lutheran, or Moravian. Otto's a Quaker.

His parents were, too, as were his grandparents. They were Moravian originally and became converts. Quakers by convincement, to use their terminology. As often happens with those who embrace a new religion as adults, they were purists who subscribed to the older, more orthodox form of the faith. The original Quakers eschewed format and ministers. Their meetings were unstructured. They simply sat and prayed quietly. Sharing the silence, I believe it's called. If someone had something to say, that person stood up and said it. Personal conviction was strengthened when others concurred. Unanimity amounted to God's blessing. That's the kind of religion these people practiced.

"I attended one meeting where Otto's father talked about the 'Inner Light,' the Quaker belief that there is that of God in every man. All humanity expresses the divine. All men are equal, as it were. They don't take it lightly. This is not the empty verbiage of some preamble no one is intended to read, but rather the very basis for daily life. Quakers were antislavery *before* the Revolutionary War. The day after *Kristallnacht*, a group of German Friends confronted the Gestapo and preached fair treatment of the Jews. To kill or injure someone, to act in a violent fashion, represents the greatest affront to God. It is the height of arrogance. You can harm someone only if you feel you have the right, the power, to assume control of that person's fate. A humble person cannot be violent. Violence defies the very nature of humility."

"Otto's not a humble man," Cubiak said.

"He takes pride in his work. There's a difference," Bathard said. "After the US began bombing Hanoi, his father published an antiwar brochure. Very moderate, more a treatise on love. He and the missus drove to Madison and distributed their pamphlet on the steps of the capitol. The governor had them arrested. Big headlines, good political move on his part. His issue for the day. Gave him his requisite fifteen minutes of fame.

"But here, Otto had to live with the repercussions, the ongoing small-town scrutiny and relentless disdain. A pack of high school bullies jumped him and beat him so badly he had to be kept home for a month for his own protection. Halverson's father was among the thugs. You can imagine the poison he poured into Leo about the Johnsons.

"A year later, Otto turned eighteen and became draft eligible. Most boys here were. They enlisted. He claimed CO status, but the climate was still very pro-war and the local draft board denied the request. Otto was sent to jail. The authorities held him for six months, clearly a violation of his rights as no charges had been filed. His parents both died while he was imprisoned but the judge wouldn't release him for the funerals. Claimed it was for his own good."

"All of which could have made him mad enough to strike back."

Bathard squelched a smile. "Quakers seek justice, not revenge. Otto persisted with one appeal after another until the Army formally recognized his conscientious objector status. He was assigned to public service, working with the criminally insane at a Milwaukee hospital. God only knows what he was subjected to during that time, but he never complained.

"Otto was the original flower child. Long before it became fashionable, he believed peace would prevail. Then the Weathermen bombed Sterling Hall at UW–

Madison and fatally injured a physics researcher. To Otto, the inadvertent killing of this one innocent man made the protesters no better than the most bloodthirsty general. He washed his hands of them and everything else he had associated with the antiwar movement. He was dating Beck's sister Claire, did you know that?"

"Yeah, I heard. Probably not to Beck's liking."

Bathard nodded. "At any rate, a couple months later they were driving on an open stretch of road near Fish Creek when they hit a patch of black ice and slid into the oncoming lane. A milk truck rammed them broadside and, well, you know the rest. Claire's death, combined with his sense of responsibility, broke him completely. Otto became a recluse. Nature and animals became his sanctuary."

The coroner emptied his glass. "Otto Johnson has devoted his life to peace and the environment. And what does he end up with? Friends who won't back his fight to save the park, and a genuine war hero as an assistant."

"I'm no war hero," Cubiak objected.

"Please, I know about the medals. You're a war hero whether you want to call yourself one or not, but Otto's no killer."

"You haven't proved that."

"You haven't proved he is."

On his right hand, Cubiak counted out the arguments. "Number one: Johnson had a motive. Number two: he found two of the bodies. Number three: Opportunity. He was near the *Betsy Ross* the day it exploded and less than half a mile from where Alice was killed when he ran into Barry. Number four: circumstantial evidence." Cubiak related Johnson's odd behavior, his comings and goings at unusual hours.

"What's number five?"

"Number five's a hunch."

"Not admissible."

"Fair enough. I'll even concede that none of the other four are strong enough taken individually to nail him. But considered together, they form a convincing argument."

"Interesting, not convincing," Bathard countered.

"I don't have anything else to go on."

Bathard pulled a small notebook from his inside breast pocket, scribbled across the top sheet, then tore the page out and handed it to Cubiak. "Until tonight, only three people knew about this. You're the fourth. I expect you to honor our commitment to confidentiality."

Cubiak held the paper to the light. It was a crude map with several lines of directions beneath the drawing.

"Go on, then," Bathard said impatiently.

"Now?"

"Yes. Posthaste."

Cubiak shoved the map into his pocket. "What do I find there?"

"Your comeuppance."


CUBIAK CUT A sharp diagonal across the peninsula toward Lake Michigan and the Mink River Estuary. "The naturalist's Eden," the coroner had said in describing the area.

North of the river, thick fog slowed Cubiak to a crawl. Even at that, it was sheer luck that he found the narrow passage marked on Bathard's hastily-drawn sketch. The lane was pockmarked with deep ruts. When he came to a patch of thick scrub that made it impassable, Cubiak left the jeep and continued on foot. In the inky dark, the chime of crickets rose and fell. A fox darted past, a blurred streak in the beam from his flashlight. The ground was soft and smelled of moss and rotting wood. Brambles snagged Cubiak's shirtsleeves. A low-hanging branch slapped his face. He was about to turn back when he came to a small clearing, a woodland oasis ringed by a series of unobtrusive plywood sheds. In the center was a one story log cabin with strips of light seeping from the tightly curtained windows.

At the cottage door, Cubiak knocked twice, paused, and then banged the door hard three times, as Bathard had directed. The sound of muffled footsteps came from inside followed by two brisk raps from the other side of the door. Cubiak thumped once with his fist. Several locks were undone and the heavy wooden portal pulled open a crack.

A ribbon of Johnson's rough-hewn face shoved into the opening. If he'd expected anyone, it wasn't Cubiak. Anger supplanted surprise. He started to close the door, but Cubiak put a quick hand out.

"Bathard sent me. He said to tell you I'm acceptable. His term exactly."

"He has a reason," the park superintendent said finally, more statement than question.

"Yes. I'm checking alibis." It was a stupid thing to say, and Cubiak regretted it immediately.

"In the middle of the night?" Johnson was incredulous. "Who for? Why?" he demanded.

"Beck. Because of all the people dying in the park. He was supposed to tell you."

"Well, he didn't. I thought you were through being a cop."

"This is different."

"It's always different for him," Johnson said with marked bitterness. The park superintendent went quiet, and when he spoke again Cubiak heard the note of resignation in his voice. "I'm supposed to believe you? Trust you?"

"Not me. Bathard."

Johnson snorted and jerked the door open. Instead of the stark hermit's retreat Cubiak had expected, the ranger entered a jumbled room that combined elements of a library and a research lab. Bookshelves filled with science journals and reference books covered two walls while metal file cabinets, stacked four high, lined a third. Most of the interior was taken up by four large tables shoved together to form a massive work island that was littered with microscopes, unopened boxes of slides, and racks of test tubes, most of them empty. A large steel box, lid up, occupied the center spot. Harsh but exceedingly bright lights hung from the ceiling. The only decorative element was a carefully mounted display of *National Geographic* photos near the entrance. Cubiak recognized a few of the animal subjects, but he ventured a guess they all represented endangered species.

"Please," Cubiak said. "You're going to have to start at the beginning. I don't know anything about what you're doing here."

A truce had been struck.

"You know how I feel about the desecration of nature and the park?" Johnson said.

Cubiak nodded.

The superintendent gestured around the room. "That's what this is all about."

Moving from one workstation to another, the old ranger explained the process by which he collected animal blood and tissue and plant sap and seeds from Peninsula State Park. Each specimen was catalogued, then dehydrated and processed in order to preserve the DNA for study, and possible regeneration, in the future.

"Why?" Cubiak said.

"To protect as many species as possible from dying out. Isn't that obvious?"

"And if it doesn't work?"

"It will. It has to."

"You've been professionally trained to do this?"

"Some. Mostly self-taught. I read a lot."

Cubiak fished. Who helped him? Bathard? Johnson said he worked alone.

"I want to see a specimen."

"I can't show you the actual specimens. Once they're completed, they are stored in vacuum pacs. But I've got these." From a file drawer Johnson pulled out a thick stack of plastic sheets, each containing a series of photos that documented the specimen preparation process. Each was imprinted with the date and time it was taken. Cubiak sorted through the pile. The dates went back to the previous summer. According to the recent dates— unless the imprints lied—Johnson had been here working when the first incident occurred and the most recent killings took place. If he hadn't shoved Wisby off Falcon Tower and shot the arrow at the lighthouse or strung the wire at Ricochet Hill, there was little reason to link him with the other killings.

"The camera's here?"

Johnson unlocked a tall metal cabinet, pulled a camera from a shelf, and set it on the worktable. The camera reminded Cubiak of his mother's old Brownie, but it was nearly twice the size.

"Bathard special-ordered it from a scientific supply company in The Hague. I got the instruction booklet. You want to see that, too?" the park superintendent said.

Cubiak leafed through the well-worn pamphlet. The first section was in English. He read several pages. Date and time monitors were preset at the factory, at the time of shipping.

"Who besides you and Bathard are in on this?"

Johnson pulled at his chin. "Ruby," he said after a moment.

"But she voted against you at the meeting."

Johnson flushed. "Yes, and I don't understand why. Maybe she felt this was enough. Anyways, I haven't talked with her since. You got to understand that Ruby's sometimes got her own ideas."

"What's back there?" Cubiak pointed to two doors along the rear wall.

Johnson opened the first, revealing a neatly organized supply closet. At the second, he hesitated. "It's where I sleep," he said.

"Sorry," Cubiak said and waited.

The bedroom was little more than a cubicle, a monk's cell absent a crucifix above the bed. A muslin curtain covered the one small window. The narrow cot was neatly made, with a rough wool blanket tucked precisely under a thin mattress. A jacket and fresh shirt hung from hooks on the wall. The only decorative item was a small photo of a woman on the simple, pine bed table. *Claire*. Loyal still. Haunted still.

Cubiak shut the door and retreated back into the main room where Johnson waited. The park superintendent's face was unreadable. "Want to see the sheds?"

The smaller barn housed injured reptiles, garden

snakes mostly, that Johnson had scooped up from the paths and roadways of Door County. The larger building was filled with an assortment of mammals in various stages of recovery from accident and injury. Johnson indicated a fat raccoon that he'd found choking on a marshmallow at the Turtle Bay Campground. It would be returned to the park later that night.

"How'd Beck rope you into this?" Johnson asked as the two retraced their way across the yard. Cubiak gave him the version that didn't include Malcolm or the lost girl. The superintendent listened without comment. "Beck's a snake. Be careful," he said finally.

"I have to see this through."

"Of course."

In deepening fog, the two men shook hands.

So, CLAIRE DIED and Johnson's life became anchored in that one tragic moment. Not too unlike his own situation, Cubiak realized, as he tramped through the dark woods to the jeep. The therapist had said people could never change what had happened, but they could learn to live with it and go on from there. We must learn to forgive ourselves our worst sins, he'd said. Those who do have a stab at happiness.

Cubiak's redemption grew out of a chance encounter with a little lost girl. Had there been prior opportunities, which he'd missed? How many prompts did Otto ignore, until there were no more and he withdrew from society and began pouring countless hours and money into a venture of questionable worth? As far as Cubiak could discern, the only good to come of the superintendent's obsession was that it proved him innocent of the murders in Peninsula Park.

AT JENSEN STATION, Cubiak found a thermos of hot tea and a plate of cookies on his night stand. Dear Ruta. He slept fitfully and was easily roused by a crash of thunder after midnight. As the storm rolled past, he lay still and listened to the wind-driven rain lash the windows. Despite the deep quiet that followed, he was unable to fall back asleep. Restless, he roamed the empty hallways but the dark house yielded little comfort. He took a beer from the back of the refrigerator and retreated to the familiar worn chair in his office. The yard light had been left burning, and the glow through the window filled the room with soft shadows. When Cubiak finished the beer he opened the middle drawer and pulled out a small hinged frame. He opened the sides into a V, steadied the frame on the desk, and looked into the smiling faces of his wife and daughter.

The pictures had been taken in the fall, on the deck behind their house. In one, Lauren was seated in a black metal chair. She wore a brown turtleneck, a match for her chocolate hair. She had a gentle face, and the camera caught her in the middle of a careless laugh. If he worked at it, Cubiak could catch a hint of the jasmine perfume on her wrist. Alexis was a pumpkin in her photo, itching for Halloween in the costume her mother had sewn. She stood on tiptoe, brandishing a taffy apple at the camera, one tiny bite missing and her jaws clamped shut around the morsel.

Cubiak was slumped in his chair when the housekeeper found him. Ruta had been awakened earlier as well, disturbed either by the storm or her own night demons, or perhaps by both. Ramrod straight, gray hair long brushed back from her face, she looked over his shoulder at the photos.

"My wife and daughter," he said, and told her the story.

When he finished, the housekeeper reached into the pocket of her threadbare robe and extracted artifacts from her own past that she laid on the desk. They were sepia prints, dimmed with time and worn on the corners and edges. Photos of people from an era when picture taking was a solemn occasion. The first, her parents, killed during the war, she explained. Next, two boys, golden haired even in the stark black-and-white reality of the image. Her sons. Dead from fever. Last, her brother. He was mustachioed and young. His bearing, regal like hers, overshadowed his too-large and poorly tailored suit. "Borrowed clothes," Ruta said ruefully. She was quiet a long time. "Secretly, he gave bread to a starving man. One piece only. The Russians said the man was an agitator, no-good. So they arrest Simas and send him to a camp."

"Who told them about the bread?"

Ruta stared at the wall as if history was encoded in the plaster. Her husband had collaborated to get medicine for their sick children, she said, her voice tight. He made the authorities agree Simas would be jailed for only a few days. As a formality, they said. Just to teach him a lesson, they promised. When the soldiers came for her brother, they brought the drug. Such a small bottle, she remembered thinking as they tossed it to her. She forced herself to watch them beat her brother and drag him away. The soldiers were laughing when they left. The medicine, too little, and what was there turned out to be mostly water. Her children died in her arms. Simas died in the camp.

"Your husband, what happened to him?"

Ruta put a hand to her throat. "Gone, too," she said in a whisper.

# TWELVE

*Tuesday*

THE RANGERS WERE at breakfast when the phone rang. Ruta took the call.

"For you," she said, handing the receiver to Cubiak. It was Bathard.

Cubiak moved as far from the table as the cord allowed. "You were right. I was wrong," he said, conscious of Johnson behind him stirring sugar into his coffee.

The coroner chuckled. "You were just doing your job. That actually wasn't the reason I called." He coughed quietly. "Rather late notice, my apologies," he said and went on to invite Cubiak for dinner that evening. It was a spur of the moment kind of thing, he explained, the last chance for a few quiet hours before all hell broke loose the next day. "It's not at our house," he added; he and his wife had stopped entertaining some time back. "We're getting together at Ruby's."

"No, thanks." Cubiak's response was immediate and automatic. The autumn after Lauren and Alexis were killed, he'd suffered through too many painful evenings arranged by well-meaning friends intent on cheering him up. Despite everyone's best efforts, he could do nothing more than sit mute in their midst, heedless of their senseless chatter, offended that anyone thought it possible for him to care about anything other than the fact that while their families thrived, his had been destroyed.

Bathard talked past the refusal. "Cornelia's the guest of honor. She specifically asked that you be included." The unspoken message was clear.

Cubiak reached for his coffee but Ruta was holding the cup, topping it off for him, her manner crisp and efficient, with no trace of self-pity. As she passed it back, he remembered how he'd rebuffed that simple gesture from Lauren the morning she'd died. Nodding his thanks, he took the mug. What had Ruta said the night before? "We go on because life goes on. We go on because we must."

Cubiak cleared his throat. "What time?" he said into the phone.

"Six. Around here, that's considered fashionably late."

CUBIAK RETURNED A handful of calls and emails and then went back to the problem of Entwhistle. Remembering Bathard's suggestion, he phoned Thorenson but the reverend claimed not to have seen the old man. Evangeline Davis had been close to Ben Macklin and might know something about his friend. He called the diner three times but there was no answer so he finally drove down to Fish Creek. The restaurant was full. Serving up slices of cherry pie, Evangeline shrugged and said she'd never liked Entwhistle and had never paid him any mind.

Over a pint at Pechta's, Cubiak questioned Amelia. Although Entwhistle had been a regular for years, she, too, knew little about him. He wasn't verbose like so many of her patrons. The more he drank the more withdrawn he became. When he needed to, he'd sleep off a bender on the cot in the back room, as he did the day the *Betsy Ross* blew up. He hadn't been around since.

Amelia seemed bothered by the fact she couldn't provide any useful information.

"He's not from around here, you know," she said as Cubiak was leaving.

"What do you mean?"

"He's a transplant. From somewhere in Michigan. Detroit, I think. Not that that's gonna do you any good."

"It might be just what I need," he said.

At Jensen Station, Cubiak found Ruta in the kitchen chopping onions.

"I need your help finding Buddy Entwhistle."

The housekeeper looked up, her knife poised above the cutting board. "Me? I don't know this person," she said as she scooped the onion into a bowl of ground beef, cracked an egg over the edge and started mixing the ingredients by hand.

"I don't know him either. What I want you to do is to call the information operator for Detroit and get the numbers for every Entwhistle in the area. Then call each of them and see if anyone knows where Buddy is staying."

"Bah," Ruta protested. Her English. The cost.

"Your English is fine, and the calls are official business." Cubiak pulled a pen and notebook from his pocket. "Here, I'll print the name out for you so you'll have the correct spelling. All you have to do is write down anything anyone tells you about him."

The housekeeper patted the raw meat into a cast iron pan.

"Okay? Do this for me, please?"

Ruta wiped her hands in a striped towel. "Okay. Yes. I will try," she said, finally.

AT A QUARTER past six, Cubiak pulled into Ruby's driveway. It had been dark the time he'd chauffeured Cate back from Beck's party, and he'd seen very little of the house and grounds. He expected that someone from a moneyed background who had a national reputation as an artist would live elaborately and was surprised by the simple, unpretentious homestead. The only building substantial enough to be Ruby's studio was a squat, weathered barn at the rear of the yard. There were two storage sheds and a grape arbor on one side and a small pen with three plump sheep on the other. A large garden plot sat nearer the house. A spreading elm shaded an old picnic table, and along the garage there was a low wall of neatly stacked firewood. The grounds were surrounded by a forest of white cedars, and both the house and garage were covered in cedar siding that blended almost seamlessly into the setting.

The back door sprang open and Cate emerged. Her hair was tinged pink and pulled back, and she wore pants and top in monochromatic gray.

As she stepped off the porch and advanced toward him, Cubiak felt increasingly self-conscious. They'd both been in their cups at Pechta's. He couldn't remember all that had been said and wasn't sure if the confidences they'd shared would embarrass either of them in the sober light of day.

Cate reached for the wine he carried. "Glad you could make it," she said, her tone was neither warm nor cold but she didn't pull back as her fingertips grazed his wrist and her calm neutrality put him at ease.

Cubiak followed her to the door and into a rear hallway cluttered with outdoor gear. The passage opened into a wide, colorful kitchen, scented with the jumbled bouquet of fresh-baked bread and fried onions and garlic. Green and yellow ceramic bowls lined a red-tiled counter. Copper-bottomed pots and pans hung over a blue workbench. Cookbooks spilled from a narrow bookcase. Jars of home-canned beans, peaches, and tomatoes filled two long shelves that had been hung to accommodate the reach of a tall person. A rectangle of windows opened onto the forest of fir trees.

Cate disappeared with the wine. Ruby, her face tinged from the heat, stepped away from the cast iron stove and gave him a solid handshake. Her hair was twisted into a single, jet-black braid. Her long skirt and top were rich-hued, flowing suede.

"Evelyn you know, of course, and the lovely Cornelia." At the built-in dinette, Bathard's wife floated on a throne of pillows. Her pale pink turtleneck and stylish white trousers seemed to envelop little more than air.

"Thank you for coming. I'm sure you're terribly busy at the park these days," she said in a surprisingly strong voice. "Evelyn was on the committee that drew up many of the hiking trails. It's such a wonderful place. A refuge from the world."

A glance from Bathard told Cubiak that the coroner had spared his ill wife news of the recent tragedies.

"You're happy there?" Cornelia said.

Cubiak was spared answering by Cate who reappeared with goblets of wine. Talk fell easily to local history and peninsula politics, and he relaxed into the undulating wave of conversation. From the stove, Ruby gave out the occasional directive, and in a while, a timer rang. After the bustle of plating, they moved into the dining room for a meal of roasted venison, braised root vegetables, hot rolls, and a salad of wild greens.

For coffee and dessert they drifted into the living room. While Cate tended the fire and Bathard settled

Cornelia into a low, stuffed chair, Ruby handed Cubiak servings of homemade cherry strudel to pass. The room was comfortable and informal, with three long skylights on a vaulted ceiling and a span of windows that looked out over the eastern approach to Death's Door. Shelves piled with art books and Navajo pots flanked the stone fireplace. A handful of small weavings and three large abstract paintings hung on one white stucco wall. The other, facing the sofa, was filled with stark black-and-white photos of elderly women with infants.

"Grandmothers and grandchildren," Ruby said, noticing Cubiak studying the pictures. She set a fresh bottle of wine on the coffee table and then sat on the sofa with him. "Some of Cate's work. She's quite a good photographer, you know. *National Geographic. Smithsonian* magazine."

"Well," he said, surprised. He'd assumed Cate's job was more a rich woman's way of keeping busy than a profession.

Cate reached for another log, her back to him. "Yes, well," she said and dropped the wood onto the fire. Cubiak started to make room for her on the sofa but shifted back when Cate sat on an upholstered hassock near the hearth.

"Talented family," Bathard interjected. He was perched on the arm of Cornelia's chair, one foot on the floor, the other casually twined around his ankle. "There's Cate, of course, following in the footsteps of her famous aunt. Ruby's latest weaving, Tree of Life, will be unveiled tomorrow evening, isn't that right, Rube?"

"Yes, and you're welcome to come. Six thirty at the Birchwood."

Cubiak wasn't sure if the invitation was sincere. Ruby

had barely glanced his way when she spoke. And Cate had remained silent.

"And then there's Dutch," Bathard went on. "A man with his own special skills. Built most of the house himself, for one."

"Dutch?" Ruby's voice softened as she looked at Cubiak, the glow of a happy memory playing across her face. "My late husband. A former cop, like you. They called him the 'Legendary Dutch.'" She looked around the room, as if expecting to catch a glimpse of his shadow. What had Cate said at Pechta's when Amelia showed him the Survivalist Club photo? That Ruby had taken it real hard when Dutch died. Cubiak recognized the longing in her eyes.

"How's the book going?"

Ruby scowled at the coroner's question and then gave a quick laugh. "Slowly. Very slowly."

"About three years after he retired, Dutch started compiling a natural history of the county. I believe he was working on it right up until the time he died," Bathard explained. "I was after Ruby for some time to finish it. Finally convinced her last winter. You are working on it?"

"Yes, I am, but it's hard. Hard to pick up where he left off." Her tone had a sudden, sharp edge but she squared her shoulders and assumed a light, breezy air. "A wonderful man, Dutch. Unflappable. Never afraid—not of anyone or anything."

"Certainly not bear," Cornelia said.

The others laughed. Cubiak looked up from refilling his wineglass—his third drink of the evening, already one past the limit he'd set for himself. "Bear?"

"It's an infamous story, part of local folklore,"

Bathard explained. "Dutch and Ruby were mushrooming one day when a young black bear popped out of the woods, rambled up to Dutch, and for no apparent reason clamped its mouth around his forearm. I wouldn't have believed this tall tale myself, except that Ruby called the next day and insisted I come by and take a look at Dutch's arm. By then the tooth marks had faded and become distorted but they were still clearly discernible."

Ruby patted Cubiak's knee. "Dutch wore that bear like a bracelet," she said with certain smugness.

"I love hearing the old stories," Cornelia said wistfully, resting against her husband. "Tell us, Ruby. Tell us again about Dutch."

"It's getting late…" Ruby started to protest, but Bathard signaled his assent, and Cubiak realized that for the dying, some things were more important than rest.

RUBY WALKED TO the window. Hands clasped, she stared into the fading light for a beat and then turned toward them. Her face was serene as she started speaking.

"Beck introduced us. I was twenty and Dutch a year older. He'd just finished his junior year at the UW campus in Green Bay and wasn't sure if he would be able to return to school. His father was seriously ill, and if he didn't recover from surgery by fall, Dutch would have to drop out and work full time in the family grocery store in Sturgeon Bay."

"What about your education?" I asked, but he just shrugged and said it wasn't a birthright.

"I thought it was."

"That summer the five of us—Dutch, Beck, Eloise, Claire, and I—practically lived on Beck's boat, a thirty-eight-foot yawl. Sometimes Otto came along, too."

Cubiak stirred, amused by the notion of a young, carefree Johnson out on the water.

"One afternoon in late August, we followed a famous racing route from the Coast Guard Station up around the tip and into the bay, trying to beat the best time.

"I rode the prow and watched for landmarks. Eloise plotted the course. Dutch worked the mainsail. Claire, the jib. Beck was captain. He was always captain. We passed the old Ridges lighthouse in record time and were through the Door and into Green Bay well ahead of schedule.

"We were passing above the skeletal remains of hundreds of lost ships, laughing where others had suffered frightful and violent deaths, dancing over the graves of ghosts.

"At the finish, we celebrated with champagne toasts, all of us saying the usual silly things, until it was Beck's turn.

"'To honor among friends,' he proclaimed, all very solemn and serious-like. He raised his glass, emptied it, and flung it as far as he could into the bay. Dutch repeated the toast and the two of them shook hands, almost as if sealing a pact.

"On shore, the trees were turning. Dutch pointed to the splotches of red and gold and said we must always be aware of the sure and quick passage of time. Then he started to sing: *Should auld acquaintance be forgot and never brought to mind...*"

Ruby looked around as if surprised that the room was filled with guests. "'You know the song,' he said, and we all joined in: *We'll drink a cup of kindness now for auld lang syne.* Oh, we were so young, so drunk on ourselves. Youth is joy, sentimental in ways age cannot fathom. Naive in ways that later seem almost absurd.

"A few weeks later, I went home to Milwaukee and Dutch went to work in his father's store. But the war in Vietnam was escalating, and he was drafted. He could have asked for a deferment, because of the situation in his family, but he didn't. He was inducted in 1968, a year after the bombing of Haiphong and Hanoi had started.

"The next summer, I went out west to a Lakota Sioux reservation where I taught the mechanics of art to kids who didn't have enough food to eat, while I learned the spirit of art from a woman who…who understood life.

"In the fall I went back to school, and in October, Eloise wrote saying that Dutch had been injured and was in the veterans hospital outside Milwaukee.

"Dutch's ward was at the end of a long, pale green hall. It was a narrow room with seven beds. The patients were all young, all heavily bandaged. Arms and legs in slings. Ropes, pulleys. None of them looked brave or soldierly. They all looked like lonely little boys.

"Dutch had been hit by shrapnel; his right shoulder and leg had been shattered and then put back together. He was bandaged and bedridden. Yet, he was cheerful. He held out his good arm and set his deep blue eyes on me.

"By April, he was able to get around. I took him away from the hospital as much as possible. We went to the zoo and the little German cafés downtown. Mostly we walked along the lakefront and talked. He never asked me to marry him. One day we just started planning our life together."

A log on the fire dislodged and sparked onto the grate.

Ruby waited for Cate to rearrange the wood and then she continued.

"Dutch was still home when Claire was killed in that awful car crash. I came up for the funeral with my family and introduced him to my parents. We told them we planned to marry the following summer. They wouldn't hear of it.

"In the end, I packed my things and returned to Door County, alone. We were married in a nondenominational chapel outside Ephraim. My sister came. My parents didn't. A month later, Beck married Eloise. They had five hundred guests, a lawn covered with tents, and strolling violinists. Dutch was the best man. I was the matron of honor.

"He was a fine man, Dutch, and the people here admired him. He'd been decorated for bravery in Vietnam, and later when he ran for sheriff he was elected handily. After he rescued a little boy trapped in an abandoned well, he became a local celebrity. Dutch always said anybody could have saved the child, but the point is, no one else even tried. The brick walls of the pit were weak and had started to collapse, and there was a nest of pine snakes on the bottom. Dutch couldn't take a chance on shooting them with the boy in there. The poor kid was crying for his mother, who was getting drunk at some bar. It broke my heart. We could never have kids, Dutch and I. Well, he got the boy out. The child was unharmed but Dutch had seventeen snake bites on his legs.

"About a year after Dutch was elected sheriff, a woman was beaten to death and set on fire in her living room. The house was ransacked and some money and jewelry stolen.

"There'd been a series of burglaries near Green Bay

that spring, and everyone thought this was another random act of violence, probably committed by the same person. Dutch was sure the killer was someone who knew the victim. He had no proof, just a hunch. Local officials tried to discourage him. Said he was keeping things stirred up, painting the county in a bad light and all that kind of nonsense, but Dutch persisted. He made up charts with the names of everyone who knew the dead woman or had been seen near the house. He checked every detail of their relationships with the victim, tracked down every bit of information he could. Something like this happens, there's a reason for it, he said. Eventually, he figured it out. It was the victim's twin sister. About a year before she'd had a fleeting acquaintance with the man who later became engaged to the deceased.

"Dutch showed me pictures of them as kids. Two beautiful little girls on an old tire swing. Then to end up like that. How sad the underpinnings of people's lives."

As Ruby stood transfixed against the black backdrop of the windows, the wind came up and began butting against the glass, a signal like a curtain falling. Cubiak picked up the wine bottle and then put it down again.

"You should look at them," the coroner said to him.

"What?"

"Dutch's notebooks. From the murder case. Quite impressive in their own right." Bathard spoke over his shoulder. "Could he, Rube?"

"Well, if he wanted to, of course." The tempo of the evening had slowed and no one noticed Ruby's slight hesitation, least of all Cubiak. He wasn't interested in the musings of a deceased small-town sheriff but felt awkward refusing.

Ruby left the room and returned with a stack of pocket-size notebooks. "Leo's the one who should read these," she said, handing them to Cubiak.

"Now, Ruby, he's had a tough life," Bathard said.

"No excuse for incompetence," she retorted.

Cate and Bathard helped Ruby clear the room, leaving Cubiak with Cornelia, who seemed to grow increasingly pale in the fire's fading light.

"We were all honored to know Dutch. He was a man of principle, the best," she said. Cornelia's voice was reduced to a whisper, and Cubiak had to lean forward to hear her.

"When he recovered that first time, he went back, after they were married. To Vietnam. To be with his men. He asked to be sent back. Can you believe it?"

"I can. I'd seen it happen, many times."

"Later, there was a rumor he'd been killed in action but it turned out he'd been badly wounded and taken prisoner. Ruby doesn't like to talk about it. I always wondered if his war experience didn't affect his health and contribute to his early retirement," Cornelia said, every word an effort.

"Halverson couldn't begin to fill Dutch's shoes. Not that anyone expected him to. It was common knowledge that he'd gotten the sheriff's job as payback for his father's accident at Beck Industries."

"Frank Halverson worked for Beck's family?"

Bathard reappeared. "Indeed. Most people did. Still do," he said as he fussed with the pillow at his wife's back. "What do you think?" he indicated Dutch's journals.

Cubiak hadn't bothered with the notebooks yet. To

be polite, he picked up the top one and flipped through several pages. He was about to put it down when something stopped him. Dutch had drawn an elaborate chart similar to the simple one he'd sketched out the previous morning. "Interesting," he mumbled.

"I should think so," Bathard said. "Dutch threw out a wide net, considered everyone a potential suspect until they were proven innocent. Played out his instincts. Always needed to know *why*."

# THIRTEEN

*Wednesday Morning*

CUBIAK STRADDLED A chair and watched Bathard stack boxes of bandages and gauze in the temporary first aid station at the Ephraim Village Hall. It was midmorning. The muffled noise of the waterfront crowd mixed with the smell of hot dogs and popcorn that drifted in through an open window.

"Any luck with Entwhistle?" Bathard said.

"Not yet. Thorenson hasn't seen him lately. Amelia said he had family in Detroit so I've got Ruta calling every Entwhistle in the metro area, on the chance he's holed up with a relative. I'm sure she'd rather be baking pies but she'll be thorough." Cubiak yawned. "Sorry."

"You getting any sleep?"

"Enough." He flexed his shoulders. "What time do things get going, officially?"

"Ten." Bathard glanced up at the wall clock in the small back room. "Fifteen minutes to bedlam," he said as he continued organizing supplies.

"I've been thinking," Cubiak said eventually, "that maybe the deaths don't have anything to do with the park. Could be the purpose is to sabotage the festival."

Bathard paused. "An interesting reason *why*, but who would want to do something like that?"

"Some crazy who hates the tourist hoopla or someone with a heavy grudge against people like Beck who benefit from the festival's success. In terms of prestige, it seems Beck has the most to lose if the thing flops. If I were to follow Dutch Schumacher's line of reasoning, I'd have to suspect everyone who knows the man either personally or through business dealings."

The coroner looked up. "Including me?" he said, his tone light and mocking.

"Correct."

"No one above suspicion."

Cubiak laughed. "I guess. Actually, the only person I wouldn't suspect is Cornelia."

The physician said nothing and went back to his task, working steadily until he finished. Then he opened a folding chair and sat facing Cubiak. Taking his time, Bathard crossed one leg over the other and pulled his pipe from his pocket. "No smoking in here, but…" He stuck the stem into his mouth. "I've been giving this a lot of thought. It seems that whoever's behind it—if it is one person—is deliberately generating an aura of confusion. There's no question that Alice Jones was murdered. In the case of Wisby and Macklin, on the other hand, it can be argued that accidents happen. Same with Delacroix: arrows do go astray. Not that I agree with Beck," the coroner added. "The business at Ricochet Hill is more difficult to discern. Those two deaths weren't necessarily as simple as they looked. Piano wire stretches taut easily, but when it's hit forcefully it sags. Anders weighed over one hundred seventy-five pounds. He hit the wire with his neck, not torso, but that's still a tremendous impact, considering the road incline and speed he had to have been traveling even if he weren't pedaling strenuously. After he hit, the wire would have sagged considerably."

Bathard set the pipe back on the table. "I spent an hour in my backyard early this morning pitching a concrete block against a strand of piano wire tied between two trees. Every time I hit the mark, the wire loosened and drooped. Based on my rough calculations, the wire should have cut Pithy across the chest, but she got it in the neck as well."

"Meaning?"

"Someone was in the woods, watching. After the first rider came through, this person reset the wire ensuring that it was in place when the second rider came along."

"There wouldn't have been much time."

"No, but it could have been done."

"You tried?"

"Of course. At first it seemed an implausible theory. If the wire is properly tightened around the tree, there's precious little time to make any readjustments, but I devised two ways someone could have made this work. In the first method, the killer—we'll use that term rather than Beck's 'joker'—ties the wire around two trees, one on either side of the road. After the first rider slams into the wire, the murderer doesn't have time to untie and retie it, or to loosen and retighten it, before the second bicyclist appears. Instead, the killer slides a slender solid object—a small crowbar would suffice—between the wire and one of the trees and rotates it approximately one hundred and eighty degrees. The maneuver pulls the wire taut again. With practice that can be done in seconds."

"No chance the bar would fall out?"

"Not really. The wire secures it in place. Of course, afterward, the killer has to remove the bar. Unless there was something found at the scene of which I am un-aware."

"There wasn't anything. And there was always the chance the person could be seen that close to the road. What's the other method?"

"It's a little more complicated but for some people, an accomplished sailor, for example, it would be the obvious choice. This time the killer ties the wire around one tree—let's call it tree A for the sake of discussion—and then strings it across the road, winds it once around the trunk of tree B. Instead of tying a knot, the perpetrator wraps the wire around the horns of a cleat, the same way you or I would secure a sail or one of those bamboo roll-up blinds. The wire stretches after the first hit, and the killer resecures it to the cleat."

"How quickly could that be done?"

"I can do a rope in a couple of seconds. A wire wouldn't take much longer."

"We didn't find a cleat on the second tree or evidence of one either."

Bathard picked up the pipe again and punched the air with the stem "It wasn't necessarily on tree B. In fact, it would have been easier to work if it were on a different one, tree C as it were. In any case, after the second victim hit, the killer pried the cleat off and positioned the wire just the way you found it."

"Could you have done it? I mean, could someone of your stature have tightened that wire using one of these techniques?"

Bathard regarded his arms critically. Even with the long-sleeved shirt it was obvious they were thin and un-muscled. "Hardly seems likely, but, yes, I think so, if I remember my physics correctly. It certainly wouldn't take some kind of muscle man, if that's what you're getting at. In either situation, the killer is using what's called a simple machine, a device that functions without a motorized element, to make a job easier. You're looking for intelligence or experience rather than brute strength."

"For these two."

"Yes, and for the others as well. Wisby, surprise. Height would help. Macklin, access to the *Betsy Ross* and a sharp instrument, a screwdriver would do, assuming the cause was a puncture to the tank. Jones, surprise again and familiarity with human anatomy. Delacroix, hunting or competitive archery."

"A professional bow is nearly impossible to string."

"Only if you're inexperienced. There are thirteen-year-old girls out here who could beat either one of us at the task."

"And the bikers," Cubiak said, thinking out loud. "Basic mechanics or sailing, depending on how it was done."

The coroner rubbed his shoulder. "That's how I see it."

"There's something else, though. The killings themselves became increasingly gruesome. There was a callousness to them that seems out of place here."

"The city dweller's romantic notion of the country," Bathard countered. "You forget that the man who killed his neighbors and then made lamp shades from their skin lived in a small town not too far from here."

"I remember hearing about that. The guy was certified crazy."

"Maybe this one is, also. Normal on the outside. Coming apart inside."

"Whoever it is, whatever the motive, there's something we're missing. A message we're not getting."

Bathard started to speak when a horn blared and shouting erupted outside. He looked at his watch. "Ten o'clock. Right on schedule," he said. The coroner took his time getting up again. "We may as well go and watch," he said.

Cubiak followed him down a short hallway and through the narrow lobby to the front doorway.

"Look over there. The helicopter." Blinking into the bright light, Bathard pointed to a black dot over the harbor.

The crowd spied the chopper as well, and with a loud whoop, a riptide of humanity surged toward the water.

"This is it then, the official start of the fest?" Cubiak said. He had to shout to be heard over the tumult.

"Indeed. One thousand ping-pong balls get dropped. Two hundred marked for prizes. Gimcrackery mostly. But there's one worth five hundred dollars." Bathard raised a hand against the glare. "When the drop first started, it was actually a reasonable activity. Self-contained, controlled. Now it's a wonder someone doesn't get seriously hurt."

"Can't you put a stop to it?"

"Not to something Beck's etched in stone."

The helicopter circled over the water, teasing the crowd. Once. Twice. Three times it made false passes toward Ephraim and then veered away. Suddenly, without warning, the chopper roared inland toward the town. The thwacking blades swirled dust and bits of sand above the sea of uplifted faces and waving arms. Several children screamed but their cries were drowned out by the cheering throng.

On the reviewing stand, Beck grabbed the microphone. "Ready?" he yelled, his free hand thrust into the air, urging on the crowd. "Ten! Nine!" Several thousand voices took up the count. "Two! One! Zero!"

A gong thundered, and the balls were released. Cascading downward, bright red, like ripe cherries, they dripped from the sky, unleashing a free-for-all, mad scramble below. In a scene of wild bedlam, summer visitors and locals alike pushed and shoved in a determined frenzy to grab the balls from the air or, failing that, to snatch them as they bounced and rolled on the ground.

"Jesus, this is nuts," Cubiak said.

"We'll get our share of business from it, that's for certain," Bathard said, stepping back inside.

IN TWENTY MINUTES the scramble was over, and Bathard's first patient arrived, a preschooler with badly scraped knuckles on both hands. Cubiak left the doctor to his bandages and worked his way down the waterfront, kicking through a layer of discarded ping-pong balls. Ephraim pulsed with activity. Clowns wandered the crowded streets, juggling oranges and passing out suckers. Outside the Village Hall, a bearded man in denim overalls shoed a workhorse while two women in long calico dresses and bonnets dipped candles from a vat of melted wax. On the main stage, a dog trainer coaxed a dachshund through a series of hoops. Next to Milton's the local high school band played exuberant marches, while the line for ice cream snaked across the parking lot and out onto the main road. Sunbathers lounged along the beaches while sailboats and kayaks drifted across the shallow bay. Happy children and adults maneuvered bright yellow paddle boats near shore, while farther out a half dozen wind surfers tried to catch a whiff of the erratic breeze. Up the hill at the Christiana, the hotel guests took in the view from a horseshoe of white Adirondack chairs on the front lawn.

Cubiak backed the jeep out of a narrow slot near the docks, made a sharp U-turn, and drove back to the park. If Bathard was right about the wire being secured with a cleat, he'd find the tell-tale puncture marks in the trunk of a tree not far from the one the coroner had dubbed tree B.

At Ricochet Hill, where the cyclists had died, the forest was especially thick, and it took the ranger considerable time to check the nearby tree trunks. Finally he reached a giant oak some ten feet in from the road. A strong windstorm a week earlier had littered the forest floor with broken branches and leaves, but at the base of the oak, the brush had been shoved aside, revealing a patch of mossy undergrowth. As soon as Cubiak knelt down, he spotted the tell-tale holes. The puncture marks were three inches apart and chest high, just the right height for an average or tall adult. Despite the density of the forest, there was a clear line of sight between the oak and tree B, to which the wire had been strung.

Boaters used cleats. But people who sold nautical hardware or hung around the docks would be handy with them as well. Bathard's theory helped explain how the two cyclists had been killed but did little to narrow the field of suspects.

At Jensen Station, Cubiak checked in with Ruta. Armed with a legal pad and several pencils, the housekeeper sat at a card table under the kitchen wall phone.

"I have no news," she said before he could ask.

"Have you reached everyone?"

The housekeeper pointed to a list of names, each one followed by a complicated code of X's, check marks, and circles. "No," she said.

"You're leaving messages?"

"If there's a machine, yes. But some people have no machines."

Cubiak nodded.

"I keep trying."

Cubiak grabbed an apple from the fruit bowl. "Yes. Please," he said.

THE WATER SHOW started at noon. Cubiak found the sheriff in Ephraim wolfing down a brat at a waterfront grill. The ranger took him by the elbow and steered him toward the jeep. "Leo, we need to talk," he said.

"What's up? Where we going?" Halverson said as they climbed aboard.

"We're not going anywhere. I need some information, that's all."

"Information? Like what?"

"The personal kind."

"What do you mean?"

Cubiak pulled out a notebook and pen and turned toward the sheriff. "Where were you the morning of Larry Wisby's death?" he said.

Halverson glared. His shoulders jerked and he lurched forward as if to grab the pen from Cubiak's hand. Instead, he settled back down and wiped a smear of mustard from his mouth. "What the fuck? You know damn well I was dealing with that tree that came down outside Ephraim."

"And before that?"

"At home, asleep."

"The day Ben Macklin got his?"

The sheriff glowered.

"Or how about the night of the full moon when Alice Jones was killed?"

"Where the hell do you get off? I don't have to stand for this…"

"Everyone stands for it. Like with Dutch." Cubiak paused and then went on. "I'm doing what Beck asked me to do. You don't like it, talk to him."

Halverson puffed his cheeks, and then he exhaled slowly and sang out his alibis. "Gun show in Two Rivers. Poker game in Carlsville."

"Witnesses?"

"You bet."

Cubiak closed the notebook. "Sorry, Leo, but I had to do this. I'm working this theory that the real objective is to get at Beck by ruining the festival. If I'm right, you've got a great motive."

A ridge of sweat cut across Halverson's forehead. "Beck? What kind of bullshit is that? And what kind of bullshit trying to tie all this crap to me?"

"Is it? Considering what happened to your father?"

The sheriff bit his lip.

"No thirst for revenge?"

Halverson went sickly white. With a sinking feeling, Cubiak realized that he could make a pretty good guess at the truth. "I need to know," he said quietly.

When the sheriff spoke, his voice was hard and strained. "Ask Bathard. He'll tell you why not."

"I will," Cubiak said. He closed the notebook. "I'm sorry, Leo, but it had to be done."

The sheriff blinked hard and watched a group of teenagers crossing the road in front of them. "Yeah, well. Now we got work to do."

"You got that right." Motioning for Halverson to do the same, Cubiak stepped out of the jeep and leaned against the hood. "Plenty of people will be watching the water show from here, but it's too wide open for our perp," Cubiak said, pointing to the shore where spots were staked out with striped towels, lawn chairs, and umbrellas. "Our killer likes operating in smaller, more confined areas. It's the bleachers up there in the park along the ridge that I'm worried about. Nothing but trees behind them. That's where we'll put most of the men." He glanced at his watch. "We got forty-five minutes to get them in position. You keep five or six of your guys with you down here and send the rest up to the park."

The bleachers were nearly full when Cubiak got back to the park. The prime spots were taken by locals and the more savvy tourists who preferred watching the water show from atop the palisade where they could sit in the shade and still enjoy a clear shot to the bay.

The Thorensons pressed together in the middle of the first row. Behind them, Martha Smithson struggled to save a few square inches of space. She waved to Cubiak. "If you see Cate, tell her to hurry. I can't hold her spot much longer."

Floyd Touhy strolled past with his black-strapped Nikon dangling from his neck. Nearby, Bathard waited in the shade of a towering American elm.

The coroner's brow was furrowed with worry. But he often looked like that. "I left one of the nurses at the first aid station. Had to come up for my niece. She's in one or two of the waterskiing acts," he said.

Near the ridge, Cubiak intercepted the sheriff's re-

cruits. He dispatched half the men into the woods behind the stands and assigned the rest to mingle with
the crowd.

"Fan out and keep alert," he directed.

"What are we looking for?" one deputy said.

"Anything or anyone that shouldn't be there. Anyone
acting suspiciously."

The show opened with an explosion of fireworks that
brought the crowd to its feet, roaring its approval.

Sixty minutes of aerial and waterskiing acrobatics
followed. For the finale, six statuesque young women
formed a human pyramid on the shoulders of four waterskiing Greek gods while five parasailers floated overhead, nylon ribbons of neon pink, purple, and yellow
streaming from their shoulder harnesses. It was quite a
show. Physical strength. Technical exactness. Skimpy
suits. The audience loved it.

Cubiak sat through the spectacle, seeing only imagined disasters.

The performance went off flawlessly. The biggest
challenge was unsnarling the traffic that jammed the
roads after the show ended and the spectators dispersed.

# FOURTEEN

*Wednesday Afternoon*

CUBIAK WAS HEADING back to Jensen Station when a silver Corvette cruised through the park entrance and halted in a patch of bright sun. Despite Wisconsin plates, the vintage car shimmered like an apparition from a Beach Boys song.

The driver's window lowered, and a woman turned and waved. Her blond hair combined with dark glasses and khaki jacket to evoke the image of a surfer girl on safari.

It was Cate. "I forgot to check supplies for the kids' photo class I teach. I do it whenever I'm around for the festival," she said as Cubiak approached. "Where you headed?"

"Lunch."

"I know a place. You want to go? Get away from all this whatever for a little while?"

Later, Cubiak would wonder why he didn't say no.

THEY TRAVELED EAST from the park and quickly left behind the tourist side of Door County. Barely a quarter mile inland, cherry orchards and dairy farms took the place of gift shops and restaurants. Cubiak closed his eyes.

The 'Vette was a smooth ride and Cate was a good

driver. At the junctures, she downshifted to second, rolled to an easy stop, and then moved back up through the gears in a rhythmic, fluid motion that allowed the thoroughbred vehicle to surge forward effortlessly.

"Someone told me once that if you drive a car a hundred miles an hour and blow the horn, you won't be able to hear it, 'cause you'd be going faster than the sound waves. I tried it when I was sixteen. It worked. I didn't hear a thing." Cate laughed. "Now I get safety awards from my insurance company."

Cubiak dozed. When he woke, they were nearing the northern tip of the peninsula. He assumed they were going to eat in Gills Rock but Cate blew past the fishing village and hung a right. Were they heading back to Ruby's? Before they reached the Schumacher homestead, Cate turned into the forest and stopped before an imposing metal gate.

"Where are we?" Cubiak said.

"The Wood."

"The what?"

"You've never heard of The Wood?" Cate scowled at him. "I thought everyone knew about The Wood. It was my grandparents' summer cottage. Ruby and my mother practically grew up here but no one's lived here since Grandfather died. The house exemplifies his curious and eccentric ways. I haven't been back for years. Wonder if it's changed."

Cate pulled a large skeleton key from her bag. "You mind?"

The gate was elaborately scrolled and spiked and loomed like a barrier against the world. But when Cubiak turned the key, it swung open effortlessly.

"What kind of place is this?" he said when he got back to the car.

"You'll see."

A quarter mile into dense woods, they pulled into a large clearing.

Cubiak whistled under his breath. "Jesus. Some cottage," he said, taking in the stately residence across the yard.

"Yeah, right," Cate said.

The Wood was an old money summer retreat. Out front, marble nymphs and deer spurted water in a large fountain surrounded by quadrants of formal rose gardens that were encased by a wide ribbon of Kentucky bluegrass, which in turn was girded by a white stone driveway lined with life-size statues of archers with drawn bows. The huntsmen faced away from the house, a three-story Bavarian hunting lodge that managed to look both ostentatious and comfortable, with its gently sloping roof, dark-stained wood, and red shutters. A balcony ringed the second floor, and lush red geraniums bloomed in the window boxes.

"A bit much, I know, but Grandfather knew what he liked," Cate said, sounding apologetic.

She led him past the flower beds and around the house to the front lawn, then down a brick path to the edge of a high cliff where a wooden deck cantilevered into the air.

"You first," she said stepping aside. "I have vertigo. I need a minute."

Cubiak hesitated. He wasn't fond of heights either and had to think his way to the far side of the platform where water and sky made up the only visible universe.

"The 'Door'?" he said, indicating the white-capped blue spread out before him.

"Yes. But that's not what I wanted you to see. Look there." Gripping the rail, Cate pulled herself onto the deck and pointed northeast to a white lens-shaped mass spiraling into the azure sky. "It's a lenticular cloud above Washington Island. Locals claim it's a unique meteorological phenomenon triggered by a land mass between two bodies of cold water."

Cubiak scoffed. "Sounds apocryphal."

"Maybe. Those kinds of clouds usually form only at high altitudes. I've seen them a couple of times in different places, but there it is. You can see for yourself, and it happens here only during the summer. Has something to do with the wind currents, I believe."

As she spoke a draft of cool air blew across the deck. Cate laughed and held up a second key. It was brass and half the size of the one that operated the gate. "Now the house," she said.

They entered through a rear door.

"Hello." Cate shouted twice into the heavy silence. "See, I told you. Nobody home," she said.

The vacant house had an eerie, lived-in feel. The back porch smelled of fresh paint. Rain jackets and boots were set out in the mud room. A set of earthenware dishes was displayed on open shelves in the kitchen. Fresh daisies filled a vase on the rough-hewn table by the windows. The pantry was stocked with canned goods and bottled water. The refrigerator held perishables and a bottle of Riesling chilling on its side. Cate picked it up and showed Cubiak. "German, 1918."

Cubiak looked around. He couldn't imagine such extravagance. "Why all this?"

"Paranoia? Grandfather always expected the worst and wanted his family to be prepared. He even added a special codicil to his will establishing a fund to pay for the upkeep of the house, in case any of us ever needed to get away," Cate said.

"Away from what?"

Cate raised her hands in a gesture of helplessness. "Who knows? Pretty crazy, huh?"

She kept talking as he followed her up the rear stairwell. "You'd think 'The Wood' refers to the trees outside, but it doesn't. It's for the floors. Each room has a different kind of wood floor made from lumber that was locally grown and milled. The hall is birch from Washington Island. The kitchen, maple from a grove near Ephraim. There's oak in the living room."

On the second floor landing, Cate stripped off her jacket. She wore a black tank top and smelled of sweat and suntan oil. "One more," she said and started up the next flight. Close behind her, Cubiak was suddenly aware of her long bare limbs and the fact they were alone in this strange, isolated place.

"Grandmother's painting studio," Cate announced, stepping into a large room that faced the water. The salon was airy and full of light, with stretched canvases and folded easels stacked in a corner.

"Here's my favorite, the nursery," she said, crossing the hall. The nursery was a storehouse of childhood treasures. Antique toys and games. Delicate porcelain dolls. A three-story Victorian dollhouse. Intricately carved wooden cars. On a table under a high window, an elaborate electric train that circled a village of wooden cottages and shops.

Cate turned over a miniature pink house. "Look at the

inside, how tiny and perfect everything is." As she set it down, the front of her shirt fell away, revealing the soft mounds of her breasts. Cubiak felt a stirring.

"I loved hanging out here when I was a kid. Even school was fun," Cate said, as she set the house down.

"School?" Cubiak snapped from his reverie. "You went to school at The Wood?"

"I played school. Mother and Aunt Ruby *went* to school here." Cate swept aside a beige curtain, revealing a miniclassroom with two old-fashioned desks bolted to the floor. "Two hours every day, all summer. Grandfather was their teacher. He considered schools in general too lax and developed his own instructional methods." Cate pulled down a large wall map, its world view hopelessly outdated. "Odd as he was I liked Grandfather. He was always nice to me."

"And to your mother and Aunt Ruby?"

"To them, he was the law. Mother sometimes forgot her lessons and got her knuckles rapped with a ruler. But not Ruby. Aunt Ruby never forgot anything."

It wasn't all drudge, she explained, as they returned to the first floor. They had fun, too. Parties and friends. "From what I heard, Beck was a regular guest when the girls were teenagers. He had grandfather's imprimatur. Grandfather felt the two families came from the same mold. His had made a fortune in breweries; the Becks got rich with their stone quarry. Beer and bricks, grandfather liked to say. He probably envisioned one of his girls marrying Beck."

They were in a room with burgundy walls, dark leather furniture, and an iron fireplace. The fireplace was flanked by heraldic sconces and the mounted heads of deer and moose. In the corner, a Kodiak bear reared upright on its hind legs, its teeth and claws glistening. A small brass plaque put the animal at nine hundred pounds, taken in Alaska a half century earlier.

"Grandfather's study. He was a hunter." Cate patted the bear. "Grandma was furious when he taught Ruby and Mother to shoot. The guns are all still here, locked up, of course."

A black-and-white photo on a side table showed the proud father holding a Weatherby Mark V and standing between his daughters. "Ruby and Rosalinde." Cubiak read the inscription. They were beautiful young women, relaxed and smiling, cradling their own rifles in their arms, preserved forever in a portrait of patriarchy and privilege. "They look like twins."

"A lot of people made that mistake," Cate said. As she moved alongside him, Cubiak caught a whiff of her perfume. "But they were totally different. Ruby was stubborn and strong like Grandfather. My mother was fragile, always doctoring with one thing or another. Nerves, mostly. That's why I came up here for the summers. I liked to run around, do things, and Ruby and Dutch didn't seem to mind the racket.

"My mother always said that Grandfather loved Ruby best, but after she married Dutch against his wishes, he cut her off completely, wouldn't even allow her to see Grandmama when she was dying. My mother sneaked her into the hospital late one night. Mother said Ruby never understood how her father could be so faithful to a wife he didn't love and so easily discard a daughter he adored."

They had moved from the study to the living room. "I promised you lunch, didn't I? Make yourself comfortable, and I'll pull together something to eat," Cate said.

Cubiak sank into a soft overstuffed chair and looked out at an unblemished expanse of trees, water, and sky, a view reflected in the soft watercolors and oils on the walls. Mirror images. Double images.

He wished he'd asked for a beer. That should be okay, he thought, as he held out his hand, amazed at how steady it was.

He was nearly asleep when Cate padded in and set a plate of sandwiches on the coffee table. "Here," she said, as she nudged his knee and handed him a glass and a chilled bottle of Pilsner. Then she poured one for herself and sat on the sofa facing him, her bare feet tucked up under her.

They talked easily, and, later, each would remember that it was the other who had reached out first across the table. There was longing and familiarity in the touch, an acknowledgment of unspoken attraction and need as they came together. Pressing into Cate, Cubiak escaped the sexual limbo to which he'd been confined since Lauren's death. He had forgotten the sweet sorrow and joy of complete surrender, and when it was over, he lurched away a happy man. Intimacy affirmed not just his masculinity but his humanity. It confirmed a belief in life and hope and the future. He felt whole again, but his exhilaration was short lived. Guilt waited patiently in the corner, and as he relaxed against the soft cushions, it stole forward and claimed him once again.

When Cate finished in the kitchen, she found Cubiak on the deck, a lit cigarette in his hand and two butts crushed at his feet.

"Dave?"

A twitch in his shoulders signaled that he'd heard her, but he didn't turn around. Keeping her eyes down and stepping lightly, Cate approached him.

"Dave?"

Cubiak remained with his back toward her. He'd been unerringly faithful to Lauren, had withstood frequent sometimes mean badgering from other men on the force because of it. After she died, he never imagined wanting anyone else. How could he even look at another woman after that last spiteful remark he'd made to his wife?

"We have to go," Cate said. She reached out and touched his arm.

Cubiak jerked away. Had he anticipated this happening? Was that why he'd come with Cate? He knew he was being unfair to her, but he couldn't help it.

"Ruby's unveiling is tonight. I have to drive you back and get ready."

THEIR EASY COMPANIONABILITY had disappeared, and they rode back in an awkward silence. "You can't go on like this," Cate said at one point, but he didn't respond and she kept her thoughts to herself for the rest of the drive.

"This is fine," he said at the park entrance. Cate hit the brakes.

"I'm sorry," he said, as he got out.

"For what happened? Or the way you reacted?" The questions were quick and arrow sharp.

He reddened. "I don't know. It's complicated."

A wave of something like sympathy passed over her face. "I know."

He wanted to say more but someone behind tooted a horn. He closed the door and Cate drove away, just as he had the night they met.

CUBIAK HAD BEEN gone longer than expected and it was nearly half past five when he reached Jensen Station.

The table wasn't set but Ruta had prepared a cold supper. "No time to cook," she said apologetically.

Cubiak wasn't hungry but took a ham sandwich to please her. "Entwhistle?" he said.

"I find no one."

"That's okay. There's time." He wished he believed that.

Cubiak ate without thinking and then went up to shower and change.

By the time he arrived at Birchwood Lodge, the lobby and two front parlors were full. He saw Bathard talking with a couple across the room and recognized more than a dozen locals with prominent names. The other guests were artsy types, outsiders. Women draped in silver jewelry. Several men wore cashmere blazers and silk ascots.

A beaming Martha Smithson grabbed Cubiak's wrist. "Like old times," she said, her face shining despite a fresh layer of powder.

"Where's Ruby?"

"Probably throwing up somewhere. She gets horribly nervous before these things." Martha nudged him conspiratorially. "Artistic temperament."

Cubiak couldn't tell if she approved or not. He murmured something noncommittal and then slipped off. At the bar, a waiter offered white wine. He asked for tonic with lime, and as he waited , Ruby materialized in the main lobby. She appeared without fanfare and so simply dressed in a long fawn tunic, she made the others look garish by comparison. Nonplussed, she welcomed her admirers with handshakes and air kisses as a cadre of greeters ushered the audience into the grand ballroom. On the far wall, a silky cream tarp hung from the ceiling to the floor.

Cubiak hardly noticed the display. He was remembering the afternoon and looking for Cate. Whom did he think he was kidding? He'd wanted her. At least that much he could admit.

Martha reappeared at Cubiak's side. "That's funny," she whispered.

"What?" he said. It's complicated, he'd told Cate. But wasn't that true of life? Wasn't everything complicated?

"I'd heard it was a two-sided weaving. So why's it hanging against the wall like that so you can't see the other side?"

"I don't know," he said as Ruby stepped onto the dais. Beck and several others were waiting and Ruby was smiling broadly. "She doesn't seem to mind."

Martha snapped a bra strap. "Go figure."

Beck waited for the room to quiet and then introduced the director of the state cultural association, who gave a short but flattering speech about the guest of honor. Asked to say a few words, Ruby simply thanked everyone for coming.

When she finished, Little Miss Cherry Blossom was escorted to the front of the stage. Beck handed the eight-year-old a cord that extended to the top of the sheeting. With Ruby on the far side, the child tugged and the tarpaulin slipped to the floor.

"Ladies and gentlemen, 'Trees of Our Lives,'" the curator intoned. Ruby did not correct him. The audience's appreciative murmurs swelled into polite applause.

Beck said a few words in closing, the principals stepped down, and the stage was quickly moved aside, giving the audience a chance to approach the featured piece.

The weaving was abstract, irregularly shaped, and

large, at least eight feet high and five feet across at its widest point. To Cubiak, it looked like something Picasso would create if he were a weaver. Great blobs of dirty sheep's wool were superimposed on chains and loops and braids of yarn in rich shades of dark green and red that flowed in random streams from top to bottom with ribbons of blue and gold interspersed. In the entire piece, there was only one recognizable image: a large bird woven into the upper right-hand corner of the tapestry. It had the hooked beak of an eagle or thunderbird; turquoise beads dripped like tears down its face.

At his side, Martha provided her own running commentary. "The warp, the part you don't see, has hundreds of yards of thread, and has to be set up just right to achieve the desired effect, the pattern, that's in the weft, the part we see. Ruby's outdone herself this time for sure. I've counted at least twenty-five colors and a dozen different textures. Then she had to add the heading. Backbreaking work. She'd done a little with that before. This is the most. But it's really effective. Dramatic impact."

The weaving was not the kind of art Cubiak appreciated. He liked things literal: trees that looked like trees, for one. There was no discernible tree image in Ruby's work. If anything, she'd produced a desolate landscape seemingly devoid of life, except for the Native American bird figure. Unless the dark smudge in the bottom left corner represented a tree. The first tree? Life's beginning? Cubiak appreciated the intricacy of Ruby's work; he only wished she'd made something he could recognize. Cate would understand it.

He spotted her in the doorway and raised a hand but she'd already turned aside and was talking to a well-dressed couple. Had she seen him? Cubiak excused himself. He was halfway through the crowd when Beck grabbed his elbow.

"Anything?" he said.

"Not yet."

"Which may be for the better." Beck pursed his lips and gestured toward the wall hanging. "Something patriotic would have been more fitting," he complained sotto voce. "But I should have known better. Too mundane for Ruby. Instead we get modern art and fucking Indian shit."

When Cubiak looked again, Cate was gone.

WHAT RUBY DID not provide in her weaving, Beck made up for at the festival fish boil that followed. During the afternoon, the town had been transformed into a faux colonial village. Stars and stripes fluttered from every flagpole. Doorways were draped in patriotic colors. Balconies and porches bore garish decorations. Greeters wore Uncle Sam hats. A roving fife and drum duo played endless rounds of "Yankee Doodle." With traffic diverted from the waterfront, the area around the Village Hall was cordoned off with red, white, and blue bunting and packed with tourists waiting for Beck's festival fish boil to begin.

The fish boil was a Scandinavian tradition imported to Door County as an efficient and economical way to feed settlers, logging teams, and fishing crews at the end of the workday. It became a popular tourist attraction, and at the festival it was transformed into high culinary art. This was no small undertaking. On a long, narrow stretch of sand, ten campfires burned, each one straddled by a raised metal frame that held an oversize black iron kettle filled with salted water. A crew of men directed by Les Caruthers fed pieces of dried wood into the flames to heat the water.

Outfitted in a yellow slicker with matching pants, tall heavy boots, and a fisherman's cap pulled tight over his ears, Caruthers waved a flag. When the water began to simmer, he blew on a sailor's whistle. At the signal, the boil masters, twenty burly men in white chef's hats, emerged from the shadows. The cooks bowed to the crowd, then paired off and carried in ten large metal baskets filled with small red potatoes. One container was ceremoniously lowered into each cauldron. While the potatoes cooked, the chefs stood arms akimbo and sang sea chanteys to entertain the hungry diners. They had just finished one of the numbers when Caruthers gave another toot, a signal for onions to be added to the broth. After more songs and another blast from Caruthers, the men carried in a second set of smaller baskets, brimming with chunks of locally caught whitefish, and set them into the kettles.

The cooking fires whipped up and licked the sides of the kettles. A gray foam of fish oil formed over the surface of the roiling water. Caruthers blew a long and two shorts. "Boil over," he yelled as the chefs tossed kerosene onto the fires. Flames skyrocketed into the air. The supercharged water bubbled over the sides of the cauldrons, spilling fish oil onto the burning logs and sending plumes of black smoke into the air. The crowd cheered. When the last whistle sounded, the boil masters, still working in pairs, slid heavy metal poles through the wire handles and lifted the heavy baskets from the kettles. Water streamed off the fish—the thick fillets, sweet and delicate, cooked to perfection—as the cooks carried the baskets from the beach to the tents where they were set on solid wooden tables that bore the scars from past boils. Using red, white, and blue plastic dishes, the local ladies served up the potatoes, onions, and fish, the famous Door County fish boil dinner—each meal complete with a slice of cherry pie.

Cubiak didn't eat fish. He bought a hot dog near the docks and wandered back toward the tent, still intent on the weaving. Ruby had titled the work "Tree of Life," which implied a positive connotation, so why the tears? Unless the bird was weeping for joy, but Cubiak didn't get that feeling.

"How's it going?" one of chefs called out to him.

Cubiak recognized the man as one of Halverson's deputies from the afternoon. "No problem."

The man wiped his brow. "Some show, huh?"

"Yeah. Guess."

The man turned back to the job of rekindling his fire for the next round. A coworker must have said something because Cubiak heard a sharp chorus of disagreement. Moving away, he thought about Beck's nasty remark about Ruby's weaving. Given the long history they shared, Cubiak had assumed they were close friends. Maybe he was wrong.

WHILE THE FISH boil prepared for a third seating, another audience of visitors began filing into Peninsula State Park's outdoor theater for the evening's performance by the Door County Folk Troupe. Children and adults tramped the wooded trails, arms loaded down with blankets and jackets to protect against the inevitable cool night air that would later engulf the forest.

Cubiak stationed a half dozen of Halverson's men

around the facility and checked out the obvious potential problem spots. The theater was a plain but serviceable facility. Trees felled to make the clearing had produced enough lumber for benches to seat one hundred fifty comfortably as well as the stage, complete with trap door and portable platforms, and a plain wooden fence for a backdrop. As with most of the troupe's productions, scenery was minimal. Little more than the forest's dark shadows and the thin moonlight filtering through the forest canopy was needed to generate the mood for the group's new musical, a production of ghoulish folk tales and songs. Given recent events, Cubiak found the selection macabre. It was a full house. The curtain was delayed ten minutes and extra seats brought in to accommodate the overflow crowd.

The audience loved the show. Cubiak didn't. Nighttime in the woods was eerie enough without skeletons popping up from wooden coffins and anguished screams in the dark. When a trap door slammed in the middle of act two, he grabbed for the gun he no longer wore. Afterward, people filed out, trailing the aroma of bug spray. Cubiak stayed an extra hour and helped the actors replace props and secure the stage.

Driving back, he checked the three campgrounds. It was nearly midnight when he reached Jensen Station. He wanted vodka and settled for tea. Ruta had baked brownies and left the foil-covered pan where he could find it. Cubiak cut two large pieces. Exhausted, he lay down and tried not to think about Cate.

# FIFTEEN

*Thursday Morning*

CUBIAK FOUND A note from Ruta on his desk. "Beck's house 11."

What the hell? Cubiak thought. There hadn't been time at Ruby's opening for him to tell Beck about the Conservation League meeting, but he couldn't imagine that with the festival moving into its second day, he'd be summoned to the house for that.

Heavy traffic made him late and ill tempered. Poised for a face-to-face encounter with Beck, he rang the bell and was surprised when a middle-aged woman opened the door. She wore a black dress and the unmistakable white-lace apron of a maid. She looked disapproving.

"I'm expected," Cubiak said.

"Yes." The hired help led him through the living room and down the rear hall to the family room where he'd first met Cate. The view by day was as impressive as by night.

"Where's Beck?"

"Please." The maid indicated a small sofa near the window and disappeared.

Ignoring the couch, Cubiak approached the glass wall, aware of the thick carpet underfoot and an intense overbearing stillness. The air inside the house was chilly.

"I'm sorry, but Beck's not here." A woman stood in

the doorway, diminutive and overdressed, her parchment complexion unseemly in a resort community that worshiped sun and placed a premium on healthy outdoor activity. She floated across the room and extended her hand. "We've met, haven't we? I'm Eloise Beck."

Cubiak remembered her from Beck's preseason party. She'd been tipsy and insouciant that evening.

"We have. I have an appointment with your husband. Where is he?" Cubiak said.

"Who knows?" Eloise eased into a chair. "Please, sit down. I insist. I get so few visitors, though you're the second today."

She raised her eyebrows at Cubiak, inviting his curiosity, but he ignored the hint. He wasn't in the mood to play games or fill out her social calendar. "I told you, I came to see Beck, but I can come back another time," he said, turning to leave.

"No, wait. Please. I sent for you, not Beck," Eloise said.

"You? Why?"

She pointed to a facing chair. "I thought it was important. There are things you need to know if you're going to work for my husband."

"I don't work for Beck."

Eloise ran her hands up and down the armrests. "Everyone works for Beck. You're working for him now, aren't you?"

Cubiak hesitated. "More like a favor."

"I see. And just how do you think you got the job at the park in the first place? Beck pulled a lot of strings to get you up here. He obviously did it for a reason."

Cubiak sat down. "You got ten minutes," he said.

"My husband is an ambitious bastard. He's good with

plans and making things happen. He lets nothing stand in his way, and he'll do anything that gives him an advantage. He married me, a girl from the wrong side of town who worked in one of his factories, because he thought he could mold me into the perfect doting wife. Didn't quite work out that way. He was desperate for a son but what he really wanted was a clone. Instead he got Barry, our late-stage miracle baby, who was more me than him. The kid never had a chance."

Cubiak glanced at his watch. "Sorry, that's of no interest to me."

"Just wait. It gets better. You know Alice Jones, the girl who was killed? Do you think Beck cares about her or who attacked her? He doesn't. Just arrest someone, anyone, which is pretty much what happened. His only real worry was that Barry caught something nasty from her. 'Stick your dick in dirt and it gets dirty,' he said to him.

"I've never known anyone with less of a soul. Maybe he doesn't have one. There's no compassion, no sense of decency. He's like a shark. He'll devour anything, even his own young, to survive."

Eloise got up and moved to the stone fireplace. "He did it to Dutch." She whirled round. "You know Dutch?"

"I've heard the name."

Eloise tittered. "Who hasn't?" She began walking around the room. "Nobody understands their rich-boy, poor-boy relationship. I think there was something genuine there on Beck's part when they were younger. He admired Dutch and wanted to emulate him. But after we came back from New York—we'd lived there several years—things began to change. At first it was like old times. We saw Dutch and Ruby often. Even went sailing a couple of times. Beck solidified his position at the shipyard and took over his father's role as undisputed spokesman for the county. Dutch got elected sheriff and solved a murder. 'The little people's hero' Beck started calling him behind his back."

"Why? Wasn't he relieved the crime was solved?"

She smirked. "Beck had his own ideas about the situation and Dutch didn't listen."

"Beck was one of those who worried about bad publicity?"

"Yes, so you've heard about this. But even more than that…" The maid entered with a tray and set it on a low table near Cubiak. A silver urn of coffee, two china cups, a small pitcher of cream and individual saucers of whipped cream, sugar cubes, and a dish of lace cookies. Eloise returned to her chair and helped herself. Cubiak poured his own.

"You could crush that cup without trying," she said, looking at Cubiak's hands. "I'm used to men with big hands. My father. Beck." The name rolled out flat and emotionless. "How am I doing on time?"

Cubiak wanted to hear more about Dutch and Beck. "Okay," he said.

"I think Beck felt threatened by Dutch's success. Beck was born into money and power; Dutch had to make his own way in life. My theory is this: when Beck compared himself to Dutch he didn't come off too well."

"And he couldn't tolerate the idea?"

She nodded. "Then the park superintendent job came up. Dutch supported Otto, and Beck hated Otto."

"Because of Claire."

"That and other things, too. Otto was a purist who believed in protecting the land above all else. Beck had grand schemes for developing the county and didn't tolerate opposition. He did everything he could to undercut Otto, but that was one time he had no clout at the top. Approval for the park job had to come from the director of the state forestry department, who was appointed by the governor who just happened to be a one-term maverick, a populist who was anti–big business and such. When Beck realized he couldn't legitimately stop Otto, he tried to discredit him. Dragged out the tired old business about the war and his CO status. Halverson was the point man on that. Anyway, the plan backfired. Dutch publicly backed Otto. Here was a decorated Vietnam veteran supporting Otto's right to be a CO."

"That was a pretty gutsy move on Dutch's part," Cubiak said.

"It gave people pause, let me tell you. But what Dutch really focused on was the park's future and Otto's reputation as a conservationist. Someone who would defend the county's natural resources. Dutch and Ruby circulated petitions supporting Otto. They got hundreds of signatures. All this played into the hands of the governor, who pressured the forestry director to give Otto the job."

"And Beck never made amends with Otto. How about with Dutch?"

"Things between them got worse. Then Beck announced plans to build a new bridge over the canal. 'Vision Bridge' he called it. Oh, he painted a glorious picture. Instead of the old bottleneck in town, we'd have a major highway leading straight into the heart of the county. Four lanes of tourists pouring in, their pockets bulging with cash. The new bridge represented progress, he said. It was forward looking. It meant prosperity and growth. Everyone would benefit. He hired a New York ad agency to conduct a promotion campaign. Posters, billboards, TV ads full of promises. By then we had a new governor who bought into the project and convinced the legislature to appropriate funds. He even lobbied Washington for money. A lot of locals liked the idea, too, but many were opposed.

"Beck asked Dutch to support it but he refused. For months, Dutch tried to persuade Beck to change his mind. Then Dutch and Ruby launched another petition drive and started a letter-writing campaign to the legislature. I suspect they knew it was a lost cause. Dutch as much as admitted to Beck that he had rallied the forces more to ensure the opposition sufficient standing so that they'd have some credibility in the future than to derail this particular project. But Beck took their opposition personally. He won, of course, but by then merely winning wasn't enough. Beck needed to punish Dutch as well. He needed to put him in his place. Eight years ago—I remember because it was my birthday—my husband came home almost silly with glee. He got thoroughly drunk and told me he'd found a way to shut up Dutch for good. The next day, when I asked him about it, he said I was imagining things. But I knew something was up. Every once in a while, I'd catch him with that gleam in his eye."

A clock chimed softly in the distance.

"Dutch was best man at our wedding, you know," Eloise said. "At the reception, Beck proposed a toast, from us to Ruby and Dutch: 'May our lives always mirror one another's.' That's what he said." She stopped abruptly and clasped her hands together.

"You never found out what Beck did to Dutch?"

"No. Whatever it was, Dutch soon retired as sheriff.

Bad heart was the excuse he gave." Eloise moistened her lips and then abruptly stood. "I've told you everything. Probably said more than I should have. I have to go now."

She left the room. The pinched-face maid showed him out as resentfully as she'd allowed him in.

AFTER THE FRIGID INTERIOR, Cubiak was glad for the heat outside. Soothed by the quiet drone of insects, he relaxed into the driver's seat and ran through the conversation with Eloise. She had plenty of dirt to shovel and seemed to enjoy throwing all of it at her husband. Cubiak was beginning to realize that beneath the peninsula's picturesque veneer, streams of animosity rippled fast and deep. Bad feelings seemed to run between Beck and a number of other people. His wife. His son. Otto Johnson. Dutch Schumacher. Who else? He hadn't had a chance to ask about Ruby's relationship with Beck. Eloise hinted that her husband had humiliated and wronged Dutch, destroying their lifelong friendship. How much did Ruby know about the falling-out between the two men? Was any of this linked to the recent series of tragic deaths?

Maybe Eloise wasn't the simple downtrodden wife she pretended to be, but would she commit murder to avenge herself on her husband? She had access to money, and if she was orchestrating a campaign to ruin Beck by torpedoing the festival, it was to her benefit to throw suspicion on others. But Otto had already been proven innocent. And Dutch was deceased. Cubiak was annoyed realizing that he might have just wasted an hour listening to local gossip.

Ready for lunch and a cold beer, he drove to Sturgeon Bay and was backing into a parking spot when he spied Barry shuffling past the bank. Barry Beck, seventeen, almost good looking, almost intelligent. The long-awaited son. His parents had called him their bonus baby and heaped all their expectations on him, a heavy burden for an infant to bear.

Cubiak caught up with the boy near the corner. "Long time no see," he said.

Barry shot him a nervous glance and kept walking.

"We have to talk." Cubiak maneuvered the sullen teen into an empty doorway.

"Lemme be," Barry said.

"Not till you tell me what's going on."

"About what?"

"Let's start with your job. The one you wanted so badly. I've had to get other people to do your work because you never show up."

Barry scuffed the ground with his expensive Topsiders. "I don't need it," he insisted.

"But you wanted it before."

Barry was tight lipped.

"Tell me what's going on."

The boy's face contorted. "The park is bad news for me," he yelped.

Cubiak took a guess. "Problems with your suppliers? That's it, isn't it?"

Barry paled. "I don't have to talk to you."

"No, you don't. But it might be useful if you did. You might tell me something that will help."

Cubiak let Barry consider the novel notion as he steered him down the sidewalk toward the waterfront. They sat on a bench near a small rose garden where a group of children ignored the large Do Not Feed the Birds sign and tossed popcorn and handfuls of crumbled bread to a flock of tame geese.

"Why's the park bad news?" Cubiak said.

Barry looked up, surprised. "Oh, man, you gotta be kidding. Some guy who just happens to be wearing the same kind of jacket as mine falls off the tower. Then a girl *wearing* my jacket gets killed. What am I supposed to do, stand there with a bull's-eye on my back?"

"No, of course not," Cubiak said, stalling. Alice had been wearing Barry's navy blue jacket when she was killed. But Wisby's jacket was black, wasn't it? Cubiak cursed silently. The coat had been soaked from the rain; maybe it only looked black. He'd never seen it dry and made a mental note to read Halverson's full report.

"Your deals went down at Falcon Tower?"

"Yeah."

"But you didn't show that one day, why? You owe them money?"

The boy turned a frightened face to him. "Promise you won't tell my father. He'd kill me if he knew."

Barry's story was the pathetic tale of a small-town kid who was in over his head to a couple of Milwaukee drug suppliers. He'd owed five thousand dollars at Christmas, and with help from Eloise he'd managed to pay off half by Easter. He'd promised full payment on the rest that Sunday morning.

"What time were you supposed to meet?"

"Five. But I didn't go 'cause I didn't have the money."

Bathard had estimated the time of Wisby's death at about 6 a.m.

"How long would they have waited?"

"My phone rang a little after six. I didn't answer. But I guessed it was them."

"No one else picked up the call?"

"I got my own line. No one else would have heard it ring."

He'd stayed in the rest of the day, he told Cubiak, and then hung by his mother's side for several more days. "They always found me before when I owed something. This time, I figured they gave up. I knew they were planning on splitting for Mexico—reconnaissance, they called it—and I thought maybe they just finally went. Then Alice was killed."

"And you thought they were after you again?"

"Sure. Next day, I told my mother enough to get some more bread out of her. I got in touch with them and paid up."

"You met them here?"

"No. Manitowoc. It's midway."

"And now?"

"They're gone. I think. I hope." Barry looked at Cubiak. "They said they'd be in touch later."

"I need names."

Barry nearly flew from the seat. "No way," he said.

Five minutes later, Cubiak had two names, probably aliases. "Where'd your mother get the money?"

"She's been squirreling away dough for years. Probably used some of that."

Cubiak offered the boy a ride home. "By the way, I saw your mother this morning," he said as they drove from town.

Barry tittered. "Quite a treat for Mom. Two visitors in one day."

Cubiak wasn't going to let this pass again. "Ruby, wasn't it?" he said, approaching a four-way stop.

"Oh, right. The vestal virgin of Door County. Not

literally speaking, of course. Nope. She doesn't come to our house anymore."

"So who was it?"

"Nobody you'd know. This old dude, Jocko Connelly. Used to be a ferry boat captain. Totally pee-o-ed, he was. Came down from Washington Island, drunk as a skunk and railing about some kind of harbor plan. 'Top secret shit,' Jocko called it. Mother didn't have a clue what he was talking about. Anyway, my dad shows up and sends her out of the room, me, too, and then tears into the old man. What did he know? How'd he find out? Had he told anyone else? Jocko just kept raving that it wouldn't happen again."

"I thought you were sent from the room."

"I listened on the intercom."

"Why was Jocko so upset about a harbor?"

"Who knows? Just another local drunk, you ask me."

"What do you know about it, this plan Jocko was talking about?"

"Nothing." The boy rubbed his jaw. "My father doesn't tell me or my mom anything. We're shit on his list." He paused. "Unlike you." The sarcasm was obvious. "Security hotshot."

"You got that wrong. I work for the park."

"Not for long. Not if my father has his way."

"What are you talking about?"

Barry shrugged. "Just something I overheard. Why don't you ask him?"

"Maybe I will."

Beck has his reasons, Eloise had said, talking about how her husband had pulled strings to bring Cubiak to the peninsula. What the hell had he gotten himself into?

Near Beck's driveway, Cubiak pulled onto the shoulder. "By the way, where is your father?"

"Green Bay, I think. He went to pick up a couple of foreign dudes. Probably for the golf tournament."

# SIXTEEN

*Thursday Afternoon*

FREE FROM THE congestion around Sturgeon Bay, Cubiak skated up the spine of the peninsula on the county's two-lane backroads. The route was marked by cherry orchards and hay fields, by cows grazing lazily in open pastures and by the weathered barns that denoted the failed farms and the occasional silo clusters that earmarked the ones that were prospering against all odds. He made good time. Near West Jacksonport he came up behind a mud-spattered, orange tractor pulling a wagonload of straw. The driver drifted onto the shallow shoulder, opening up the view of the road, and as Cubiak passed, the man raised a hand in greeting. Cubiak returned the gesture. A nice custom, he realized, and one he was coming to expect.

Cubiak was on his way to the ferry at Northport Pier. Before Eloise aired her bushel of dirty laundry, she had tried to steer his interest toward Jocko, the retired ferry captain. Cubiak didn't think anything of it until Barry mentioned the old seaman as well. Cubiak wasn't sure how much credibility to award a vengeful recluse or a spiteful son, but it was clear that Jocko was pissed enough about something to trek from Washington Island to the mainland amidst the chaos of the area's biggest festival to make his feelings known. And the something that upset him was linked to Beck. If Barry was right about the jacket and being the target of the attacks, perhaps there were dots to connect. Cubiak had to find out.

He could have called Jocko but knew it would have been a wasted effort. Cubiak remembered seeing him in Amelia's photo of the Survivalist Club. Jocko was the instructor. At the time the picture was taken, he couldn't have been more than twenty-five, but the fierceness of his eyes and the firm set of his jaw portrayed him as a man to be reckoned with. Before he left town, Cubiak had stopped to ask Bathard about Jocko and learned that during World War II, he'd parachuted behind German lines. Later, as a ferry captain, he was reknowned for the ease with which he piloted vessels through ice floes. No, Jocko didn't sound like the type who'd warm to a friendly telephone chat. Cubiak needed to confront him face-to-face.

The road to the ferry landing wound past The Wood and then Ruby's house before it dead-ended at the water. Northport wasn't even a nub of a town, just a dock with a restaurant and a parking lot cut into the forest on a rocky stretch of Lake Michigan. At the water's edge, a robust, red-haired man motioned for Cubiak to follow a beige van onto the ferry, a bilevel box that looked barely seaworthy to the ranger. In a leap of faith, Cubiak rolled over the loading ramp, pretending not to notice the boat's shuddering. He squeezed the jeep between two cars and eased out as a group of teenagers wheeled their bikes past. One flight up, he made his way to the bow. Despite the bright sun, the air was cool. Cubiak pulled up his collar and jammed his hands into his pockets. He wished he'd worn a cap and hoped the Dramamine Bathard had given him would work. As a gas truck maneuvered over the loading ramp, the ferry shimmied in response. Cubiak grabbed the handrail.

"First time across?" A heavyset man in a neatly patched denim jacket had joined him on the deck. "This ain't nothing. You should see 'em pull on them double-deckered tour buses. Now that's a hoot. Swear everybody on board thinks we're going to capsize." The passenger tapped the railing with a thick, rough hand. "But they're built solid. For the cargo and the weather."

"Just hope nobody's smoking." The comment came from a tourist with a video camera.

The first man harrumphed and shuffled away.

In a sudden flurry of activity, the ferry was loaded. Then a horn shrilled, the mooring lines were freed, and the steel ramp was raised to a vertical position, sealing in the people and vehicles. The engine revved and the 150-ton craft slid away from shore toward the open water. The vista widened at surprising speed, leaving the dock and restaurant looking forlorn and lost, two shrinking white spots pinned against the expanding stretch of trees and cliffs that formed the rugged northern shoreline. Seagulls wheeled above their wake, and the wind, dormant while they hugged the dock, stung Cubiak's face. Around him, conversations dropped off as the travelers took refuge in their own thoughts. Even the two teenagers draped over each other under the stairwell—thinking themselves hidden—pulled apart, their lust diminished by the great wash of water and open sky.

Ten minutes out, the birds deserted the ferry and carried their screeching calls back to the mainland. On the lake, there was no sound but the keening of the wind and the steady churning of the ship's engine. No world existed beyond the water and sky that stretched in every direction as they motored toward the harbor at Washington Island.

Disembarking was efficiently routine. Passengers flowed from the upper level toward their vehicles and quickly slid off the ferry as a deckhand waved them forward. Cubiak was the eighth driver out.

A waitress at the harbor coffee shop gave him directions to Jocko's place. There was only one road from the harbor, and he followed it into the interior. Washington Island was home to several hundred year-round and seasonal residents, most of them on site only during the warm weather months when they were joined by hordes of day visitors who rode the ferries over from and back to the mainland. Though only six miles from the peninsula, the island seemed remote and exotic, and the landscape rolled out lush and verdant. But nature's bounty could not disguise economic hard times. Cubiak passed half a dozen homes and businesses that were boarded up and offered for sale. Under a grove of towering elms, a fifties-style drive-in sagged in glum neglect.

At the second juncture, Cubiak veered left and passed through pastureland and thick woods before he ran into a patch of rocky coast. The road angled back sharply, pulling him away from the water, and then it bent toward a shallow inlet where a string of large frame houses and modest cottages hugged the shore.

A half mile farther, the lane ended at the disheveled two-acre plot that was Jocko Connelly's Tobacco Road estate. Belly-fat seagulls lined the weathered dock and spilled over into the yard, perched on discarded fishing dories and a junk dealer's heaven of old stoves and refrigerators. There were three vehicles on the property: the cannibalized shell of an old John Deere tractor, a splotched yellow Edsel propped on cement blocks, and a shiny teal pickup, ostentatious in its freshness. Someone's home, Cubiak thought.

Picking his way through the bird droppings and past a crumbling picnic table that spoke of happier times, Cubiak approached the daisy-chain house, four wooden shacks stacked one against the other parallel to the cove. He pounded the door, surprised by its resonance. No response. He banged again. From deep inside came a muffled bark, followed by the slow shuffle of footsteps. The door yanked open. A face marked by deeply creviced and weathered skin jutted out at him.

"Who're you?"

Cubiak gave Jocko enough information to keep him from slamming the door shut.

"Ha!" The old seaman glared and then turned and wordlessly slipped into the interior. Cubiak followed down the narrow hall that linked the cubicles. To his right, a series of dirt-streaked windows gave way to spectacular views of the water, while on the other side one cluttered room followed after another. When they reached the kitchen, the terminus of the chain, Jocko stopped and confronted his guest. He had at least two days' worth of stubble on his cheeks and his breath was heavily perfumed with alcohol.

"That old fool need someone to bail him out again?" The ferry captain waved a hand impatiently at Cubiak. "Johnson. Otto J," he hooted.

"Otto's fine."

Jocko maneuvered behind a wooden table littered with dirty dishes and empty gin bottles and dropped into a chair. He glanced suspiciously at Cubiak, then tilted toward the floor and spat a stream of black tobacco juice into a sawdust-filled coffee can.

"Glad to hear it," he said and visually skewered his visitor again. "Who sent you?"

"No one."

"I ain't so popular people go out of their way to visit. 'Specially strangers." Jocko spoke deliberately, trying to outfox the slur that dogged his words.

"You went to see Beck this morning. You were angry. Very foul tempered, I believe."

"You his stooge?"

"Several people have died lately under suspicious circumstances. I'm trying to find out if they've been killed and if so, by whom."

"You a cop, too?"

"Used to be a detective with the Chicago PD."

The ferry captain's eyes narrowed. "Chi-town police? What's any of this to do with me?"

"Nothing, if you're not the one harpooning tourists with hunting arrows."

Jocko cackled.

"I understand you know something about a new harbor being planned."

The comment had a sobering effect. Jocko plunked the spittoon again and studied the dirt-encrusted table before he looked back at Cubiak. "Read a book about it."

"What book?"

"A grandiose piece of fiction someone left laying around."

"Beck?"

"Not him, but somebody he had with him. One of those foreign-looking types."

"Recently?"

"Could have been."

"You and Beck don't get along?"

"I don't cotton to his kind."

"Why the fuss about this 'harbor' business? A modest condo development just south of Fish Creek is what I've heard."

"Hell it is," Jocko retorted.

Cubiak waited.

Jocko took his time. "It's like something in a fairy tale gone wrong," he said, finally. "The bastard intends to remake the whole north half of the peninsula. Fish Creek, Ephraim, and all the little towns north are gonna be wiped off the map. Like they never existed. Everything gone. Farms. Orchards. Cottages. Marinas. Even roads. Gone, just gone. He's gonna plow it all under and plant it all with trees, like when the Indians were here, with room for a big golf course and an airport and a monorail train connecting it to some fancy-ass new resort up north at the tip. You should see the houses he's gonna build there. Mansions, they looked like, with a goddamn castle in the middle. Who's that for? Tell me that! Where are all the regular folks gonna go?" he said with escalating rage. "And the island? Jesus! Some kind of fucking *hunting preserve*." Jocko's face was red, the veins in his forehead and neck thickly corded.

"What do you mean everything gone? That sounds impossible," Cubiak said. Was the old man hallucinating or had he lost it completely?

"For you and me, yeah, it's impossible. But with enough money, you can do any goddamn thing you please. Beck aims to turn a whole chunk of the peninsula into a playground for the rich. You should've seen the people he had out with him. An East Coast pansy—

I could just about hear the silver spoon clanging against his teeth—and a couple of foreigners whispering to each other in some weird language I ain't never heard. These people eat, breathe, and shit money."

"When was this?"

"Couple weeks ago. He chartered the passenger ferry for his little outing. Just happens the captain got sick that morning and his wife asked me to take the run. The look on Beck's face when he seen me!"

"There a name for all this?"

Jocko sniggered. "Paradise Harbor."

"And you think Beck's trying to buy up the land for it?"

"Wouldn't put it past him. Came close to doing it before on the island. Least ways his family tried. Twenty-three square miles and they own the most of it."

"But you said the harbor project was a piece of fiction."

Jocko took a deep breath and calmed himself. "People won't sell up. Not this time."

A bee buzzed outside the window.

"You seeing to it?"

Jocko ignored the question. "Look it there," he said and gestured impatiently at an aging, yellowed map of the island taped to the wall. Though the print was indiscernible, Cubiak had no trouble following the line of thick red crayon that had been clumsily traced along much of the shoreline and around large sections of the interior. On the western edge, only a thin slice of land had been spared.

"Granddaddy Beck bought it all up some sixty years ago." Jocko sneered. "Smart businessman, knew all about getting his way. Misunderstanding some calls it.

Cheating, others say. Sort of implied he was merely buying up logging rights, long-term leasing sort of crap. Civil engineers showed up measuring surface depth. Real worried about the tunnels collapsing they said the government was down in Madison."

"Tunnels? What tunnels?"

"The ones under the island. Our own little geological phenomenon. Lot of hooey. Those tunnels'll outlast the moon. You'll see. But it was a real bad time for most folks here. Couple hard winters. Barely any money coming in because of what the crash did to the fishing industry and tourist trade. Hell, there wasn't nothing happening. And old Daddy Warbucks shows up with hard cash money. Some say you can't blame the locals for selling."

"Not you."

Jocko slammed a fist against the table. "Fools, every damn one of them. Land's the one thing you hold on to, no matter what." He exhaled slowly and tipped back into the shadows. "Teach them that in school, they oughta."

"Who owned the land before?"

"People." Jocko's face darkened.

"Your family."

"Some. There were others, too."

Cubiak studied the small crescent-shaped sliver outlined on the map. "Just the homestead left then?"

"Homestead!" Jocko bellowed. "Yeah, this little piece of shit here. And my grandpa was about to sign that last teensy bit away along with the rest when he dropped dead of a heart attack and my father—just sixteen at the time—chased Granddaddy Beck off with a shotgun. Ran him all the way back to his big fancy skiff in the harbor. Later, my daddy tried to get the other families to go in with him and sue Beck for fraud, but they were all scared and wouldn't. He tried by himself but Beck's lawyers trampled him in court. Greedy bastards, all of them."

"How many families still own land on the island?"

Jocko squirmed. "Couple dozen. Maybe less."

"You could've been rich, had your grandfather not buckled to the Becks."

"Would've owned a bunch of land. Up here that ain't enough to make you rich."

"Instead, you sit here nursing a grudge."

"Wouldn't you?"

"Plotting revenge."

"Hell. I wish I could plot revenge! Truth is there's nothing I can do about all that. I don't like it, but I know it. What's done is done."

Suddenly Jocko brightened. He leaned forward conspiratorially and spoke almost gleefully. "Tell you one thing, though, it ain't gonna happen again. Little Becky Boy ain't gonna get away with it this time."

"Why not?"

"I seen to it, that's why not." He splayed a grimy hand on the table.

"You going to tell me what you did?"

"Nope. Ain't none of your business." Jocko pulled a dented tin from his breast pocket and stuffed a fresh pinch of snuff into his cheek. "Way I see it, folks got a right to know about things so they can plan. Develop a strategy."

"And you're playing town crier, is that it? Or is there more to it?" Cubiak stepped to the window. He could feel air leaking in along the sill where the wood had rotted and shrunk. "You live up here alone. Can pretty much come and go as you please, can't you?"

"Could be."

"Nobody'd know what you were up to half the time." Jocko guffawed.

"You were an instructor for the Survivalist Club. You have skills that can be used a lot of different ways."

The ferry captain sat up smartly. "Had. Had skills." His face grim, Jocko laid his left arm on the table, then with his right hand unbuttoned the frayed cuff and deftly rolled up the sleeve to the elbow. He extended the bare limb to Cubiak. "Go on, pinch it," he said.

The arm was hard plastic. The fingers immobile. Cubiak cursed himself for not having noticed.

"Boat's got power steering. I can operate it easily enough with this other one here." Jocko waved his right arm. "Can't do much else."

"Maybe. Maybe not." But Cubiak knew it was true. He surveyed the disheveled room. Testament to a sad pastiche of a life given over to resignation and neglect, a life guided by anger and bitterness fueled by a washed-out map that kept old wounds fresh.

In the dim light, Jocko appeared to be dozing. His head, on his chest, bobbed gently.

Cubiak was turning to leave when he spied a black phone on the far wall. Judging from the dull finish and discolored plastic dial plate, it had to have been one of the originals installed on the island. Next to it, a small notepad hung from a tenpenny nail. The top sheet was crowded with rough pencil scrawls of names and numbers. Except for one line, scratched in near the upper edge, whose obvious freshness made it stand out from the rest. Cubiak was too far away to decipher the number, but the crisp dark digits made it clear that it was newly added to the list.

Before Cubiak could edge closer, Jocko rumbled awake. "You don't hurry, you'll miss the ferry," he barked and pointed the way back down the cramped hall.

PARADISE HARBOR. CUBIAK didn't know how much credence to give to what Jocko had told him. The old man loathed Beck, despised the entire family. Not without good reason. And he was drunk, too. But he couldn't have made up everything about Paradise Harbor, and the outing would be easy enough to trace, or would it? A little bonus from Beck and there'd be no record of the boat charter. Beck was up to something. But what? And how far would Jocko go to stop him?

At Northport, Cubiak tried to pick up a signal on his cell and then gave up and fed a handful of coins into the outdoor phone. At the dial tone, he punched in a number from his past. Listening to the monophonic rings, he pictured the distant room where the jangling phone vied for attention. In a million years, he wouldn't have expected to ever be making this call. The desk sergeant's rough greeting interrupted his daydreaming, and Cubiak asked for Officer Malcolm. It was a holiday weekend, and he knew he had a good chance of finding his old partner on duty.

"Malcolm. You mean Captain Malcolm? He's in six."

Cubiak was surprised, but pleased, too. The sixth district. His buddy had done well and in short order. He asked for the number and dialed again. This time a soft-spoken secretary answered and asked for his name. "Tell him it's an old friend from up north," Cubiak said.

"I'm sorry. I need a name."

Cubiak hesitated. She wouldn't know who he was. Still he was reluctant to identify himself. "Jeff Hardy," he said, pulling a name from the past, a suspect from one of the early, more complicated cases he and Malcolm had solved.

"Thank you."

A series of clicks put Cubiak on hold, off hold, and then onto another open line. Malcolm, if he was there, wasn't saying anything.

"Malcolm, it's me." Cubiak spoke quietly.

*"Sweet Jesus.* That you, *Dave?"*

Cubiak heard his former partner's enormous weight shift on a creaky chair.

"Where you *at?"*

"Up north. You know."

"Things working out?"

"More or less." He hesitated. "I'm fine."

*"Good."* Malcolm didn't believe him.

They exchanged pleasantries. Cubiak learned that Malcolm's eldest daughter had recently given birth to twins and the youngest had graduated from high school with honors. His mother had died—quickly, mercifully—and his wife was toying with the idea of going back to school to become a teacher. "At her age, can you *fathom* that?" he asked.

"I need a favor," Cubiak said.

The captain growled.

"Two actually."

Malcolm roared. "Like *old times.* Shoot."

First, Cubiak explained, he needed records of all phone calls to and from Washington Island for the past four months. He could get this through the local police department, he said, anticipating Malcolm's question, but at this stage discretion was important. He pictured Malcolm scratching notes on a piece of paper.

"What else?"

Cubiak gave him the names of the drug dealers he'd coaxed from Barry. "They're supposedly from Milwaukee but operating up here as well. I'd appreciate it if you could find out how nasty they get about overdue debts?"

"I know a couple guys up there. I'll see what I can dig up. What's this all about?" Malcolm said.

Cubiak ran through a summary of recent incidents. When he finished, he knew he owed his former partner more. "The victim at the tower was Larry Wisby, the younger brother," he said.

"*Wisby*. Oh, Lord, and how you doing with that?"

Cubiak caught both sympathy and an insistence on truth in Malcolm's tone. "Getting by. I won't try to fool you, it's not been easy. I saw the parents at the inquest."

"This investigation you're working on, it's *official*?" Malcolm asked after a marked silence.

"More or less."

"And you need this *pronto*, on a *holiday weekend*?"

"Wouldn't be right if it was any other way."

Malcolm tapped a pencil on the desk. "I got a press conference with the alderman in a couple minutes, then events that'll last most of the day tomorrow. I'll do what I can after. Can't *promise* anything. Call me at ten Saturday. *No*, darn that won't work. I'll call you. *Noon*. You going to be all *right*?"

"Yes, Malcolm. I'll be fine."

"Good to hear from you, *buddy*. I'm praying for you, you know that."

"Yeah, I know that. Thanks." Cubiak dropped the receiver onto the hook. He felt better already. Halfway to the jeep, he realized he'd forgotten to congratulate Malcolm. "Damn," he muttered.

HALVERSON'S REPORT ON the tower incident lay on the front seat of the jeep. The sheriff's prose was overblown and flowery but one fact stood out clearly. Wisby's jacket wasn't black; it was dark blue.

Cubiak tossed down the document and sped away from the ferry landing. Putting aside Barry's paranoia, it was possible that the boy was the intended victim of the first and third killings. The ranger didn't buy the drug connection; Barry was too small time for that kind of retribution. Factoring in Benny Macklin's death strengthened the argument that the killer was a local. But why shift the target so abruptly from Barry to a trio of out-of-town tourists?

Paradise Harbor was significant, Cubiak was sure of it. How much of Jocko's version was fact and how much exaggeration, he didn't know. But even drastically downsized from the boatman's grand proportions, the project required immense real estate holdings. Thanks to his grandfather, Beck already owned sizable swaths of Washington Island. Still, he would have to employ extreme measures to get the land on the peninsula. Destroying the tourist trade was an obvious ploy and if Beck was behind the rampage, making Barry look like a target was a smart way to divert suspicion.

Cubiak mentally crossed off Jocko's name from his list and added Beck's.

Something didn't sit right. Was Beck playing him for a fool? Had he been put in charge of the investigation because Beck figured that as an outsider he would never sort things out?

As he neared Ephraim, a firecracker boomed. Then another. Amateur stuff to whet the appetite for the elaborate display scheduled for Saturday's Fourth of July celebration. Again thousands would throng the little village. Sitting ducks.

Cubiak frowned. Whom had Jocko called?

STREAKS OF HOT pink and orange laced the western sky as Cubiak crossed the historic steel bridge in downtown Sturgeon Bay on his way to Bathard's office. One more indistinguishable cog in a long line of traffic, he imagined the other cars filled with tourists, cameras at the ready, flocking toward the Green Bay shoreline in anticipation of another magnificent Door County sunset. In a different lifetime, he'd owned a camera, a nice one. Where was it? Probably tucked away in an unopened box in the back of his closet. There might be pictures in it of Alexis and Lauren, frozen in time. He would grow old but they would never change. He would never know his daughter as a petulant adolescent or a wistful young woman, never see Lauren with wrinkles.

The emptiness overwhelmed Cubiak. He knocked on Bathard's door, no longer remembering why he'd wanted to see him.

The coroner was equally subdued, and while the desk clock ticked through several minutes the two men sat in strained silence. Finally, Bathard spoke. "Yesterday you rather facetiously included me in your panoply of suspects and said that Cornelia is about the only person not under suspicion."

The physician swiveled toward the wall and pulled a worn Door County High School yearbook from a low shelf. "There is something you need to know," he said. Bathard flipped the book open to a double-page spread of photos and laid it down so Cubiak could see the pictures clearly. The black-and-white shots captured the fresh-scrubbed, wholesome look of a small-town high school prom. Looking at the carefree teenagers, the ranger imagined Alexis grown up. Then the coroner tapped the photo in the upper-right corner. It was a picture of the prom king and queen.

Cubiak recognized the teenage boy, good looking and arrogant even then. "Beck?"

"Yes."

"And the girl?"

Bathard exhaled sharply. "You can't tell because of the ravages of the disease, but Cornelia is considerably younger than I. That's her. The bookish beauty with the jock. Her friends nominated her on a lark. That she won surprised everyone. An intoxicating moment, no doubt, for someone always outside the limelight. But she was ill prepared, out of her league. She had no experience with the likes of Beck and the 'in crowd,' as it were. She was an innocent, a young lady who assumed her date would act the gentleman. Suffice it to say, he did not. For Cornelia, the consequences of that one night were unfortunate, if predictable. Her family took care of everything, all very quietly to avoid the hint of scandal, but the procedure was botched and as a result, Cornelia was left unable to conceive. She told me this before we married; she blames herself, not entirely but more than she should."

The coroner looked at Cubiak. "I always found it quite remarkable that she was able to forgive him."

"And you?"

"She made it a condition of our staying together. Doesn't mean I have to like him, though. Truth is, I never could stomach the bastard." Bathard slammed the book shut. "Life's not fair, son. Most times you go with the hand you're dealt. Or at least you try."

"I wish I'd known this earlier."

"Would it have altered your investigation in any way?"

Cubiak pinched the back of his neck. That afternoon he'd discovered the deep animosity between Beck and Jocko. Now this, between Beck and Bathard. "I don't know," he said.

"Of course." The coroner offered a thin, rueful smile. "You came on official business, didn't you? Shall we get on with it?"

Cubiak remembered why he was there. "I'm looking for information about a harbor."

Bathard looked puzzled. "Plenty of harbors on the peninsula, none of them especially noteworthy."

"I'm interested in a new harbor. Is there one being planned, as far as you know?"

The coroner held out his hands, palms up. "Nothing. And I'm a member of the county planning board. If someone has an initiative going, then it's only very preliminary or speculative and, possibly, illegal, given existing zoning restrictions. It certainly lacks legitimacy at this stage."

Cubiak recounted his conversations with Barry and Jocko.

The coroner scoffed. "Barry could be making it up. Or he misunderstood. You know how kids are. On the other hand, if what Jocko says is true, maybe Beck *is* up to something. I wouldn't put anything past him." Bathard tapped the desk. "Wouldn't be the first time."

"Whatever it is, I'm to be in charge of security."

"Congratulations." The coroner's hand strayed to the

pipe rack. He chose one with a dark bowl that looked like burled ash and lifted it carefully from the stand.

"Barry seems to think that's why I was hired. Claims his father was behind it."

"Could very well be."

"I don't like being used."

"No one does." Bathard opened a worn leather pouch and dropped slivers of tobacco into the bowl.

"I don't like things being done behind my back."

"I wouldn't worry, it's only conjecture."

Before he left, Cubiak asked Bathard about Halverson. The story was pretty much what he expected. As a boy and even a young adolescent, Halverson had sustained a series of suspicious injuries. Bruises, broken bones.

"His mother claimed he was just a clumsy kid, told me he fell a lot. Whenever she brought him to the office, Leo never said a word, just sat on the exam table and looked scared while I checked him over. I suspected he was being abused at home, probably by his father who was a notorious alcoholic, but the mother wouldn't cooperate—you can only imagine why—and without corroboration my hands were tied. The situation would be different, now, of course," Bathard said.

"One day Frank reported to work drunk and managed to overturn a forklift truck and get pinned underneath, sustaining irreparable damage to the spine. As it was wont to do, Beck Industries settled the matter privately with the family, no unpleasant questions asked or issues raised. If there's an upside to the whole sorry mess, it was that Leo's health improved overnight.

"So you see that in a twisted way, Leo sees Beck as his salvation. He's not about to do anything to harm the man who stopped the torture." Bathard spoke slowly. "It's not Halverson you want."

"No, I guess not."

Cubiak was nearly to the door when he remembered something else. "When you examined Anders's body, were you able to determine how long it'd been since he'd lost that tooth?"

"No question it was quite recent, maybe even that morning. The socket was swollen and bloody. It's possible he lost it on impact. I looked for it but Halverson's men had made a mess of things already, probably tamped it into the ground. Why?"

"Just wondering," Cubiak said.

# SEVENTEEN

*Thursday Evening*

WHEN CUBIAK COASTED into Beck's driveway, the only
light on in the mansion was in Beck's downstairs corner
office. Through an uncurtained window, the ranger saw
Beck. He was on the phone, striding back and forth. He
was ebullient, smiling and gesturing grandly. Why not?
So far everything had gone the way he had predicted.

Earlier, after he'd finished with Bathard, Cubiak had
stopped at the Kozy Kafe for the Thursday evening hot
beef and cherry pie special. Over several cups of coffee
at the restaurant and then a beer at the corner bar, he
worked through what he'd learned about Beck's secret
harbor plan. Bathard's assessment of the project seemed
too low key and Jocko's version overly grandiose. Cubiak needed more information and decided to try to get
it directly from the source without tipping his hand.

When Beck hung up, he knocked. The door opened
abruptly.

"You? What the hell are you doing here tonight?"
Beck said, the stink of alcohol on his breath.

"There's something I wanted to discuss."

"Now?"

"I was in the area."

Beck hesitated. "All right, come in, long as you're
here. Go, fix yourself something to drink." He moved

aside and motioned toward the bar. "Just don't tell me you're here to whine about the regatta again."

Beck's office was palatial compared to Bathard's, and as luxurious as the coroner's was sparse. A large mahogany desk matched the floor-to-ceiling bookshelves that lined two walls. The fireplace was surrounded by black marble and above it a polished birch mantel displayed a tasteful sampling of awards sculpted in crystal and brass. Light jazz purred from unseen speakers.

Only the best at Beck's bar, too. Plymouth gin, Blanton's bourbon, and a bottle of twenty-five-year-old Calvados. Cubiak loaded a glass with ice and then reached for the buffalo grass vodka. "It is about the race," he said, measuring out a few drops.

"Christ almighty already," Beck said as he snagged the half-empty Calvados. "We've been over that business a dozen times. I'm telling you there's nothing to worry about."

"The way it's organized, all the boats are vulnerable to attack. It's impossible to police the miles of shoreline, and there's no way we can monitor the small skiffs and boats that will line the route loaded with people angling for a better view. It's too dangerous."

Beck scoffed. "You've been crying wolf ever since the festival started. But look what's happened. Exactly nothing. We got through the first two days with no incidents. We'll be fine."

"There's going to be another attack. And it's going to be well planned and organized."

"You got any proof?" Beck tossed back his drink. "No? No proof. Then stop all this doomsday talk."

"We could at least alter the route. Scramble things up."

Beck laughed. "You fucking nuts? The regatta route is

tradition, and in Door County we don't mess with tradition. Up here we do things the way we always did them."

"You mean, the way you want them done."

Beck laughed again. "That's exactly right," he said, refilling his glass. He held out the bottle.

"I'm done," Cubiak said and retreated to an easy chair near the fireplace. For a moment, the two men regarded each other. Then Cubiak began again.

"I'm coming to appreciate that you pretty much run the show. Call the shots, don't you? Last week, you said things were going to happen, and that I might benefit. I didn't pay much attention at the time, wasn't particularly interested, to be honest. Maybe I'm still not. But at any rate, I'm willing to listen."

"Well, well, finally starting to wake up to reality," Beck said. He crossed back to his desk and reclined against the front, studying his visitor. "See that?" he said as he pointed over his left shoulder to a wall covered with framed photos, certificates, and news clips. "That represents four generations of family history. Four generations—" he held up the appropriate number of fingers "—to move up the ladder from immigrant status to top of the heap. People say we were lucky, but they're wrong. We were successful, and success doesn't derive from luck alone. You know what you need to succeed? First, you need to recognize opportunity and take advantage of it when it rises up in front of you."

Beck rocked back and forth on his heels. "Let me tell you a little story to illustrate my point. It starts with my great-grandfather, John Dugan Becker. He was eighteen when he came to this country, worked in the Chicago stockyards for a year, hated the noise and confusion of the city, and came up here, doing whatever and living like a pauper. In four years he had saved enough money to open a small quarry. There were dozens of operations like that around here, men breaking their backs cutting stone from holes in the ground. But Becker had a knack for business and slowly expanded the operation until he had six or seven employees and contracts with a couple builders in Milwaukee to provide stone for their buildings. He was a handsome man by all accounts and could have married any one of the beautiful immigrant girls working as maids to the wealthy landowners up here. Instead, he married one of the locals, thought it would do more to secure his position with the locals."

A tradition you continued, Cubiak thought.

"In 1871, two things happened: my grandfather was born and more than three square miles of Chicago burned to the ground. Everything was made of wood back then, not just the buildings but the sidewalks and streets even. The city fathers' decision to rebuild in something less flammable created a demand for stone that no one could ever have imagined. While the owners of the other quarries plotted strategy, my great-grandpop dug into his savings and borrowed what he could. It's said that in one weekend, he tripled the size of his crew and leased half the barges operating this side of Green Bay.

"In a decade, he shipped more hewn rock two hundred miles down the lakefront than the rest of the stonecutters put together. The man saw an opportunity and ran with it."

Beck emptied his glass. "You know what else you do to succeed? You create opportunity when there is none. At the time Great-grandpop was running stone to Chicago, every boat that left Sturgeon Bay for the Windy

City or any port south of here first had to sail *west* and then *north* to the tip of the peninsula before it could travel *south* in Lake Michigan. Just think of the time wasted when Lake Michigan was less than two miles from the east end of the Sturgeon Bay harbor. All anyone had to do to subtract a hundred miles from the journey was dig a ditch and connect the two bodies of water."

"I suppose your great-grandfather dug the ditch?"

Beck roared; he liked that. "No. He put his money in with other forward-thinking business leaders, and together they hired the men and equipment to dig the canal. Then they charged other shippers to use it!"

"The American way," Cubiak said dryly.

"Exactly. But nothing lasts. Nothing. Sit on your ass and the world marches right past you. To succeed, you also have to be flexible and willing to shift gears. When the demand for stone dried up, the family went into the shipbuilding business! For years, they built ore boats and barges. War broke out, twice, and they churned out cruisers and destroyers. Then supertankers came along. Even if we could build vessels that size there was no way to get them through the Saint Lawrence Seaway and to the oceans. What'd we do? We retooled, refocused our marketing strategy, and emerged as one of the country's premier manufacturers of private yachts, large sailing craft, and automobile ferries."

"Right."

Beck began pacing again. "Remember what I said about opportunity? It's everywhere. Keep an open mind and you'll find it. Know where I found it?"

"No idea." Cubiak retrieved his host's glass and refreshed it.

"Not here in the good old staid Midwest. No, I found

it on the global scene. Went to Princeton, did you know that? Bunch of uptight East Coast assholes but they got connections and through them, I made valuable international contacts, people with unlimited wealth."

"What's all this got to do with me?" Cubiak said. Cupping his empty glass, he reclaimed his seat.

"Plenty. I'm linked into people who have money to eat and what I've discovered is that they're fanatics about safety. Bulletproof everything. Fences. Dogs. Body guards. Metal detectors inside the front door, for chrissake. These people aren't stupid but they are scared; they know that what they've got, everybody else wants. They see a world filled with hate and distrust and violence. They're living in a time when they're the targets for every extortionist or revolutionary with a gun and a grenade. And here, hell, the yokels don't even bother to lock their doors at night."

Cubiak sat up. The conversation was finally moving where he'd intended it to go.

"Now, it's true I can offer these rich bastards top-of-the-line luxury boats, but so can a dozen other shipyards. So I asked myself: What else? What can I offer that's unique? And I realized it was the thing staring me right in the face.

"What I can provide is a little bit of Camelot. The peace of mind they crave. A secluded playground isolated from war, terrorism, disease, and deprivation. A refuge—for the elite. Here on the peninsula and on Washington Island as well. This is strictly confidential," Beck said as he handed Cubiak a large leather-bound book.

*Paradise Harbor.* The title was embossed in gold letters, just as Jocko had said. Cubiak opened the cover and paged through. Here was Door County metamorphosed into the ultimate luxury community, gated and crowned with stunning amenities. A modern medical complex staffed by physicians from the not-too-distant Mayo Clinic, an expansive health spa, stables, and even artificial hot springs. For security, an electronic underwater grid in the newly dredged Fish Creek Canal and in the surrounding offshore waters. The state-of-the art network of hidden microphones, not unlike the Navy's SOSUS system, could detect and track any manmade sound, providing early and adequate warning of possible intrusion.

"Well, what do you think?" Beck was puffed with excitement.

"Impressive."

"You haven't seen the half of it!" At the back of the room Beck switched on an overhead light and lifted a white sheet off the conference table to reveal a three-dimensional model of Washington Island.

Gone was the utilitarian ferry dock with its funky general store, family restaurant, and moped and bike rental shops. The village that had grown up along the isle's main road no longer existed. The waterfront cottages and frame houses were no more. In place of the inlet where the ferry docked, Beck had ordered up an elaborate harbor for the kind of vessels the very rich favored. Overlooking the facility was an upscale resort, similar to the one planned for the peninsula. Even more incredible was the transformation of the interior into a hunting preserve. Instead of cows and fruit trees, Beck's Washington Island was dotted with miniature statues of wild game.

"Tigers and elephants?" Cubiak said.

"A four-season hunting preserve, stocked to order according to the calendar. Black bear in spring. Moose in winter. Ah, but there's so much more. The island is a unique land formation, a true gift from nature. More than four hundred million years ago, during the Paleozoic Age, half the continent was covered by an ocean. The receding waters left massive deposits of dolomite that became Niagara Falls out east and here in the Midwest formed the bedrock of both the peninsula and Washington Island. The result: scenic bluffs on the mainland and interconnected tunnels on the island."

At Beck's touch, the island model swung open to reveal a honeycomb of underground caverns. "A man can stand upright, the tunnels are so tall. Some are even wide enough for ATVs to get through. And they're impregnable. In fact, during World War Two, the Army stored secret documents down there. When the Cold War started, a local entrepreneur tried to promote the tunnels as the ultimate fallout shelter before the state stopped him.

"A primitive venture," Beck observed dryly. "For my purpose, the tunnels will be outfitted with private living quarters, gourmet food service facilities, and a medical clinic, all to be used in extreme emergencies only." In such a haven, a person could disappear whenever necessary. Most important, he said, it was readily operational.

Beck stepped back from the table. "Paradise Harbor: Shelter from the storm."

Cubiak said nothing.

"You think I'm nuts, don't you? Who's going to invest in such an outlandish scheme? Here, look at this. It's what I give my prospective buyers to underscore the need."

He tossed Cubiak a red leather binder. Inside, a timeline and clips from the *New York Times*, *Financial Times*, and other world media. Photos of the towers coming down and people in Manhattan gray with dust. Terrorist attacks in London, Bali, Saudi Arabia, Spain, India. In Russia, twelve hundred schoolchildren held hostage by separatist extremists. Suicide bombings. Riots in Paris and China. Rogue countries with nuclear weapons. The Swedish foreign affairs minister stabbed to death in Stockholm. Assassination attempts on both the president and vice president of the United States, the president of France, the queen of the Netherlands, a British MP. Swine flu. Mad cow disease. The Doomsday Clock at five minutes to midnight.

Beck drained the last of the Calvados into his glass. "See what I mean? The post–nine-eleven world is not a pretty place. Chaos. Death. Disaster. Suddenly my plan doesn't sound quite so outrageous, does it? The people who have the money to afford what I'm offering are legitimately concerned about their safety. They recognize the serious problems facing the world and see that I offer a serious solution."

"What about the people who live on the peninsula, in all those places you want to bulldoze and build over?"

Waving his drink, Beck sloshed the two-hundred-dollar-a-bottle booze onto his hand. "They'll be fairly compensated, don't worry."

"What if they refuse to cooperate?"

Beck dried his wet palm on his thigh. "Oh, they will. Some may need a little more persuading than others, but eventually even the most stubborn will come around. Money talks, my friend. Money talks and bullshit walks."

I'm not your friend, Cubiak thought. "And my role? Where do you see me in this scenario?" he said.

"A man with your credentials? That's easy." Beck clapped him on the shoulder. "Vice president of security."

Security honcho, Barry had said. Cubiak set his glass on the floor. "I'd have to hear more," he said.

"Of course."

"Quite a project. Becker would be proud."

"Indeed, he would." Beck grinned and then grew serious. "Not a word of this, you understand. No one can know anything."

Too late, Cubiak thought, as he rose to leave.

HE NEEDED THE night air to clear his mind. Jocko hadn't exaggerated. Paradise Harbor would destroy Door County. Beck's proprietary attitude was galling, but seen in the context of family history, it made sense in the warped way the rich and powerful viewed the world. To Beck's way of thinking, he was simply following in the family's footsteps and enlarging them as he went. Land was the key. The plan could be implemented only if Beck held title to thousands of acres of prime Door County real estate.

Jocko said locals wouldn't sell, but they might if a series of murders wiped out the tourist trade and vanquished their livelihoods. Was Beck so determined to have his way that he would kill to make Paradise Harbor a reality? Up until an hour ago Cubiak would have said no. But after the man's performance that evening, he wasn't sure.

At the same time, he realized the scenario could be flipped and the opposite question posed. Did someone think that tarnishing the peninsula's reputation would destroy the harbor plan as well, someone willing to commit murder in order to thwart Beck?

Cubiak had known people to kill for less.

Had he been too quick to eliminate Johnson from his list of suspects? The park superintendent had a lifetime of reasons for hating Beck. Johnson had given his word that the dates on the specimens, which cleared him on the deaths, were tamper proof. But what if he hadn't told the truth?

Perhaps Bathard should be considered a suspect as well. The coroner claimed ignorance about Beck's plans but he could be lying, and Cornelia's illness gave him motive enough to seek revenge on the man.

Jocko and Bathard weren't alone in loathing Beck. Eloise Beck hated her husband for ruining her life and for not loving their son. Amelia Pechta despised Beck simply for who he was, and as a teenager she had learned skills that equipped her to survive or to kill. She hobbled around the bar, but what if the weakness was a feint? Even Halverson's bumbling could be an act.

Had Jocko notified one of them or did he call someone else, someone who didn't register on the radar? The old ferry captain was disabled and didn't look well heeled, but appearances could deceive. Maybe Jocko had squirreled away enough money to pay someone to do the killing for him.

# EIGHTEEN

*Friday*

AN HOUR AFTER DAWN, the grand boats began slipping into the Ephraim harbor. With a steaming cup of black coffee for company, Cubiak paced the dock and watched the windjammers motor in. Sails down and masts gleaming, the magnificent vessels strained against the water like nervous thoroughbreds waiting for the signal to let fly.

The ranger had slept poorly. Beck's assurance that nothing would go wrong had not diminished his concerns. He was sure the killer would strike again but couldn't predict where and when. The regatta was a prime target.

A throng of spectators jostled past Cubiak. And still the boats kept coming. Their combined grandeur reminded him of Paradise Harbor.

It was a plan spawned by arrogance and driven by ugly ambition. Beck said that folks in Door County didn't mess with tradition. Maybe not, Cubiak thought, maybe some like Beck just plotted to destroy it. Cubiak knew he could never be part of the scheme. After the festival, he'd work with Jocko to try to stop Beck, whatever it took.

A sudden light breeze carried snatches of conversation to shore. Cubiak listened to the mostly male voices, laced with bravado. The race kicked off day three of the festival. Boats competed for prize money, bragging rights, and trophies. Thirty vessels, including one flying the flag of Beck Industries, were registered for the event. The route ran north from Ephraim, around the tip of the peninsula through Death's Door, and then down the Lake Michigan side to Baileys Harbor. It was the reverse of the run Ruby had described after dinner on Tuesday. Shading his eyes, Cubiak followed one of the mighty boats as it jockeyed into position at the starting line. He could imagine a young Ruby on the deck, the others as well: Beck, Dutch, Eloise.

Chicago's Bridgeport neighborhood where Cubiak had grown up was less than a twenty-minute bike ride from Lake Michigan, but he had never been out on the water until he was an adult and could afford to treat Lauren to a dinner cruise. He'd expected so much from the outing. The view of the city had been stunning, but the boating experience was disappointing. The cruise ship was large and impersonal. From a deck three stories above the water, he looked down and imagined himself on a sailboat, close to the waves and working with the wind.

He envied those readying for the race. And he hoped that Beck was right, that nothing would go wrong.

At sunup, Cubiak had rendezvoused with Halverson to assign the sheriff's deputies to their stations. Those with sea legs were posted on board a half dozen power craft that would escort the racers through the course. The rest patrolled the peninsula. Given the miles of wooded cliff on the Green Bay side and open shore along the lake, it was hardly a satisfactory arrangement.

"You worry too much," Halverson said, echoing Beck.

To anyone who would listen, the sheriff bragged about the bikers he'd arrested before the start of the festival, implying that he had the situation well under control. Any additional security measures were merely for show.

At seven, the starter's pistol popped. As the boats swept past the starting point, the crowd cheered. Wrapped in a colorful cloud of billowing sails that bit the wind, the vessels flew toward the deep water. For the landlubbers, there was nothing to do but turn around and walk back to town.

Following the waterfront roads, Cubiak tracked the race from the jeep. More often than he liked, his view was blocked by patches of forest, but occasionally he glimpsed the boats and felt his spirits lift at the spectacle.

The lead boat crossed the finish line at 8:20. A new record. Cubiak lingered on the sidelines as the victorious crew hauled down the sails and made their way to shore. They were handsome, rugged, wealthy men, the kind who took winning for granted. Did they even notice him, the working stiff in the brown uniform? The guy who was supposed to keep them safe from harm? Probably not, he thought. People like him were invisible until they were needed. Cubiak tossed his empty coffee cup and reversed out of the lot.

EARLY THAT AFTERNOON, Cubiak pushed through the door at sheriff's headquarters. He had come to question Petey Kingovich. From the beginning he thought the man's quick arrest was a convenient ploy to assuage the locals and keep the festival on track. Perhaps there'd been more to it. Maybe Petey knew something about Beck's plans that Beck didn't want blabbed around. Encouraging Halverson to put the younger Kingovich behind bars was a sure way to keep him isolated and out of touch.

Halverson was none too happy to see Cubiak. "I don't have to do this," he protested as he got to his feet.

"Yes, you do."

The sheriff kept his own counsel as he led the ranger across the lobby and through a series of heavy metal doors to the jail. A one-way glass wall separated the command center from the two-tiered pod of cells where a dozen inmates in bright orange garb played cards or watched TV in the lower-level common area. "Domestic abuse, drunk and disorderly, theft, you name it," Halverson said. Kingovich was housed in a separate area for recalcitrant prisoners.

"Visitor, asshole," Halverson intoned as the cell door swung open. "Twenty minutes," he said as he swiveled aside and let Cubiak pass.

Petey lay stretched out on the bunk, arms behind his head. A reclining scarecrow, he appeared to be taking a detailed census of indentations in the off-white acoustic ceiling tiles.

Cubiak leaned into his view. "I'm probably the only person within a hundred miles not ready to string you up for the murder of Alice Jones. If you've got more than two brain cells rubbing together inside that thick skull, you'll talk to me."

He pulled back and let Petey think things over. After a few minutes, the young man sat up and folded his legs yoga style on the thin mattress. Face blank. Eyes flicking contempt and trained on Cubiak.

"You had opportunity, but no motive as far as is obvious. The two usually go together. Maybe you know someone who had them both."

No reaction.

"The axe yours?"

Nothing.

"Okay, I'll answer for you. 'Yes, sir. It's mine all right.'"

Petey glared at him.

"How many keys to the shed?" Cubiak waited. When the prisoner didn't respond, he went on. "Shall I continue in both roles?"

Petey's shoulders rose a millimeter.

"One?"

Petey's tongue pried loose from its moorings. "Maybe."

"That's better. And you had it?"

"I had all the keys." Petey yawned, open mouthed. "Wouldn't have mattered nohow."

"Why?"

"Lock's busted."

"For how long?"

This time the shoulder elevation was slightly more perceptible. "Month. Six weeks. Six years."

"Leaving the shed open to anyone who wanted access."

"Sure. No matter. Nothing in there worth taking."

"You never found anything disturbed."

"Not really. People'd go looking for oars. Tools sometimes, too. Once in a while a screwdriver's missing. Didn't matter any."

"There's a shelf full of boxes. What's in them?"

Petey grinned. "Proof we paid our taxes. Shit like that. Junk my mother put aside for posterity. Hell, we even had a box my old man was holding for Dutch."

"Your father knew Dutch?" The news surprised Cubiak but he kept the question casual, taking things slowly.

"Sure. No big fucking deal. Everybody knew Dutch."

"How did Dutch's stuff end up in your shed?"

Cubiak lifted a pack of cigarettes toward the ceiling camera and then held it out toward Petey. The inmate snatched a cigarette, jabbed the tip into the proffered match, and inhaled loudly.

"What's to say? He come by one day a couple years back when he was going round talking to people for some book he was writing. Shows us a box of shit he's collected and starts asking about Kangaroo Lake. Looking for picturesque stories on marshes and bird migration. Like we're taking serious notes for decades, ya know? My old man poured a couple of shooters, sat down, and told me to leave. Said he had private business to discuss with Dutch."

"You didn't hear what your father had to say?"

"Nah. He was just another bag of wind, far as I was concerned."

"Then what happened?"

"Hour or so later, I seen Dutch leave. He's looking kind of wild, like he'd been kicked in the balls. 'What did ya tell him?' I asked my old man, but he won't say. Just that he owed Dutch an apology for some kind of job he'd done once. Anyways, Dutch was feeling no pain when he left."

"And he didn't take the box with him?"

"Not that I saw."

"Did he come back for it later?"

Petey snickered. "Dutch? He never did nothing later."

"Meaning?"

"He bought the ranch up the road a piece, near Institute. Looked like he missed a turn. What I heard, he sailed clear over the ditch, hit a fence post, and rolled a couple two three times. Killed instantly, like they say."

"Heart attack?"

"Who knows?" Petey slid forward far enough to grind the butt into the floor with the toe of his boot. Cubiak handed him another cigarette, already lit. "My old man's pretty shook up about this. He tosses the box on the shelf and won't let nobody near it." The words flowed out on a thin plume of gray smoke that rose in a straight line to an unseen vent. Petey's gaze shifted from floor to ceiling to barred windows and back to Cubiak. He took another long hit and sagged back against the concrete wall.

"The box still there?"

"Far's I know." Petey scratched his chest.

"With Dutch's notes and maybe information on whatever job it was your father did for Beck." Tossing out the name was a calculated risk. But whatever Beck had done to harm Dutch, Eloise implied that it was underhanded, just the kind of job for someone like the elder Kingovich.

The heir to Kingo's sniggered and motioned for another cigarette. "Beck? Biggest fucking asshole on the peninsula. I got nothing to do with him."

For the moment, Cubiak believed him. "How'd you know it was Beck your father worked for?" he said, holding the pack just beyond the prisoner's reach.

"Who else? He had one talent, my daddy. He was a master counterfeiter. Hell, the man could forge anything. Did time for it a ways back. Beck knew all about his special gift. Took advantage of it, too, every once in a while."

Cubiak let Petey grab another smoke. "Sounds like maybe your old man helped Beck put the screws to Dutch."

Petey popped the knuckles on his left hand. "Guess. Shit, he probably needed the money."

"So why the guilty conscience later on?"

Petey looked up. "Man, you don't know nothing, do you? 'Cause Beck made him fuck the guy who'd saved his kid, that's why."

A story told in front of a dwindling fire flashed back to Cubiak. "You were the boy in the well."

Petey offered a lopsided grin. "Yeah. That would be me."

CUBIAK TOSSED THE remaining cigarettes to Petey. Whatever had gone down between Dutch and Petey's father was important. The ranger paused at the cell door. "I need to talk to your father. Where can I find him?"

"Go to hell," Petey replied smugly.

"You know, I've had just about enough of your bullshit."

Unperturbed, the prisoner eased himself off the cot and flexed his knees. "I ain't bullshitting. You wanna talk to my old man, you gotta go to hell."

"Meaning what? That he died and now is paying for his sins?"

"I ain't said nothing about him dying. All I says is he's in hell."

"You got an address?"

"Yeah, he's at the Green Oaks Nursing Home outside of Valmy. Notice I didn't say he 'lived' there," Petey quipped, pleased with himself.

On his way out, Cubiak let the door slam.

DUTCH DIED ON his way to Sturgeon Bay, probably to confront Beck. The former sheriff had driven off in a rage, so distraught by what he'd learned from the elder Kingovich that he left without the research material he'd spent years gathering. What great insult or injury had Beck engineered that would prompt a man known for his composure to react so impulsively and recklessly?

If Dutch took notes during his meeting with Kingovich, the answer could be in a storage box in the shed behind the tavern. From the jail, Cubiak drove straight to Kingo's Resort, trailing a thin cloud of dust through the empty parking lot. A hand-scrawled sign was taped to the bar door. Closed, it read. The house and cabins were shuttered as well. Despite the bank of tall pines that surrounded the property, the heat was oppressive.

Four boys, ten or eleven, fished off the old dock, their bikes piled against a tree. Cubiak waved to the youngsters and ducked under the yellow police tape encircling the shed. The lock was weather worn and decrepit and offered no evidence of recent use. The ground was trampled and partially caked with mud. Recent rains would have obliterated any trail that might have been left by an intruder. The door gave way easily. He waited for his vision to adjust to the dim light and then started to pull the boxes from the shelf. Petey's account was true; there were at least thirty years' worth of tax materials neatly stored in carefully marked files.

Dutch's box was not in the shed. Either Petey had moved it and lied to him, or someone had taken it.

The shed was accessible both from the road and from the lake. Anyone coming from the road took a chance on being seen, but someone approaching from Kangaroo Lake could sneak in undetected. Cubiak began circling toward the water. A hundred feet into the dense underbrush he found a nest of broken bulrushes and a patch of trampled weeds where a boat had been pulled up onto land. Could have been kids. Or someone looking for a back-door entrance to the storage shed.

Figuring the boys on the pier for regulars, Cubiak asked them if they'd seen anyone snooping around. They shrugged and said the only guys they ever saw were Petey and his friends.

The lake shore south of Kingo's was undeveloped, so Cubiak headed north. About half a mile up he turned in at a sign for Archie's Resort. The resort was a shabby fishing compound of eight one-room shanties and a single narrow pier where several dugouts and canoes were tied up. The sound of a car door slamming brought a white-haired man with an ancient face out the door of one of the shacks.

"Howdy, mister," he said.

"You Archie?"

"All day. Every day. You looking for a room?" He sounded hopeful.

"No, but I might need a boat later this week. You rent them out?"

"Don't need to. Most people here are fishermen. They bring their own." Not like you pansy city kind, he implied. Wouldn't know an earthworm from a garden snake.

"Then who are those for?" Cubiak gestured toward the pier.

"Wives. Kids. Gives the family something to do. Quality time." The sibilants whistled through the spaces between Archie's narrow, pointed teeth.

"You take reservations, for the boats?"

"Nah. Got enough paperwork without worrying about that, too. Them's all first come, first serve. They always come back. Local kids use them, too, sometimes. They think I don't know. But I do. I just don't say nothing, being as they come back in one piece."

The old man coughed and then went on. "Funny, though, had one disappear for a couple of days not too long ago." He rubbed his chin and grinned. "It made its way home eventually."

"Remember when?"

"Two. Three weeks maybe."

"Rowboat?"

"Nah. Canoe. Probably some teenagers spooning under the full moon." He paused. "They still do that?"

"I guess."

ANY HOPE CUBIAK had that the elder Kingovich would be able to tell him about Beck's scheme to undo Dutch evaporated when he arrived at the nursing center. Neither the woodsy setting nor the antiseptic corridors could disguise the fact that the facility was a warehouse for the dying. When he was shown to Mr. Kingovich's room, Cubiak found pretty much what he dreaded—the skeletal frame of a man lying motionless on a high bed rimmed with safety rails. Massive stroke on top of everything else, the nursing director announced matter-of-factly but not without compassion.

"Any chance he'll ever recover enough to talk?" It was an inane question, but one Cubiak had to ask.

"Oh, no. Unless there's some kind of miracle. It's been more than six months. Unfortunately, Mr. Kingovich's window of opportunity has closed," she explained.

The old man moaned and Cubiak started. But the nurse had already anticipated what he would ask next. "We have no way of knowing what, if anything, he hears." She skewered Cubiak. "At any rate, he can't chit-chat, if that's what you wanted."

Cubiak edged toward the door.

"We turn him every two hours to prevent bed sores," the director went on cheerfully as she reached over and fluffed the pillow that framed the vacant, ravaged face. Before she had the chance to say any more, Cubiak was gone.

Outside, he fished a stale cigarette from his breast pocket and lit up. Petey's assessment about his father had been right on the money. Whatever sins the old man had committed against Dutch, he was paying for them now in his own private earthbound hell. According to Petey, his father resented being forced to do Beck's dirty work against Dutch. The younger Kingovich didn't seem overly fond of his father but that could be an act. If Beck had put the arm on the old man more than once, there could be a catalogue of longstanding wounds festering between the two. Enough to prompt the younger Kingovich to try to avenge his father by torpedoing the festival and undermining Beck. How ironic, Cubiak thought, if Halverson had been right all along in blaming Petey for everything bad that had happened.

# NINETEEN

*Saturday Morning*

CUBIAK ROSE WITH the crows and ran an abbreviated track through the woods near Jensen Station. The forest was cool and quiet save for the birds, and the treetops shone like ebony against the wash of bright sky. Peninsula Park Golf Course was groomed and trimmed, ready for the festival tournament later that day. Below, the waters of Falcon Harbor lay blue and still. Along the shore, the quaint village of Ephraim waited to reprise its role as perfect summer host for the final two days of the celebration.

It was the kind of summer day that resort brochures hyped and the county tourism board coveted, the epitome of nature in prime, A-one condition. The kind of day that ensured large crowds at every festival event.

In his room, Cubiak retrieved his police service revolver from his worn Army duffel. Trying hard not to overthink what he was doing, he secured the holster around his right ankle and slipped the .38 Smith & Wesson into place. The gun felt all too comfortable in the familiar hollow above his foot.

Dressed, he followed the aroma of breakfast sausage and fresh-baked rolls into the kitchen. Johnson was pushing food around his plate while his nephew inhaled a molehill of eggs and sausage, seemingly oblivious to any but his visceral needs. Cubiak limited himself to coffee and toast. While Ruta fretted in the background, the park superintendent and his furloughed assistant went over the day's staffing logistics. Six part-time workers had been hired specifically to help during the festival. One of them was Barry Beck, who had yet to show up for duty at the Nature Center. Assuming he wouldn't be on the job that day either, Johnson had slotted his nephew into Barry's spot.

"You need anything from us, you just let us know," he said to Cubiak.

After the two left, Cubiak asked Ruta if she would stay in that morning. "I'm expecting a long distance call at noon and I need someone here to answer the phone. You'll miss the parade, but it's important," he said.

"It will help, with this?" The housekeeper pointed toward the window and the forest beyond.

"Yes, I think so. I hope so."

"Then I will stay. I do not need parades," she said, brushing toast crumbs from the table into her cupped hand.

Cubiak was rinsing his mug when Beck called.

"Didn't I tell you not to worry? Imagine the fiasco if we'd canceled the regatta and cut back on things like you wanted," he taunted.

"Day's not over."

Beck chortled. "You keep up this happy patter, we're going to have to start calling you *Grumpy*. But you're right, the day's not over. Except it's a magnificent day. Look out the window, you don't believe me," Beck said and hung up.

ALL OF DOOR COUNTY seemed caught up in Beck's feelgood mood. After the dreary spring and the tragedies of early summer, a feeling of civic pride and optimism reverberated over the landscape. The peninsula would reclaim its fine reputation. The festival promised to continue in its traditional sterling fashion and to go out in fine style. Only Cubiak could not shake free from the gloom that had dogged him for the past three days.

The day's events kicked off in Ephraim with the parade. Macklin had died in Fish Creek, along the south edge of the park, and the other deaths had occurred in the park. If the killer wanted to complete the symmetry, Ephraim was a logical choice for the next attack. The previous day, Cubiak had established a dozen checkpoints in the town and instructed Halverson to station a man at each by 8 a.m. At thirty minutes past the deadline, when Cubiak cruised through the village, the posts were vacant. He found Halverson and his squadron of deputies hunkered around two picnic tables outside the town's pancake breakfast tent. The men were devouring stacks of buckwheat cakes awash in syrup.

"What the hell is this? Why aren't these men on duty?" Cubiak said.

Halverson lifted his fork in protest. "It'll get done. This here's tradition. I can't ask my boys to work on empty stomachs."

Cubiak bent to Halverson's ear. "You got ten minutes. That's it. If they're not ready, I hold up the parade. And it'll be your ass in the fire."

In the hostess tent, two lines of tourists snaked past locals who cheerfully handed out plates of food. At one of the service tables, Cate arranged a small mountain of crisp bacon. She wore the ubiquitous red-checked apron and wielded a pair of oversize tongs. Ruby, another of the volunteers, spied Cubiak in the entrance and motioned for him to come eat. He waved off the invitation and slipped away. Outside, the hungry horde stretched to the beach. "People come eat, then get a prime spot for the parade," Caruthers had told him.

The roadway through town was rimmed with camp stools, lawn chairs, and a maze of towels and blankets. In the bay, a flotilla of sunfish, wooden rowboats, and cabin cruisers assembled off the shore, ignoring the half dozen noisy jet skis that buzzed past. The crowd at Milton's stood three deep.

At the northern edge of Ephraim, traffic was detoured off Route 42, leaving a stretch of vacant highway where the floats and marchers could assemble. Most faces were unfamiliar to Cubiak but none seemed out of place. He talked with several of Halverson's men, but they hadn't noticed anything out of the ordinary either.

AT TEN O'CLOCK, the siren at the Ephraim Volunteer Fire Department shrieked, announcing the start of the parade. The town's new fire truck led the procession, its bright red metal sides and bumpers polished to a hard sheen and draped with bunting. Three volunteer firefighters and their families, selected by lottery, clung to the side and rear straps and waved to the crowds massed along the parade route.

Cubiak watched the entourage wind around the first bend in the road. The parade was rough edged and homespun, a small-town combination of charm and kitsch: A trio of bagpipers loud, but not precisely communicating with each other. A high school marching band that strutted out of step and out of line. In loose formation, the members of the local VFW who had all but outgrown their starched and pressed uniforms. Straggling behind in piecemeal, hodgepodge fashion, three Vietnam veterans wearing remnants of jungle camo. Local celebrities ran to Girl Scouts bearing handmade pot holders, a bevy of Miss Lynn's preschool ballet students in pink tutus, and an acned cluster of shy 4-H representatives brandishing homemade birdhouses and home-canned cherry preserves, one leading a reluctant heifer by a leather halter.

The audience applauded them all: the youngest descendants of the town founder who sat nervous and self-conscious in the front seat of a vintage restored Buick Roadmaster; the contingent of greeters who tossed flower petals into the street; the irrepressible Bay City Cloggers, who click-clacked their cleated shoes down the pavement as if determined to pulverize the roadway. One group after another was warmly welcomed: the ladies auxiliary of the Moravian church; the Door County Lions, Moose, and Rotary; Cate and Ruby, arm-in-arm with other members of the Door County Conservation League. In honor of the Native Americans who had owned the land first, the two women wore traditional fringed, fawn-colored shifts fashioned from deerskin. An intricately beaded band sparkled around Cate's long hair. A red smear marked Ruby's forehead; a black feather dangled from behind her left ear. Among those receiving the loudest cheers were the royalty spawned by the celebration itself: a five-year-old town princess and a preteen king and queen.

At the reviewing stand, the entrants paused for special recognition from Beck and other officials. Then they moved on, scrambling to catch up with the rest of the parade.

An attack on the procession would have been easy to

plan and implement. The parade route was a half mile long, and marchers and onlookers were vulnerable for the entire distance. They could have been targeted from the ridge or the water or even from the immediate area. Yet the event passed without incident. Cubiak doubted the increased police presence was the deterrent. He was on his way back to the park when he realized there was another possible reason there hadn't been an attack on the parade: the killer was one of the participants.

# TWENTY

*Saturday Afternoon*

AT TWELVE NOON, the phone rang in the kitchen at Jensen Station. While Ruta jotted down the information provided by the soft-spoken gentleman at the other end of the line, a piercing air-horn blast heralded the start of the annual Peninsula State Park Golf Tournament. On the clubhouse patio, the crowd of spectators stood and cheered. Cubiak jumped to his feet with them. Unlike the onlookers, he'd heard more than just the screech of the air horn. With a singular clarity honed by years of training as a soldier and police officer, he'd also registered the sharp ping of a distant rifle report, and it reached him as one of Beck's foursome crumpled to the ground at the first tee box.

"Quick get inside! Someone is shooting," Cubiak yelled as he zigzagged between the tables. A middle-aged couple in matching pink golf shirts glanced up from their mimosas and regarded the park ranger as if he were crazy. A woman in a straw hat pointed toward the fallen golfer. "Look, the man's had a heart attack," she said. Cubiak shoved two teenage girls toward the clubhouse entrance. "Get the fuck out of here," he shouted again as he reached for his .38. At the sight of the weapon, onlookers screamed and scattered.

Certain the shot had come from the ridge above the

course, Cubiak leapt into an empty golf cart and drove toward the fairways, keeping his head down and his foot pressed to the accelerator. The tournament was sold out, and the other players were not yet aware of what had happened. Caught up in the excitement of the game, they had heard only what they wanted to hear, the familiar signal that marked the start of play.

A burst of gunfire shattered the last vestiges of the day's equilibrium. Bullets tore into one tee box after another, startling the players and generating explosive ripples of confusion that quickly fanned out across the rolling terrain. In a wave of mad motion, terrified golfers dispersed. Many ran to the trees, propelled farther into the woods by high velocity bullets that nipped at their heels. Others raced toward the clubhouse, speeding recklessly in their carts or sprinting on foot. Gunfire peppered their paths and punctuated the air around them. There were so many shots it sounded like a semi-automatic had opened fire.

Cubiak knew that wasn't the case. He recognized the gun as a bolt-action rifle and knew the person handling it was an expert. One weapon. One shooter. Numerous targets. He among them. His only hope of stopping the attack was to reach the top of the ridge and find the sniper.

Maneuvering the golf cart onto a little-used service road, he travelled along the base of the cliff and then up into thick brush until a fallen tree forced him to get out and claw his way up the punishing vertical rise on foot. Burrs bit into his cheeks and neck, and the calloused pads of his hands shredded on the rocks. Near the top, he slipped and broke the fall on an outcrop of rough boulders. With a final toehold in a narrow crevice, he grabbed hold of a low-hanging branch and pulled himself up onto level ground. The gunfire ceased. The shooter was reloading or repositioning. The respite was brief—he estimated it at only about forty-five seconds—just enough time for a sharpshooter to attach a second clip.

During the lull, Cubiak ducked into a narrow clearing that provided a view to the clubhouse below. A fresh round of gunfire erupted, blowing out a wall of windows on the clubhouse restaurant. Busboys and patrons streamed out, swelling the crowd of terrified players, caddies, staff, and spectators. Several sheriff's deputies were directing people into carts and cars; screams and shouts punctuated the air as the vehicles competed for room on the narrow road leading out of the park. The barrage continued but Cubiak realized that the shooter was no longer aiming at people. Beck's party had been the only human target.

On the ridge, the eerie whine of the bullets ricocheted off the limestone cliff, making it impossible for Cubiak to pinpoint the attacker's exact position. Crouched low, he made his way toward the highway, figuring the shooter was counting on the road to provide a ready escape.

Between the outcroppings of trees and bushes, he glimpsed the bay and the town. So far, neither had been attacked and activities at both seemed obscenely normal. The first of the caravans from the park rolled into town to the upbeat sound of a tuba band practicing near the bandstand. At the sight of the frenzied golfers and their bullet-riddled vehicles, the crowd laughed and applauded. They think this is part of the postparade entertainment, Cubiak realized.

A fresh volley of bullets shredded the bunting on the grandstand, and dazed silence gave way to hysteria. The shooter was behind him. As he doubled back, the attack intensified. Rapid-fire gunshots riddled the water and sliced through the hedges along the waterfront park. One shot hit the wrought iron weather vane atop Milton's and sent the decorative peacock spinning. Another tore through the flag on the front lawn of the Christiana.

In the confusion, a car rammed a food stand behind the Village Hall. A tank of propane ruptured and burst into flame, setting the bunting on the historic building on fire. Clouds of black smoke roiled through the square. People screeched and scattered.

The gunfire intensified again. Cubiak picked up his pace. Suddenly several bullets smacked the ground nearby. He dropped to his stomach and snaked off the path into a clump of brush. More shots splayed behind him. Two rifles were being fired. One aiming down from the ridge. The other up toward it.

The last shot he heard—fired from the ridge—was a tracer bullet. As Cubiak scrambled to his feet, a police vehicle near a private dock exploded in a fireball of blue and green flames, and the man standing near it toppled into a shallow marsh.

Below in the village of Ephraim, the fire department siren screamed, but on the cliff, there was a complete absence of sound. Not the normal hushed quiet of the woods but a ghostly unnatural stillness. In a low crouch, Cubiak plowed forward. He sensed that there would be no more shots from below. But he made a handy target to anyone still up on the ridge. It took him five minutes to traverse the rest of the path, but he found nothing. There was only one spot, other than the trail itself, the sniper could have used.

Several hundred yards in, Cubiak slid down an overgrown footpath onto a narrow ledge. The landing was deserted, but someone had been there. Cubiak scooped a handful of shell casings off the packed dirt and dropped them into his shirt pocket. Climbing back up to the path, he searched for the sniper's escape route. Not a single bent branch. Not a scuff mark or rock kicked aside on the trail. Whoever had been on the ridge had left no further trace.

The attack was over.

CUBIAK SCUTTLED DOWN the cliff and jogged across the course. Near the first tee box Beck huddled under a tree. He was in shock. Traces of vomit ran down his shirt, reminiscent of his son at an earlier scene of carnage.

Nearby the sole victim of the onslaught lay motionless in the bright sun. Blood pooled around his shoulders; brain matter spattered on the freshly cut grass. Beck's golf partners knelt on either side of the body. Arms lifted in humble supplication, they filled the air with the piercing wail of an ancient prayer offered over their dead companion.

"Who?" Beck repeated the question as he staggered to his feet.

"I don't know," Cubiak said.

"Why?"

Cubiak wanted to punch the man. "I think you know the answer to that better than anyone," he said and walked away, leaving Beck spitting a barrage of protests into the wind.

AT THE CLUBHOUSE, Cubiak pointed the medics toward the dead golfer. As the ambulance rolled up the fairway, he sucked down a beer at the deserted bar.

The park jeep had disappeared, probably used as an escape vehicle by someone who knew how to jump wires. Cubiak found an old bike in a storage shed and was about to set off when the sheriff arrived, abusing a vintage pink Thunderbird he'd commandeered from a tourist.

Halverson was dripping wet and bloated with excitement. "The bastard got me. But not before I got some good shots off," he said. No number of parking tickets could match this for a pure adrenaline rush.

"You were shooting at me," Cubiak said dryly.

"Fuck! You were up there! What did ya see?"

"Not much, but I found these." He produced the shell casings.

Halverson sniveled. "Hell, these could be from anywhere."

"Maybe." Cubiak gave one to the sheriff and dropped the rest back in his breast pocket.

"The director of the state boys bound to be calling my office soon—maybe right now—wanting to come in."

"Good. Tell him we'll need help with traffic. The roads will be jammed."

"What about roadblocks? They could help set them up."

"For what?"

"You know. To stop the sniper."

Cubiak mounted the bike. "You don't need roadblocks, Leo. The killer's either long gone or blended into the background. We have to keep the roads open and help people leave safely. Don't you understand? It's over. The festival's gone. The season's ruined."

Halverson blinked hard and looked away.

And Paradise Harbor is destroyed, Cubiak thought,

the dream vanquished before the first shovel of dirt was turned. He waited for the sheriff to regain his composure. "There's bound to be plenty of people trying to get off the peninsula. I'm going to Ephraim, then back up to the park to help. You'll have enough to do with the crime scene here but you might send a couple of men to Sturgeon Bay to make sure there are no tie-ups on the bridges."

Keeping to the shoulder, Cubiak bumped unsteadily down toward town. Traffic poured past him in the opposite direction. The day guests were fleeing first, sunburned and solemn behind the windshields, ignoring whimpering children in the back seats, their collective hysteria and panic propelling them south and away from Door County.

They had been betrayed. Promised fun and relaxation, they had instead been subjected to brutal, random terror. Those still marooned in town wandered the waterfront and narrow streets trying to organize, regroup, and get out. Their fear was palpable, caught in their tense voices and sharp quick movements.

Ephraim was in shambles. Village Hall smoldered. Flags and bunting torn and tattered. Flowerbeds crushed. Store windows shattered. Picnic tables and garbage cans upended. Litter and food strewn on the ground.

Near the grandstand, a dozen deputies were organizing for a manhunt. They were angry, frightened men. Cubiak shouted them down. "A posse's not going to do any good."

There were protests. "The sniper could still be up there and start shooting again," one man insisted.

"Whoever it was got what they wanted. It's over,"

he said. "We need to restore order and help these people here."

He told four of the men to round up any injured and take them to the Moravian church. He posted one man by the deserted shops to deter looting and another to keep the curious away from the town center. The rest he assigned to traffic detail, instructing them to open up both lanes of the highway for people streaming south away from the peninsula and to divert northbound traffic around town.

Cars and vans scraped and bumped against one another as their drivers, the lucky ones who'd reached their vehicles, maneuvered for openings in the flow of traffic. Bottlenecks formed as people tried to move from one part of town to another. A woman with blood streaming from a cut on her arm dragged a young toddler behind as she spun around, disoriented and unsure where to seek refuge.

On the waterfront, dozens of fishermen and swimmers huddled in chest-deep water under the long piers and watched, ashamed, as a man wearing street clothes thrashed wildly into the water for a frail, young girl—a frightened preschooler with a shocking pink suit and inner tube of dancing mermaids—whom the others had deserted in their selfish haste to find safety beneath the docks.

Along a slip of white sand, lifeguards from the Chris evacuated guests off the beach; on the hotel's long expanse of porch, a gaggle of elderly women clutching croquet mallets huddled in a knot and watched as a crush of younger, more vocal patrons shoved through the front doors into the lobby and demanded refunds for their ruined vacations.

On the steps of his church, Thorenson organized

greeters to retrieve lost children and directed visitors into the inner sanctuary for juice and cookies. Having shielded Cornelia from the chaos and by some small miracle pushed her wheelchair into the back room of the Christmas Shoppe where two elderly sisters comforted her, Evelyn Bathard administered emergency first aid in the small dining room of Milton's. Wielding a garden hose, Ruby Schumacher and Amelia Pechta helped the volunteer fire department water down Village Hall.

Near the fudge shop Cubiak encountered a teenager with a group of seven youngsters in tow. She looked fragile and terribly young, yet she'd had the presence of mind to tie a length of bunting around the kids' waists, to keep them together. Incongruously swathed in gaiety, they stumbled after her, faces run with tears and smeared with ketchup and ice cream.

Cubiak offered to help, and the girl almost wept with relief. They were from Algoma and had been on a church outing, she explained. Their van was parked up the hill—blue with a large sun painted on the side.

Ten minutes later, Cubiak delivered the van and loaded the children onboard. "Use the back roads," he urged.

In town, Cate worked the old pump and offered cups of cold water to passersby. Cubiak waited his turn in line.

"You okay?" he said, when he reached her.

She nodded, but fear shone in her eyes. "This has to stop, Dave. You have to find who's doing this and stop them," she said, her mouth pinched with strain.

Cubiak squeezed her hand, wishing he could do more for her, for everyone.

He needed to get to the park. The bike was gone, so he borrowed a police car and steered it into the flow of traffic streaming out of Ephraim. Cars and vans jammed the park entrance. Cubiak pulled under a mulberry tree and went in on foot. The information booth was empty. Twenty yards in, he found Barry Beck directing the exodus from the southern rim.

Near the day lot, Ruta managed the flow of cars, motorcycles, and bicycles toward the highway. Her tall, commanding figure was made even more formidable by the official ranger's shirt she'd buttoned over her housedress and the wooden staff she grasped in her right hand. When a car full of teenagers tried to muscle ahead, Ruta smacked the hood with the stick. "You wait your turn," she ordered and stepped defiantly in the way.

"Where's Otto?" Cubiak said.

"Bluestone Bay. He said to tell you he blocked the north road." That explained the absence of traffic on the ridge.

At the station, Cubiak tried and failed to raise Johnson on the radio. He reached Turtle Bay Campground on foot and found it in turmoil. The campers had had to battle outgoing traffic to get back in, and most had just recently made it through. The few veterans were able to disassemble their tents quickly and efficiently, but the majority were soon tangled in tether ropes and outwitted by the yards of fabric they had to reduce to a two- or three-cubic-foot bundle. In their hurry, they tripped over loosely rolled sleeping bags and piles of aluminum cookware. "Stay calm," one father shouted at his three quivering children. "And hurry up."

Cubiak moved through the crowd, doling out reassurance and help. "There's no reason to rush. It's all over," he said.

"For now, maybe," a tall, stout man in a green T-shirt countered.

"We're sitting ducks here. They could start shooting at us now!" That from a muscled, young man with a mustache.

"No. The danger's past. No one's going to shoot at you. You can take it easy. I'll stay and help. In fact, everyone help each other. You'll get done faster." The roads were gridlocked, he explained. They might as well use their time wisely.

Grudgingly the vacationers returned to their tasks, and gradually the tension eased. "Wait'll I tell the guys at school," a lanky sunburned teenager said to another. "How many gunmen does it take to ruin a picnic?" a freckled boy teased a younger brother. His mother boxed the older boy's ears and told him to shut up. The campers wolfed down leftovers, covered ashes with dirt, and slowly stuffed their gear and themselves into their comfort-equipped vans and deluxe four-wheel-drive vehicles before joining the exodus home.

Cubiak hitched a ride with one of the last families to leave. The man hunched over the wheel had grudgingly allowed him to squeeze into the vehicle. The woman who sat between them clutched her hands and gulped down air in short, anxious breaths.

"I'm sorry," the ranger said, as they dropped him off near the station.

"I want my goddamn money back. A whole week's worth of camping fees." The driver's mouth was screwed up in anger.

Cubiak pulled three crumpled twenties from his wallet and shoved them at the open window. "This is all I got." The man snatched the bills and peeled out, kicking up dust from all four tires.

# TWENTY-ONE

*Saturday Evening*

BY DUSK, A ridge of dark clouds had blown up over Green Bay. The gray gloom blotted out the sunset and cast a pall over the peninsula. The day visitors had fled, along with many of the weekly and long-term guests. Those who hadn't yet left huddled behind locked doors at their cottages, hotels, and condos. Ephraim was deserted. So, too, were Fish Creek and Sturgeon Bay and the other resort communities that dotted the pristine shoreline.

The first rampaging tourists had ignited the panic, driving through the streets of the other towns, windows down, shouting inflammatory words—sniper, shooting, madman. The relentless wave of frightened vacationers had fueled the egress, drawing others from their picnics and festivities until they created a vortex of momentum that drained the famed vacation area of all visitors, all gaiety, all hope of pleasure. Many hyped the situation, enlarging their roles in calls and texts to hometown radio stations that replayed the news throughout the day until finally they hit the jackpot with live reports fed to sister stations in Milwaukee, Chicago, and Minneapolis. With its vulture-like appetite, the news media sensed a fresh carcass to be picked clean and assigned reporters to the story.

Across the peninsula, shops and restaurants were

dark. Shades were drawn, windows shuttered. The locals lay low. Bathard gave Cornelia a sedative and put her to bed, gently tucking a soft down quilt around her ravaged body. Afterward, he sat alone in the vaulted living room with a snifter of brandy and brooded over the day's events. He'd hoped, assumed even, that Cubiak would halt the string of murderous deaths that had plagued the area. Perhaps that was too much to ask of any one man, a stranger at that. Perhaps there was more that he—or any of them—could have done to help.

In the modest parsonage uphill from the Moravian church, Waldo and Gladys Thorenson sipped hot tea. Earlier they had tidied the church and meeting hall, and then knelt side by side before the altar in silent prayer. Good souls, they forgave the attacker and beseeched the Almighty for mercy. Later, snuggled in bed, Gladys admitted to her husband that rejecting vengeance was the hardest thing she'd ever done. "Me, too," he'd whispered as he pulled her into his arms.

In Sturgeon Bay, a somber Floyd Touhy prepared a special edition of the *Herald*. He had hard news to report, and some residual trace of the newsman he'd once been kicked into play and reminded him how to do it. He'd had several reporters, a handful of stringers, and three photographers on the scene. "Play up the 'Death's Door' angle whenever you can," he'd directed them. The page one headline read simply: DOOR COUNTY UNDER SIEGE: TRAGEDY STRIKES PENINSULA.

At his waterfront mansion, Beck bolted his study from the inside and telephoned Caruthers, who raved drunkenly about lost revenues. Beck cut him short with an order for an early morning emergency meeting of the Tourism Board and then banged the phone down. Slowly he looked around the room. The walls were hung with the documented history of his predecessors' victories. The conference table held the monument to his own ill-fated wonderland, the project that would have outshone them all. Still in his golf attire, Beck carried the remaining copies of the Paradise Harbor plan to the fireplace and laid a match to the paper and kindling on the grate. As the fire began to take, he ripped the pages from the bound books and slowly fed them to the flames.

Surrounded by bodyguards, Beck's international guests waited at the Cherry Valley Airport to begin their trip home. Earlier, the potential investors had allowed Beck's assistance in acquiring the official approvals needed to remove their companion's body. Afterward, in a public gesture of humiliation, they had symbolically turned their backs on Beck and walked away in complete silence, relegating the scion of Door County to oblivion.

In the north end of the peninsula Cate cleared away the remains of the snack she'd hastily prepared for herself and Ruby. Though Cate had forced herself to nibble at the food, her aunt had attacked the meal ravenously and then insisted she couldn't sleep as her niece trudged upstairs. Cate dropped into bed fully clothed, only vaguely aware of Ruby's nervous pacing downstairs and the reverberating sound of an Indian chant being played full volume on the old stereo.

At Peninsula State Park Cubiak watched the last of the visitors leave. Then he sent Barry home, mixed a hot toddy for Ruta, and presented Johnson with a preliminary damage assessment.

THE RANGER WAS under a scalding shower when he remembered Malcolm's phone call. Damp and bone tired, he found Ruta's message on his desk. Malcolm had left two numbers. Cubiak dialed the first. A machine took the call, and a crisp voice informed him he'd reached the office of the Door County Welding Company. If he left a message they would get back to him as soon as they were able. Cubiak hung up and tried the second number.

The call was answered on the third ring "Hello? Who is this?" a voice demanded.

"Hello!" Then a click.

An aching hollowness ballooned in Cubiak's chest.

He knew the voice.

Outside, a cold rain fell.

# TWENTY-TWO

*Week Three: Sunday*

UNDER A LEADEN, windswept sky, Cubiak headed north. The roads were empty, the resort towns unnervingly still.

"I am sick at heart at what I must do now. There is no satisfaction in solving this crime," Dutch had written in his notebook when he'd identified the killer. The same heavy, unhappy sentiment dragged at Cubiak. Late the previous evening, he'd talked with Johnson and Martha Smithson, then Bathard and even Buddy Entwhistle, whom Ruta had finally located. Cubiak was up past midnight weaving the threads of who and why into a cohesive theory. At five that morning, he dragged Halverson out of bed and had him roust Petey from his cell. The additional details he coaxed from the reluctant prisoner seared the information into a nightmarish knot.

Burdened by the truth, the most Cubiak could do was to drive slowly.

Even then he was brought up short when he reached the junction at the top of the peninsula. He had no choice, really. He understood this as he crimped the wheel to the right and turned down the narrow blacktop that led him under the by-now familiar arching green canopy toward land's end. Crawling around the last bend, he cut the engine and coasted into the circular driveway of the house

Dutch had built. The yard was empty. Near the house a bed of bright red azaleas sparkled with misplaced gaiety, but beyond the clearing, the dark forest cedars stood mute and guarded.

"RUBY? CATE?"

The names echoed through the stillness, then faded to silence. Cubiak tried the barn first. The door was locked. He peered through the four-paneled window. The walls had been emptied of their great loops of yarn. The looms were stripped and barren, naked in the thin light.

The ranger approached the house. The back door was ajar.

"Ruby? Cate?" he called as he stepped inside, and again, no answer. Only the faint sound of classical music from deep inside. Violins. Something melancholy and familiar he couldn't place.

He mounted the bare, wooden stairs. A small rear bedroom he assumed was Cate's was casually thrown together. The other two had the comfortable look of rooms lived in and carefully tended. Downstairs was the same. The living room curtains had been pulled shut. The fireplace swept. A short stack of photo albums sat neatly piled on the coffee table. He flipped through the top two. Pictures of Ruby and Dutch from long ago. A striking pair. In the kitchen, a cup and saucer rested in the drain by the sink. Cubiak ran his finger over the bottom of the cup. Still damp.

From the front hall, he stepped out onto a wide porch that seemed to open onto the very end of the earth: all trees, water, and sky. He followed a stone path through a yard landscaped with native plants and bushes. The path led to a cliff where a steep staircase plunged down to a narrow dock. A lemon yellow rowboat bobbled alongside the pier. A woman sat in the boat; she faced the water and held a slender brown pole. At first glance Cubiak thought it was an oar. He gripped the handrail and took his time descending the narrow steps.

"Ruby."

No response. Cubiak was about to call out a second time when Ruby lifted her feet and, with the agility of someone half her age, swirled around to face him. As she turned, Cubiak glimpsed a red gas can under the seat.

"I need to talk to you," he said.

Ruby pointed the brown pole at him. The oar became a skeet gun, probably twenty-gauge.

Cubiak advanced to the middle of the dock. "Target practice?"

"Maybe." Ruby balanced the shotgun across her knees and took his measure. "Rather early for a social visit."

"I have something important to show you."

She waited, a mix of amusement and skepticism on her face.

Cubiak reached across his chest and into his shirt pocket. His hand came out with the fingers tightly clenched.

Ruby motioned him forward.

When he was four feet from the boat, she put up her hand. Cubiak halted and slowly opened his fist to reveal four .300 Weatherby Magnum cartridge cases.

"I found these yesterday in the woods above the golf course. On the rock ledge, to be exact."

Ruby's face was inscrutable.

"Your father owned a Weatherby, custom-made with gold inlay. I saw it in a picture at The Wood. You were

in the same photo with him. You and your sister, Rosalinde. The gun's gone. I looked."

"I'll have to report it missing."

"You learned to shoot with your father's gun, didn't
you? He taught you everything he knew about hunting
and the outdoors."

Ruby stroked the barrel of her weapon.

"You should never have shown me the notebooks,"
he continued.

"You've lost me, I'm afraid, David. My mind's not
so quick anymore." She called him by his full name, as
had his mother.

"Something like this happens, there's a reason for
it." He quoted Dutch. "You did it, Ruby. You killed all
those people."

She said nothing.

Cubiak edged toward the boat. Ruby hoisted the shotgun and pointed it at him, and he took two steps back.
"I did what Dutch would have done, Ruby. I talked to
everyone. I followed all the threads. Some went a little
further than others. But they all fell short. Then you answered the phone last night and provided me with the
thread that led to the motive. It took some digging but I
finally figured it out."

"Go on," she said as if humoring a bothersome child.

"It began a long time ago, after you had Cate." He
waited for her to react but Ruby remained like stone.
"You needed a birth certificate for her and went to Beck
for help. He did as asked, but unbeknownst to you he had
a second birth certificate forged, one that named him as
Cate's father. That's the one he used to blackmail Dutch
into retiring to protect your name. After that, Dutch was
never the same. At the time, you may have suspected that

something wasn't right but you couldn't say anything. So you decided Dutch was depressed. A plausible notion. He'd had a major life transition. His health was failing. To keep up appearances and give Dutch something to do, you hit on the idea that he should write a book about Door County, never realizing where it would lead."

A flicker of recognition swept across Ruby's countenance.

"It was worse than you imagined, wasn't it, Ruby? Having Beck reveal your secret was bad enough, but then for him to claim he was Cate's father was unconscionable. For six years, your husband was forced to believe the worst, that while he was trapped in some stink hole in Viet Nam you were carrying on with his best friend. When he talked to Kingovich, he learned the truth about Cate but maybe more importantly, he learned that you hadn't been unfaithful to him with Beck. Knowing this should give you some comfort, Ruby. Dutch was driving to Sturgeon Bay when he went off the road. It's not hard to imagine he was on his way to confront Beck."

"How'd you ever come up with such a fanciful tale?"

"Dutch recorded his conversation with old man Kingovich just like he had all the interviews for the book. This morning, I got Petey to admit he'd listened to the tape. He told me the whole story."

"Pure conjecture. You think Kingovich ever told the truth about anything? Hah! He was a thief and a liar."

"After Dutch died, Bathard encouraged you to continue your husband's work on the book. You refused at first, but he persisted. Last winter you finally agreed and started looking for Dutch's notes. You must have thought it strange that you couldn't locate the material he'd accumulated. You knew some of the people he'd interviewed and eventually, you followed his trail to Kangaroo Lake. The old man was in a coma by then, but you knew about the papers and documents the family kept in the shed. That's where you found Dutch's box, and discovered Beck's treachery.

"Eloise told me how Beck toasted you and Dutch at their wedding: 'May our lives always mirror one another's.' You held him to it, didn't you? Beck destroyed your husband, so you decided to destroy his son, not because Beck loved Barry like you loved Dutch but because it was important to him to have an heir. You tailed Barry and knew when and why he'd be at the tower. But that fateful Sunday morning, Wisby was in the park instead. Same height and build and wearing the same kind of jacket. You killed the wrong person, Ruby. When you realized Benny had seen you that morning, you killed him, too. Two nights later, in the park, you got Alice, who was wearing Barry's jacket."

"Is this how big city cops solve crimes? Fiction one-oh-one?" Ruby said.

"Then Jocko phoned, ranting about Paradise Harbor. You realized the project meant more to Beck than anything, even his son, and your tactics shifted."

Ruby said nothing.

"The attacks began again but instead of targeting Barry, you killed tourists to try to scare away Beck's investors. Yesterday at the golf course, you could have shot Beck, but you murdered one of his guests instead, knowing such a blatant act of violence at the culmination of the festival would panic the entire county and finally, once and for all, destroy the Paradise Harbor scheme."

"My, that's quite an elaborate plan you credit me with. You have proof, I presume?"

"The research material that Dutch had accumulated would prove everything, but, of course, you took that. There's also Petey's version of what was on the tape, which you've no doubt destroyed. So it's your word against his."

Ruby rolled her eyes.

"That leaves the weaving."

"The imaginative musings of an old lady. That's what they said about my last show. That I was losing my touch."

"At the unveiling, Martha Smithson seemed upset that the hanging was displayed with only the front visible. I didn't think much of it at first, but then I got curious and wondered if there was something on the back that you didn't want anyone to see. This morning, I went to the Birchwood and looked."

Ruby shrugged. "It's an unconventional piece."

"More than that. A true double weaving would have a reverse of the Tree of Life on the other side. You wove a different picture entirely, a Tree of Death."

"Artistic license."

"It's not unheard of for a killer to maintain an elaborate diary that details the crimes committed. You told your story through the image you created on the back."

Ruby shifted her weight on the narrow seat. "Still with you," she chirped.

"There aren't many books left in the library at Jensen Station. But I did find several on the Lakota Sioux. A fierce bunch, they were. When they went on the warpath, they brought back souvenir scalps and hung them from their lodge poles. A little wartime contest they held to see who could kill the most. There were seven scalps on your death tree, each one of them with a clue.

A piece of fabric from Wisby's jacket. A fragment of rope from the *Betsy Ross*. Alice's broken nail. The tassel from the cap of the man you killed at the lighthouse. A tooth from the male cyclist, and an earring from his companion. Then, finally, this."

Cubiak pulled another bullet casing from his other pocket. "It matches. I checked," he said.

"And there's only your word it came from the weaving. That wasn't very smart. No," Ruby said, wagging a finger at him, "it won't wash. Do you think anyone would believe that I—that a woman—could do such things?"

"Why not? You were raised to be a skilled hunter and outdoors expert."

"You flatter me."

"You knew Sioux traditions from your summers on the reservation. The men did the fighting, but the torture and death of prisoners were left to the women."

"You've shared this theory with other people. Bathard, perhaps? Halverson?"

"No."

"So just the two of us are privy to this fantasy of yours."

"For now."

Ruby's look was dreamy and distant, her voice quiet. "You do the Lakota a disservice with your narrow focus. They are one of few cultures to recognize women's strength and to honor them for it." Ruby bent forward and came up with the shotgun aimed at the prow. Snapping the butt to her shoulder, she pointed the nozzle at the terrain beyond the dock and then slowly guided the weapon toward Cubiak until she held him directly in her sights.

"Funny thing about this place. So beautiful and yet so isolated, so treacherous. There's no accurate count of the number of people who've drowned in the entrance to the Door. Few of those who've gone down have ever floated back to the surface. The bottom currents are too swift, that's one theory. People drown and their bodies are carried out to the deeper depths where they snag on the boulders that cover the lake bed and eventually get picked clean by the bigger fish."

"You won't get away with it, Ruby."

"You left a note. You told Otto—someone—you were coming to see me."

"You know I didn't." He paused a moment. "They were all innocent, those people you killed."

"Dutch was innocent, too. So was I, once."

"You need help, Ruby."

"Help! From whom? You?" She clucked scornfully. "You can't even help yourself."

"Yesterday, in the parade, you walked past Beck wearing a Lakota war symbol. You wanted him to know. Oh, Ruby, why didn't you try to stop yourself?"

Ruby said nothing.

Cubiak looked past her, toward the massive white funnel spiraling upward over Washington Island. "You should have told Dutch the truth," he said, finally. "He would have forgiven you anything."

"Would he?"

RUBY STIFFENED, HER features rigid. Only the twitch in her left eye betrayed her internal struggle.

"Dutch was a man of honor," she said, eventually. "You have to remember that he was quite young when all this took place. Life teaches us to forgive, but when you're young…" The thought trailed off.

"There'd been a storm late that afternoon and the air was fresh and filled with the scent of pine. I was standing at the back door when the two men arrived," Ruby said. "It was dusk and they apologized for coming so late. They were new to Door County and had miscalculated the amount of time needed to traverse the length of the peninsula. The drive had taken them nearly an hour longer than planned. They were done up in dress blues, all spit and polish. Parade clothes. Death clothes.

"I'd eaten an early supper, watching the storm, and as the men talked, I had to struggle to keep down the food.

"The words were gibberish, garbage, bullets that split my heart. They told me Dutch was killed in an accident near the DMZ. One of four American soldiers." Details were sketchy. Dense fog. No man's land. An innocent mistake—if a mistake at all, more likely, an aggressive response to an attack. Grenades thrown. Rockets launched. "I couldn't keep up; there was so much they were saying. They kept telling me I needed to rise to the occasion. The US was still trying to recover from the disaster at My Lai, and the Paris peace talks were underway again. this time with some hope of resolution. The government's hands were tied; the State Department was in no position to make demands, too much hung in the balance. They pleaded with me to see their side of it. Surely, I understood, they said.

"I understood nothing.

"I asked them if it could be a mistake, aware that this was the question everyone in my situation asked and the one the men dreaded most.

"There was no mistake. Their response was firm,

resolute. Dutch's death was confirmed. The enemy had provided dog tags.

"I could re-create him with my hands. I knew the ripple of every muscle, the solid bend of his shoulders. I knew they were talking rubbish. Dutch pulverized by a mortar and bullets? It was all nonsense. Dutch can't be dead, I insisted. He couldn't be dead because he was talking to me, his voice was in my ear."

Ruby faltered, and Cubiak blinked at the mounting sun. He knew. He had lived the same horror and had felt himself go ice cold as she must have.

"They wouldn't stop talking! All I wanted was for them to go away so I could pretend they'd never been there, that it was all a nightmare. But they wouldn't leave. They kept talking. They told me that I had to keep the terrible news a secret. I could not plan a funeral because the remains—I gagged at the word—would not, could not, be released. It might be months, the younger one cautioned. Perhaps it was the older one who spoke.

"It was dark when they finally left.

"Their taillights were like a rat's eyes swimming in ink. I stood in the doorway until the two red dots disappeared, and then I began to shriek and cry. I beat my breast until my fists were numb.

"I had nothing," Ruby explained. "I had given up everything for Dutch, and now he was gone.

"By morning, I had devised a plan. I left before dawn and drove west to the reservation where I had worked summers during college. In the vast forgotten emptiness of the prairie, I thought I could be disappeared, like Dutch."

"You've never told this to anyone, have you?" Cubiak said.

Ruby lifted her chin. "No, never," she said.

"Last week when you came for dinner, I mentioned how Dutch had to drop out of school to operate the family store when his father got sick and how he didn't resent it, because he didn't feel he was entitled to an education.

"He was so different from me in that. I felt entitled to everything. Call it the arrogance of privilege and wealth or youthful naiveté, but..." Ruby squirmed on the narrow seat. "It's the way I felt, and there was nothing I could do to change it. When Dutch died, I felt more than grief for a life lost and a love lost. I believed to the very core of my being that I had been cheated, that fate had unjustly stolen the one thing I most wanted and deserved. My rage was absolute. I drank beyond all reason. I fucked every man who crossed my path. My friends on the reservation tried to stop me, but I scorned them and went on day after day, living a life of despair and debauchery.

"The following spring, I found myself pregnant." Ruby looked at Cubiak and laughed, though there was no mirth in it. "I never ever considered the possibility," she said.

"From somewhere in my moralistic past came the clear directive of what I had to do. Sober up. Stop the degenerate behavior. Figure out a way to make a living and raise the child. I decided to stay out west. I wanted the haunting vastness of the Indian lands to be our home, a bleak world to match a bleak life.

"I bought a secondhand trailer and moved it to a desolate valley near the north edge of the territory. I quit drinking and painted bright colorful clouds on the walls of the tiny living room. I even planted a garden. At night I sat on the wobbly metal steps and listened to coyotes howling in the distance. In the empty landscape, the sound was eerie, but I found it soothing. One day followed another with no change but in the girth of my body. When the baby was due, an ancient midwife came to help. She arrived two days early and camped behind the trailer until it was time. It was not an easy birth.

"Cate was five days old when I had a visitor. A rangy, pockmarked man in pressed jeans and a black bolo tie pulled to the trailer and handed me a telegram. The envelope was tattered and worn, its seams sealed with cheap tape. I waited until his car vanished over the horizon and the dust settled on the dry, narrow road. Then I tore open the message.

"Dutch was alive.

"I must have fainted. It was the baby's crying that brought me back. Dutch was alive! I screamed and danced. I threw things in the air. There *had* been a mistake! He was badly hurt but safe. All life's blessings were back. I fell to my knees in thanks. And then, I caught myself. Because everything was wrong, and it was my fault. Dutch was coming home to a life I had destroyed."

In her despair, Ruby admitted, she almost allowed that it would have been better if Dutch had been killed or if she'd terminated the pregnancy as some had suggested, but she defused the notions before they could be fully articulated.

"My husband was alive, and I needed to act.

"I held my infant daughter to my breast and paced back and forth in the constricted space that defined my life. I had to consider my options. I had to think straight.

"I could hide everything I'd done but I couldn't hide the child. If I'd been guilty of a single indiscretion, I could have lived with the consequences. I could have begged forgiveness. But I had debased myself beyond redemption. It came down to the simple fact that I could not name the father. It came down to the realization that I had sullied myself with countless men. It was more shame than I could bear, more forgiveness than I could grant myself or ask from Dutch."

Trailing her hand in the water, Ruby told Cubiak how she had swaddled the baby into a worn blanket and left the reservation in the middle of the night during a freak spring blizzard. "I drove nonstop through swirling snow and thick darkness. By dawn, I was in Sturgeon Bay where I presented myself to Beck and asked his help. I provided few details beyond the pathetic story of an unmarried teen I'd befriended and the sad tale of my younger sister who was desperate to adopt, that half of the fable true. 'I need a birth certificate,' I told him.

"A few hours later, Beck produced the requisite document, one that named Rosalinde and her husband as the parents. The next morning, I went down to Milwaukee and gave my darling Cate to my sister. Then I boarded a plane to Washington where my hero husband was very quietly being returned home after more than a year as a prisoner of war."

"Hey! Hey, you guys!" A shout erupted at the top of the stairs.

Cubiak and Ruby looked up simultaneously and saw Cate waving energetically. Ruby turned ghostly pale and lowered the weapon again.

"Tell her to go back. Stop her," she commanded.

Cubiak moved toward the steps. "Stay there. Wait," he bellowed up the ridge. But Cate was already on her way down, hurrying, leaping the steps two by two, one hand sliding loosely along the railing, her hair bouncing, cupping her head.

"She mustn't know, for her own sake. Promise me that much. You won't ever tell her," Ruby said, pleading.

Before Cubiak could reply, Cate was with them, nearly breathless, her face flushed from the running descent. "I can't believe I made it without getting dizzy."

Neither Cubiak nor Ruby spoke. Cate spied the gun in her aunt's lap and glanced anxiously from one to the other.

"What's going on? What are you two doing down here?" she said.

THEY FORMED AN uneasy trio. A human triangle linked by time and circumstance.

Cate stamped her foot. "What's going on?" she demanded again.

"We're talking," Cubiak said.

Ruby interrupted and addressed Cate directly. "David came to tell me his theory about the recent deaths, the murders. It's an intriguing concept, really, with just a touch of whimsy about it. Especially the notion that the weaving provides proof that I'm the killer."

Cate gasped and whirled on Cubiak. "What the hell are you talking about?" Her fury erased any trace of intimacy that might have lingered between them.

"I told him it wouldn't wash. But then it's just guesswork on his part about my wanting to derail Beck's latest scheme. The dedicated environmentalist gone mad. A familiar theme." Ruby went on, steering the story to her purpose. "As it is, I have a theory of my own, which is at least as interesting. There were two killers at large who functioned quite separately from each other." Ruby fixed on Cubiak. "But you were the one to start the process." She hesitated, and then went on in a rush. "The first victim was Lawrence Wisby. You knew him, didn't you?"

"I knew who he was," Cubiak said. He turned toward Cate. "His brother was the man who killed Lauren and Alexis."

Cate inhaled sharply. "You knew he was in the park?"

"No."

"He had a campsite!" Ruby said.

"He reserved a campsite at the beginning of March. A month before I arrived."

"You could've known then, that he was coming to Door County?" Cate said, floating nervously between the other two.

"Maybe. But I didn't. I had no reason to look at the bookings."

Ruby rose to her full sitting height. "Which of us are you going to believe, Cate? Who's telling the truth? Him or me? David, the sometimes dipsomaniac, the man with the troubled past, or sweet Aunt Ruby who gave you piggyback rides up and down those very steps when you were a wee child."

She banged the butt of the firearm against the floor of the boat. "Stand still and listen to me." Cate froze. With the attention to detail and pattern that she gave to her work, Ruby talked, pulling together the threads of her tale. How Cubiak hurled Wisby from the tower and then spied Macklin's boat in the bay. He assumed the old man had seen him and then killed him as well. Cubiak was in Fish Creek at the time the *Betsy Ross* exploded.

"I saw him coming out of the post office," Ruby said.

"Across the street, there was a shortcut to the docks. David could easily have slipped down to the water be-

tween the vacant cottages and tampered with the gas
tank without being noticed. Probably that would have
ended it all, but then Petey killed Alice. Nasty son of
a bitch with a temper like his always ends up hurting
somebody, usually a woman. After her murder, David
figures why not keep the streak going. Petey had already
been arrested for Alice's death, and at the meeting of the
Conservation League, he heard Otto present his plans
for the park and figured he could pin the rampage on the
superintendent. When David realized he couldn't target Otto for the killings, he hit on me. I had the means,
there's no denying that. He found his motive when he
learned that Jocko had told me about Beck's plan to turn
Door County into some kind of international playground
for his jet set friends. It's no secret that I have a reputation for standing up to outrage and greed.

"Unwittingly, I played into his hands with the weaving. The back depicts the Tree of Death, not a true
reverse of the front, which Cubiak interprets as an ad-
mission of my culpability." Ruby paused. "But you know
better than that."

"It's true," Cate told Cubiak. "For years, Ruby's
talked about doing an unconventional double weaving."

"Then by sticking in tricked-up clues, he planned to
make it foolproof."

Silent until then, Cubiak finally spoke up. "The clues
don't mean much. The key is in what Benny told Entwhistle."

Ruby scoffed. "That he saw someone else on the
tower? I doubt Macklin could make out any identifying
characteristics from the bay."

"You're right, he couldn't. I took a boat out there myself and looked. But I checked it the other way as well.

From tower to boat. It's a good distance. A harsh angle. Whoever was up there with Wisby couldn't see enough detail to identify the boat. They had to know that it was Benny's and had to be someone Benny could identify and connect with Wisby's death."

Ruby cut him off. "The sheriff theorizes that the alleged second person was a friend of the victim. A female companion, perhaps, whose situation would be compromised if her presence with the young man came to light. In any case, she's never been located."

"I talked to Buddy Entwhistle," Cubiak said. "What he told Halverson about Benny remembering someone else on the tower is true. But there's something else, too, something Buddy never bothered the sheriff with because he didn't think it was important. Although Benny couldn't identify the second person on the tower, he did know who it was he saw earlier that morning making a beeline for the park."

Ruby's eyes stayed on Cubiak.

"After Benny sold his catch, he motored into town. It was Sunday, the day Martha Smithson bakes pecan rolls. Macklin'd had a good haul and had decided to treat himself to a sack of fresh rolls. He stopped by the wharf to eat a hot bun and from there he saw you coming downhill through Ephraim and turning toward the park.

"Normally, of course, you wouldn't need to go through Ephraim to get there. You could take 42 to Town Line Drive. Once past the village you'd circle around to the north entrance. But that day, the route was blocked by a fallen tree, forcing you to cut through town."

"You're weaving a loose web. Full of holes. Suppose I had detoured through the village and was heading toward the park, intent on murder. It's a bit much to assume I'd even see old Macklin on the dock," Ruby said.

"You didn't have to. But you would have noticed the boat from the tower. And later when you and Cate stopped at the bakery for pecan rolls, Martha would tell you about Benny coming by earlier that morning and how she saw him on his boat tossing bits of roll to the seagulls and bird-watching up the hill. He saw an awful lot through those binoculars, more than was good for him."

The spark of triumph drained from Ruby's face, replaced by a look of calm resignation.

"Dave, what are you saying?" Cate was rigid with anger and fear.

"He's saying that I'm guilty as charged, sweetheart."

"No!" Cate cried. "Why?"

"Someone had to stop Beck. He was going to destroy Door County. The peninsula. Washington Island. The Wood. My home, the lovely home Dutch built. Everything. I couldn't allow that."

Cubiak looked at Cate. "It's true," he said, and started reciting the highlights of Beck's plan.

Ruby interrupted. "I must take my leave now," she said. Without their noticing, she had freed the mooring line from the pier and started to drift away from the dock.

The boat was still within reach. Cubiak catapulted forward.

Ruby raised the shotgun and fired. A spray of pellets ricocheted off the wood. Cate screamed. Cubiak hesitated and then advanced further. Ruby fired again, peppering his legs. He dropped to the dock, helpless as Ruby pulled the engine cord and the small motor caught.

"Wait! What are you doing? Where are you going?" Cate cried as she raced forward.

"Consider this my final act of contrition," Ruby said.

"No, Ruby, don't!" Cubiak staggered to his feet.

"Please, Aunt Ruby. Listen to me. I'll get the best lawyers. They'll figure something out."

Ruby gave a half smile. "It's too late for any of that," she said.

"Aunt Ruby, please, I love you."

"My dear child," Ruby said.

The yellow boat never faltered. Bent on its own pre-determined mission, the wooden skiff sliced through the water.

A hundred feet from shore, Ruby cut the motor. The engine sputtered, and for an instant, Cubiak thought she might turn back.

Instead, she called out to them "Don't judge me too harshly. Dutch would understand," she said.

As the launch pivoted toward the open water, Ruby stood and waved. Behind her, beyond a calm expanse of blue water, a billowing cloud tower massed over Washington Island. Against the backdrop of this silent, menacing witness, Ruby began to speak. Her words were clear and self-assured.

"All men, all women shall be held accountable for their actions. We suffer the consequences of our own deeds. I hold Beck accountable for his deceit. I hold myself accountable for my response."

Ruby picked up the red can.

"No!" Cubiak yelled. Cate collapsed against him, sobbing.

Splashing gasoline on herself and the boat, Ruby

sang: "Should auld acquaintance be forgot and never brought to mind…"

Cubiak didn't see the match struck. The inferno seemed to spring from the frigid waters beneath the old rowboat and engulf the tiny vessel and the solitary passenger.

For one dreadful moment, Ruby remained standing, her outstretched arms forming a burning cross against a brilliant blue curtain of sky and water. Then she emitted a single, solitary cry and fell headlong into the channel at the spot where she had buried Dutch at sea. As the flames consumed the last remaining shards of the wooden boat, her soul swam down toward him, oblivious to the curious, screeching gulls gliding over the water and the anguished pair on shore.

Seeking only Dutch.

Wanting only him.

Even as all around her, the ghosts wept.

# TWENTY-THREE

*Lastly*

RUBY'S BODY, WHAT remained of it, was recovered by divers and dispatched to Madison for autopsy. As officials awaited the results, the peninsula pulsated with harrowing stories of her misdeeds. Bathard called a hurried preliminary inquest to quell the worst rumors and ease the public's fears, but wild tales lingered like shadows in the evening light. The stories spawned more fear and talk of accomplices, despite repeated assurances from the sheriff and the coroner that Ruby had acted alone.

Cubiak secluded himself at Jensen Station and compiled a complete report for the sheriff. He was determined to give a full accounting not only of Ruby's motives and actions but also of Beck's duplicity and his Paradise Harbor project. The fire that killed Ruby had destroyed Cubiak's emotional distance as well and left him raw with pain. Pain of loss for Ruby's death, despite the evil she'd committed; of regret for his role in naming her as the killer, even though he could not have done any less; of concern for the future of the peninsula, even though the cycle of misfortune that had linked two of its leading citizens had finally played out.

THREE DAYS AFTER the incident at Death's Door, Cornelia died. Certainly her demise was expected, but such unfortunate timing. Two funerals, complete opposites, in the span of one week. Standing room only for Cornelia's send-off. An inspiring homily by Pastor Waldo Thorenson, elaborate and tasteful floral arrangements created by the likes of Anne Cooper and her retinue. Everyone in the church teary eyed when Bathard finished the eloquent tribute to his dear wife. Afterward, leaving the cemetery, the mourners commented on the bright sun, the beautiful day that Cornelia had enjoyed, had so richly deserved. Heaven smiling on her. Despite the highly charged emotional setting, Cubiak was unable to cry or take solace in the fine weather. Death was death, and only hollowness ensured.

Ruby got more the bum's rush than a ceremony. The day of her funeral dawned cold and rain sodden. Cubiak got to the church early. He was worried about Cate and anxious to comfort her. When she arrived, she was sickly pale in her funeral black. He went to her immediately.

"Cate." Cubiak held out his hands, but the emptiness in her eyes kept him from touching her. "I'm so sorry." Though he meant well, the words sounded hollow, like the look she gave him before she moved on.

Sitting alone in the back, Cubiak grieved—for Ruby and for all those she had killed, for Lauren and Alexis, for his parents, for the soldiers he'd known, for Cornelia. Other than Cate and her mother, Rosalinde, only Otto, Jocko, and a handful of others were scattered in the pews. Save for Amelia, no business owners were present, but then Ruby had been very bad for business. Bathard came, which surprised many, but he was such an honorable man people reasoned that the noble gesture suited. Thorenson struggled mightily with Ruby's homily, did his best, but barely knew what direction to take and ended saying little very poorly. Even the lovely wildflowers that graced the altar drooped in step with the faltering service. Of course, Anne Cooper and her group had tried to stop the proceedings, paltry as they were, from occurring at all.

No burial. Cremation, and Ruby's ashes scattered where she would have wanted them. With Dutch.

"HAVE YOU SEEN CATE? Since the service?" Late one afternoon, Bathard and Cubiak huddled at a back table at Pechta's. The dreary surroundings suited their collective mood. Bathard worked on his second Manhattan. Cubiak nursed a beer, his one-a-day. Neither had touched the plate of sandwiches that Amelia had prepared.

"I've driven past the house a couple of times, meaning to stop, but I don't have the nerve." Cubiak glanced at his friend. The coroner looked haunted, exhausted. His shirt was uncharacteristically rumpled, his hair curled over the collar. "Cate blames me for Ruby's death."

"She will for a while. She's in shock. She needs time. Think of all she has to take in. She hasn't just lost Ruby—there's everything that Ruby did, too. But, please, you mustn't blame yourself. Ruby was set to take her own life whether you showed up or not."

"You think the choice was deliberate, to try to atone for her sins?"

"Knowing Ruby, yes, I'm sure of it. Self-immolation is one of the most horrible ways to die. I'm sorry Cate was there to witness it."

Bathard pulled an envelope from his pocket and methodically turned it over in his hands. After several minutes of indecision, he laid it on the table. "Final autopsy report." He paused and then continued. "There's evi-

dence of both pregnancy and live birth. Ruby had a baby."
Bathard cleared his throat. "Cate?" he said, finally.

"Yes. But she doesn't know. Ruby didn't want her to know."

"I remember more than once remarking on the resemblance between Cate and Ruby, but then the sisters looked so much alike, I never thought anything more of it. Who… ?" Bathard couldn't go on.

"It wasn't Beck, although he wanted Dutch to believe that." Cubiak relayed the entire story to the coroner. "When Beck saw Cate as a young woman he would have realized the truth."

Bathard punched the table. "Damn them both to hell."

"Ruby'd already damned herself to hell. Giving up Cate was her penance but even she didn't think it was enough."

Bathard wilted. "Poor Ruby. Her sense of right and wrong warped by the pain of loss."

"It can happen to anyone. For months, I obsessed about killing the man who ran down my wife and daughter."

"But you didn't. The truth is vengeance was yours for the taking. You could have created your own opportunity, you know that. Covered your tracks and outwitted any of your colleagues who would have investigated."

"I was too cowardly to act."

"No! You were a man who recognized the fundamental difference between right and wrong, and who refused to cross the line no matter how strong the desire for revenge."

Cubiak slumped in his chair. "You make it sound more than it is."

"No, I think I make it sound exactly what it is. Ruby lost her moral compass. And now Cate. Poor Cate. What are you going to tell her?"

"I don't know," Cubiak said.

Two weeks after Ruby's rampage, an unemployed security guard walked into a fast food restaurant in Southern California and began shooting. Armed with a semiautomatic rifle, shotgun, and pistol, the man left twenty people dead and sixteen wounded. In Door County, people stopped talking about Ruby and began wondering about a world gone mad. At Pechta's, Cubiak consoled a distraught Amelia. The photo of the Survivalist Club hung over her shoulder. All that youthful optimism and vigor tarnished or erased. What would become of those who were still alive? What would become of him?

Fall arrived early that year. With autumn, a few tourists trickled back, unable to resist the spectacle of the brilliant colors. Across the peninsula, life slowly assumed a familiar rhythm. Understandably, however, many lives had changed.

Cate Wagner ignored Cubiak's messages. In October she left Door County and moved back to Milwaukee where she again picked up working as a freelance photographer and began traveling widely. Cate had inherited two substantial properties—The Wood and the house where Ruby and Dutch had lived—a fact that fueled speculation that she would eventually return to the peninsula.

The three members of the J. Dugan Beck family also departed the area. Eloise entered an exclusive alcohol-abuse treatment program in Palm Springs, California, and filed for divorce. Barry defied his father's wish that he matriculate at Princeton and enrolled at the University of Wisconsin at Madison. After a national business magazine published a cover story about the Door County murders that portrayed Beck as a greedy, self-serving civic leader, shareholders in Beck Industries forced Beck to resign as president. The ouster destroyed any hope he had of reviving even a modest version of Paradise Harbor. Beck relocated to New York where he eventually resurfaced as a successful real estate management consultant.

Facing the wrath of angry voters, Wisconsin legislators passed strict regulations limiting development on the peninsula as well as in resort areas throughout the state. The governor, long a proponent of growth, ran for reelection on a platform pledged to preserve Door County.

Otto Johnson, the cantankerous park superintendent, became a local hero. During the public inquiry into the murders at Peninsula State Park, word got out that at the first sign of trouble, Johnson had tried doggedly to shut the facility and halt the festival. For his actions, people treated him with new respect. When it was announced that Ruby, in her will, had bequeathed the one hundred acres of pristine shore land adjacent to The Wood to the Door County Conservation League as a wildlife preserve, Johnson was named to direct the project in response to public demand.

Following his wife's death, Evelyn Bathard retired as coroner and withdrew from public life. Restless and with too much time on his hands, he eventually took on the job of completing the history of Door County started by Dutch Schumacher.

Leo Halverson resigned as sheriff. Ensured of a county job that secured his pension and provided a government car, he began working as a supervisor in the highway department. Pleased with the regular hours and the financial arrangement he'd negotiated, he often bragged to locals that he'd gotten the better part of the deal.

After Halverson stepped down, Dave Cubiak announced his candidacy for the office of sheriff of Door County. He ran unopposed in the next general election and won handily. Shortly after he was sworn in, he moved from Jensen Station into a rented log house on a stretch of rocky shore on the peninsula's Lake Michigan side.

ON A CRISP EVENING, Cubiak was stacking wood in the stone fireplace when he heard a high-pitched whine outside. The new sheriff grabbed a flashlight and stepped onto the small, open porch. Clouds obscured the stars and intensified the darkness. Cubiak hunched his shoulders against the sharp northeast wind and listened over the crashing waves. The sound came again from the woods behind the house. It was an eerie cry clearly audible over the roar of the surf. Cubiak remembered what Cate had said about ghosts. As he eased off the porch, he heard a rustling in the underbrush. A coyote perhaps.

Something bumped Cubiak's knee. He swung the light down into the startled black eyes of a skeletal mutt.

"Shit," Cubiak said.

The mangy animal dropped onto its haunches. In spite of himself, Cubiak laughed. "I didn't say *sit*." At the sound of a human voice, the dog's ears lifted, its shoulders straightened to attention.

"I hate dogs. Go away, beat it. Scram." Cubiak shooed his arms. The dog whimpered but didn't move.

"I don't want a pet," Cubiak said and tromped toward the house. When he gained the porch, he glanced back and saw the dog gimping after him on three paws, its right front leg lifted at an awkward angle.

Cubiak groaned. "Okay, but just for one night," he said and opened the door.

Two days later, Cubiak took the dog to the vet.

"Name?"

"Cubiak."

"Not yours. The dog's."

"The dog doesn't have a… Butch. The dog's name is Butch."

The vet looked up, amused. "Unusual name. For a girl."

Cubiak grimaced. "How'd you know who I was?"

Pushing back a mountain of brown curls, the vet peered into the animal's floppy ears. "Everyone knows who you are." She kept up her inspection. "Butch isn't spayed. You want her fixed?"

"No." He answered automatically.

"You sure?"

"Yeah," he said, wondering if he really was sure.

Butch needed a splint, a full regimen of immunizations and preventive medicine for fleas. "The free ones always end up costing the most," the vet observed dryly as Cubiak wrote a check for the total. On his way out of town, he bought a dog bed and matching orange bowls for food and water.

As often happens in late fall, Door County enjoyed a brief interlude of unseasonably warm weather. Temperatures reached the low seventies in the afternoons and continued mild long past dusk. After supper one evening, Cubiak fed the dog, tidied up the kitchen, and cracked a beer. Navigating by starlight, he carried an old aluminum chair to the patch of scrubby lawn between the house and the water.

The lake was black and flat. As Cubiak watched, a giant hunter's moon crested along the horizon and released a line of liquid silver over the water. Drifting upward, the moon illuminated an increasingly larger segment of the shoreline, unmasking trees and rocks and welcoming spirits from the shadowy universe they inhabited. Ghosts from Cubiak's past and ghosts from pasts too long gone for him to know walked the damp sand. The luminous land made room for all and eased the pain of remembering. Transfixed, he sat quietly and thought of Lauren and Alexis. For the first time since they had died, he felt more love than sorrow, more peace than despair.

"Thank you," he whispered into the night, sure that they were listening and could hear him.

Butch floated through the stillness and rested her chin on Cubiak's knee. Happy for the company, he scratched between the dog's ears.

After a while, he pointed to a bright dot low on the horizon. "There's Venus," he said. "Or Mars. One of the two. Big Dipper's behind us." Cubiak twisted around to make sure the constellation hadn't drifted from view. "North Star's up there, too. And the Milky Way. Not that easy to see tonight but it's there. You just have to believe me and take it on faith." He lifted his chin in the general direction of the celestial roadway. "That's it. All I know."

Butch sighed, deeply content.

Lulled by the shushing of the water over the shoreline pebbles, they fell into a companionable silence. When Cubiak finally rose, the moon had crossed to the west. The evening's glittery magic had faded, and the air had chilled. It was late.

"Come on," he called to the dog. "Let's go home."

\* \* \* \* \*

# ACKNOWLEDGMENTS

ONE EVENING DURING an early visit to Door County, Wisconsin, I sat on the Lake Michigan shore as a deep mysterious quiet settled over the peninsula. Anything can happen here, I thought. Indeed, much did. Cozy Thanksgiving celebrations. Summer days of long walks and kayaking and creating castles and candles in the sand. Beach fires with wine and good friends. Nights tracking the moon's silvery path across the rumpled surface of the water.

When I began to write this book, there was no question of the locale. It had to be set in Door County. I learned much in the process and have many people to thank.

First, my dear Ray, whose belief in the story and my ability to tell it never wavered. Then, my daughters, Julia and Carla, who provided unfailing support and encouragement.

Others who have critiqued and helped shape the work include both friends and colleagues. My deepest appreciation to all: B. E. Pinkham, Esther Spodek, and Jeanne Mellett, the talented members of my writing group; Barbara Bolsen, Anna Fallon, Rachel Shefner, Jeanne Zasadil, Maura Kiley, and Betty Giorgi, the outstanding women of my book group; and the many others—Max Edinburgh, Tom Groenfeldt, Lisa Dresdner, Norm Rowland, Lee Somerville, Kevin Desinger, Pat Shaw, Carol Moffat, Jeffry Salyer, Lauren Phillips, Russ E. Stoll, and Jenny Lindsay who either read the manuscript in its various stages or simply cheered me on. Your input was invaluable.

Special thanks to Door County Sheriff Terry Vogel who graciously explained the workings of local law enforcement and understood my need to occasionally bend reality to fit the story—and who bears no resemblance to the fictional sheriff in my book. Also to Fred Shafer, whose editorial comments and suggestions always pointed in the right direction; the late Ruth Talaber, a woman of many talents who urged me to get on with my work because life is short; the Authors Guild, for help with the business side of being a writer; and, Off Campus Writers Workshop, for a steady flow of inspiring programs and lectures.

Finally, my sincere gratitude to the staff at the University of Wisconsin Press, including Raphael Kadushin, Sheila McMahon, Carla Marolt, Elena Spagnolie, Matthew Cosby, and Bronte Weiland, for their thoughtful and generous assistance.

Thank you all. Because of you, there is this one and there will be more.

# Get 2 Free Books,
## Plus 2 Free Gifts—
### just for trying the *Reader Service!*

 HARLEQUIN
# INTRIGUE

# Get 2 Free Books,
## Plus 2 Free Gifts—
### just for trying the
### Reader Service!

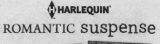

HARLEQUIN
ROMANTIC suspense

# Get 2 Free Books,
## <u>Plus</u> 2 Free Gifts -
### just for trying the Reader Service!

STRS17R